One For the Reason of Love

Shubricca L Bell

ISBN: 069268946X
ISBN 13: 9780692689462
Library of Congress Control Number: 2016906556
Glass Therapy, Cameron, NC

1

*I*t was a gloomy winter day and unusually slow at work for Caroline. She took the opportunity to start on other plans and projects that didn't need immediate attention, but she had all of her other tasks caught up. So, she kept herself busy by getting an early start on plans for next winter's art fundraiser, which benefits the nonprofit television station Caroline works for, named GPSG. Work was Caroline's life, and she didn't have much of a life outside of work. She spent most of her time at home watching every episode of Gangsta Files, which was packed with drama about the mob, their businesses, paper trails, strippers, the Feds, and people who get tangled up in the chaos of the fast lifestyle. Caroline had a mundane life, to say the least, no kids, no pets, no friends, and the only action in her life was her dramatic neighbor next door, who was always cursing and yelling at her husband about something.

Caroline thought that either this man was no good or the wife was just crazy; either way, they made the otherwise too quiet neighborhood a little interesting. All of this was five years ago, and on this day five years ago, her life suddenly changed. As Caroline made her way home from that unusually slow day at the office, she pulled into her driveway and noticed her neighbor's car wasn't parked next door. "Good, I may actually get to watch my soaps in peace, today," Caroline said as she hit the lock button on her key to her Audi. Caroline slipped off her shoes that resemble clogs and slipped into her house shoes.

"Man, my feet hurt," Caroline said, looking down at the two-inch heel shoes that looked like shoes from the early nineties. Caroline popped her dinner into the microwave and went into her room and turned on the TV, just in time for Gangsta Files. Beep, beep, beep, beep, the microwave went off, just as Caroline was getting to the good part of the soap opera. "OK, ok, I'm coming," Caroline said as she headed to the kitchen to get her food. "Yummy, there's nothing like some good old mac and cheese."

"Bang, bang, bang." "What the..." Caroline placed her dinner on her night stand next to her bed and rushed towards her front door to see who was knocking on her door like the police. "Excuse me Ms., I'm sorry to bother you, but can I use your phone?" It was the cute little kid from next door that Caroline saw almost every day, outside riding his bike.

Usually, the cute little kid was riding his bike through Caroline grass.

"Um, where are your parents?" "My momma is at work and my daddy won't wake up." Caroline had on her pajamas, so she quickly ran into her room and threw on her trench coat and went over to see what was going on with the child's father. Caroline got to the house and saw the man shaking violently on the floor.

Caroline gently lifted the man's back off the floor and put him on his side. Caroline loosened the man's neck tie, and after a couple of seconds, the man became conscious again.

'Sir, are you ok?" The man nodded. "I am going to call an ambulance. You just had a seizure, and I'm pretty sure it lasted about three minutes." The man looked up at Caroline as if he was beholding an angel. Caroline had her natural wavy hair tied back into a ponytail and a single strand hung on the right side of her face. "Am I in heaven?" The man said, smiling up at Caroline. Now, I see why his wife is so crazy; he's barely conscious and he's flirting.

Ignoring his question, Caroline said, "How do you feel, are you ok?" "I'm fine, and no please don't call an ambulance. I'm quite alright.

Thank you Ms.?" "I'm Caroline from the house next door, but are you sure that you're going to be ok?" The cute little boy ran to his father as soon as Caroline helped him off the floor, and he sat on the couch.

"Daddy," the little boy said sadly, while wiping the tears from his eyes. "It's ok Michael. Daddy is fine. I'm sorry that I gave you and Ms. Caroline a scare, but Daddy is going to be ok." Just as Caroline was walking out of the house, her neighbor's wife was walking in the door. She saw Caroline in her pajamas and a coat and she went crazy, like a mad woman.

"What are you doing at my house?" The crazy lady said with her eyebrow raised and a frown on her face. "See, that's it Mike. I am so done with your BS. Get out!" "I'm sorry," Caroline said, attempting to interrupt and resolve the confusion, because obviously, the woman had Caroline mistaken. Mike threw up his hands in surrender to the mad woman and advised Caroline not to say anything, because his wife is a ticking time bomb, ready to explode.

"No Daddy, please don't go," Michael grabbed his father around the waist as he wiped his eyes on his father's slacks. "No, no I don't want you to go Daddy, please." It broke Caroline's heart to see this. Caroline left her neighbor's house, and Mike left the house behind her. "Caroline, I'm sorry to be a bother, but can you give me a lift to the train station? I guess that now I'm officially kicked out of my own home, I will have to suck up my pride and go back home to live with my parents." Caroline hesitated for a second before answering. She thought to herself, I just got caught up in you and your Looney Toon of a wife's drama, and now you want her to see me drive off with you in my car? No sir, I don't think so. Then, Caroline thought to herself that maybe she should take him to the train station, seeing that he'd just had a seizure not even thirty minutes ago.

"I have to get up really early in the morning," Caroline lied.

"How far away do your parents live? I can call you a cab. Are you sure that you're ok?" "I'd rather take the train, but if you can't take me, I understand. You've done more than enough for me already." "Well to be honest, you can thank that brave little boy of yours for that. He came

over here, banging on the door and almost scared the life out of me."
"Yes, that's my little man, my pride and joy." "Well, look," Caroline
said, rubbing her hands against her arms, trying to stay warm against
the January night breeze.

"I'll tell you what, if you promise to go see a doctor in the a.m., I will
take you to your parent's house." Mike smiled the biggest smile, showing off his perfect pearly whites and then he put his hands into his pant
pockets and said, "Yes ma'am, by the way, can I use your phone to call my
parents to let them know that I'm coming?" Mike's wife started banging
on the living room window from inside their house. "Do you need for
me to meet you up the street say, in about 10 minutes?" "No, I'm not
afraid of your wife; however, she is your wife, and I don't want to stir up
any more trouble than what I've already caused." "Oh, trust me; Angel
is no angel; however, she is all bark and all bite." "Gees," Caroline said
as she glanced at the window to Angel cursing and fussing and telling
Caroline and Mike to get out of her yard.

Caroline shook her head and rolled her eyes. "Yeah well, I may be
small, but I can throw a few punches."

"Ha, ha, I hear that," Mike said, while smiling and admiring
Caroline's small, but tight and firm frame. Caroline is five foot two
inches and she's a size two with a nice round bottom and a pair of thirty-
four c cups. She looks tiny, compared to Michael's six foot seven inches
and two hundred and sixty-pound frame, which looked as if most of his
weight was the muscles in his arms. Mike's skin tone is milk chocolate,
like a Snickers candy bar, with abs of steel. He looks like a walking cover
of GQ magazine.

The drive to Stone Mountain to Mike's parent's house was fifteen
minutes, and he slept ten minutes of the ride there. Caroline looked
over at Mike, who was sleeping so well that he was drooling. Well, thank
goodness I have a GPS, because he is knocked out over there, she thought
to herself. Caroline had to shake Michael a few times when they'd arrived at his parents' house to wake him up. Michael's mother ran to the
car to greet him; apparently, she'd been looking out of the window and
waiting, ever since Mike had called to ask could he sleep over.

The next morning, Caroline was exhausted. She went to bed the night before at her usual time, between nine thirty and ten, but she was still tired. "Caroline, I need these reports proofread and on my desk before lunch," her boss said, stacking a pile of paperwork on her desk. It seemed like every one needed her today. Her coworkers were coming into her office left and right. She had what seemed like a million emails to answer, and she still needed to book her boss's flight to Chicago, all by lunch time. "Looks like no lunch for me, today," she sighed.

It was Friday evening, six o clock to be exact, and Caroline was just finishing up her work for the day. Usually, on Friday, Caroline leaves her job early, along with the top executives and her boss the COO of GPSG, General Public Station of Georgia. "Gosh, my feet hurt," Caroline said as she was locking the office door. A woman who looked like she belonged in a super model ad came strolling by, giggling, with another woman, who wore entirely too much make up, and Caroline couldn't tell if the lady was really a woman, a man, a drag queen, or what. "No, she didn't in those heels," the drag queen looking woman said, while rolling her eyes at Caroline and her two inch heels.

Caroline twitched her nose and rolled her eyes at the woman and proceeded to get her house shoes out of her purse and put them on. "Ah, that feels much better," Caroline said as she walked past the two women with her bunny slippers on. The two women burst into laughter as Caroline walked by. "No, she didn't girl, not with the bunny slippers," the drag queen looking woman said to the super model looking girl, before they started laughing even harder. "Excuse me sir, but one of your tracks just fell on the floor," Caroline looked at the piece of twenty-inch hair extension that had fallen on the side of the chair where the woman sat.

The supermodel looking lady just stood in disbelief with her mouth open at Caroline's comment. The drag queen looking lady hurried to pick her weave off the floor and looked around to see if anyone was looking. Caroline then took her hair out of the usual bun she wore to work and rubbed her fingers through her hair and let her natural wavy jet black colored hair flow down her back. Caroline reached in her purse and took out her sunglasses, put them on, and proceeded to walk out the door, making sure that her natural hair was bouncing, and as the double doors opened, the wind blew in her hair, making the two women turn up their noses, pissing them off even more. "Ha, ha, ha, ha," Caroline heard the front desk receptionist laughing as Caroline walked out the door.

2

"Hey wait up." Caroline turned around to see who the receptionist was talking to. "Yes, you, Ms. Caroline," the receptionist said as she approached Caroline. "Dang lady, you walk fast," the receptionist said as she placed her hands on her knees to catch her breath from running a few steps. "Look, those two had it coming. It's been a long time coming, if you ask me, and I'm glad somebody besides me grew some balls to say something to at least one of them."

"I'm so sorry, but who are..." The receptionist interrupted Caroline and said Tangerine." Caroline gave the receptionist a confused look and said, "Like the fruit Tangerine?" "No, Tan-ger-re-nae with an acute accent on the e. You know, like French?" Caroline tried to hide the laughter inside, because there was nothing French about the name Tangerine.

"Nice to me you, Tanger-re-nae, I'm..." "Call me Tangie and I already know who you are, Ms. Caroline. I may be new, but the first thing I always want to know is who's in charge of my money, so that if I have any issues, I'll know who to see. Look, you did all us a favor by telling that hussy off, so I owe you one. A couple of my home girls and I are going out tonight, so you should come hang out with us. You look like you are dying to have a good time." "Um, no thanks, Tangie, but thank you." "Aw, why not? You know you want to. You need to loosen up a little girl, relax and have fun, and besides, my home girls and I are supposed to meet some guys at the club tonight, and we need an extra girl, because one of my home girls backed out at the last minute. Please, please Caroline. I will owe you one, anything you need. Girl, I'm trying to get some free drinks. Everybody isn't big money like you." Caroline smiled at the comment, big money. "Well I don't know about big money, but I do alright," Caroline said, while lifting up her handbag and getting her cell out. "I will think about it, but I'm definitely not making any promises. What is your number, and what club are you all going to?" After Caroline got Tangie's number, she walked to her car and drove straight home. As Caroline pulled into her garage, Michael was, once again, cutting through her yard on her grass to get to his house. Caroline noticed that no car was parked in her neighbor's driveway, which was nothing out of the ordinary. Usually Michael's mom has the car for work during this time, but the dad is usually home with Michael.

"Michael is your dad home? He left his license in my car, and I'm sure that he'll need it."

"No ma'am. My mama said that my daddy is never coming back or the police is going to lock him up." "What, what happened? Did he come back?" "No, mama said that daddy hit her, and he can't come around anymore, because if he does, the police is going to get him,"

Michael said, while sitting on Caroline's porch step. "What time does your mama get off work, Michael?"

"I don't know. Usually she comes whenever her job lets her off, but my dad is usually at home with me." "Do you know any kids around here you can stay with until your mom gets home, so that you're not all by yourself?" Caroline opened her front door and went inside with Michael following behind. "Nope."

"Can I stay over here until she gets off?" "No sir, you cannot. Look, I'm sorry Michael, but I have plans. There must be at least one kid you know whose house you can stay over." "Well, I do have one friend, but I don't like going over his house, because all he wants to do is stay inside and play his game. I like to ride my bike and check out the girls at the playground down by the lake." "I tell you what, if you call your mom, right now, and ask her if you can stay over your friend's house when she's at work, then I promise to get you a gift of anything that you want for your birthday."

"Yay, wait; how did you know my birthday was coming up?" "Well, your dad talked about you a lot before falling asleep in my car to the drive over to your grandparents' house last night, but I can tell that you two are close, and he loves you a lot." "Yes, he's the best dad ever.

Too bad mama doesn't think so, though." "Yeah, I'm sorry, Michael." "Yeah, me too, but maybe it's for the best."

Caroline turned around, shocked that Michael had made that comment. Caroline hung up her coat on the coat rack in the living room as well as her purse. In curiosity, she turned to Michael and said, "Michael, why would you say such a thing?" "I'm tired of them fighting, and I'm tired of my mama coming home late, and Daddy is always sad." Caroline knew it was none of her business, but since she had gotten tangled up in her neighbor's mess, she thought she'd ask.

"Michael, have you ever seen your dad hit your mom?" He sat at the dining room table as Caroline placed her TV dinner into the microwave. Michael poked out his lip and said, "No, but mama said he does it when I'm not around." Something didn't add up about this whole situation with Caroline neighbors, but she thought that she'd just leave the whole situation alone. Caroline thought to herself, I've done my good deed, and now, I'm done, and there is no way that I'm getting even halfway involved in what these people got going on.

Michael took off his coat and sat it on the chair in the dining room. "What are you doing?" Caroline said, with one hand on her hip and pointing a finger to the house phone, so that Michael could call his mom. "Please Ms. Caroline, I'm hungry, and my dad usually brings home take out, but since he's not here, I'm going to starve. You don't want me to starve, do you Ms. Caroline, please?"

Michael pleaded with his puppy dog eyes and pouted. Caroline brushed her fingers through her hair and scratched her head and said,

"Nice try, but business first and play later." "What does that mean?" Michael said with a slight frown. "It means, young man, that you handle business with your mom first to see if you can stay over your friend's house, and then we'll play your little game later that you're trying to run on me."

Michael just smiled and shook his head and called his mother. Shockingly, the mother didn't curse Caroline out for having Michael over. She did, however, tell Michael that she wasn't getting home until late and to ask his friend's mom if he could stay the night. Caroline felt sorry for Michael, but again, it wasn't really any of her business, and she kept telling herself to mind her own... Business that is.

I would mind my own business if I had any, she thought to herself. "Is your mother going to call and talk to your friend's mom?" "No, my friend's mom is pretty cool. This isn't the first time my mama has put my daddy out, and I've had to stay over there." Then he held his hands together with his fingers between each other and held his head down. This is the first time she has gone to the police on him, though, and Daddy don't play with the Po Po's, so I know he's not coming back, even for me.

Caroline wanted to lighten the mood, so she gave Michael the food out of the microwave and told him to go wash up and come and have dinner. Michael and Caroline sat at the table and talked about things he wanted for his birthday, school, and even the little girls at the playground. Caroline walked Michael down the street to his friend's house, and before they got there, she even stopped by the store to buy them some snacks. Caroline enjoyed the walk, which was only a total of twenty minutes. Surprisingly, Caroline had a burst of energy when she got back home and was debating whether or not to meet Tangie and her friends at the club.

It was midnight by the time Caroline arrived at Black Diamonds ATL, which from the outside, looked nothing like a diamond at all. The only thing that was sparkling was the bright neon sign outside, along with the men with gold teeth or diamond grills. The club appeared to be a hole in the wall on the outside, but the line was wrapped around the building, with people trying to get in. When Caroline arrived, Tangie met her at the door and found it hilarious that Caroline wore a pinstriped pant suit to the club. Tangie shook her head, and when she saw her with some short wide heeled shoes on that reminded her of clogs, she hurried Caroline into the restroom to try to fix her up.

"Caroline, what do you," Tangie couldn't even finish her sentence, she was so amused by Caroline's no fashion sense style. "Look Caroline, you have to loosen up. This is a club, not a business meeting.

You got the job already, girl, now it's time to get you a man, and you're not going to get one looking like you ready to fire somebody." Caroline looked at the body length mirror in the restroom and thought that she looked fine. She didn't know what Tangie was talking about.

"Come here, sista, and let me see what magic I can work on you, because I refuse to let you walk out there like that." "What, what's wrong with this? This is Prada ma'am, thank you very much."

Tangie looked at Caroline like she was crazy, and said, "and this is Nada," making a serious face and shaking her pointer finger side to side, indicating the outfit was a no go for the club scene. "Why do you always wear your hair up in a bun anyway?" "Because I can't deal with it. It takes hours to straighten, and even when I do, it frizzes up." "Girl bye," Tangie said as she took Caroline's hair out of the bun. "Look, you're not giving me much to work with, but I'm going to do my best."

Tangie used water and a wide tooth comb on Caroline's hair, but she looked as if she'd just left the salon, and then she grabbed her makeup kit out of her purse and applied light blush, eye shadow, and mascara to Caroline's face. "Do you even own at least one lip stick, lip gloss, or something?" Tangie looked down at Caroline as she stood over her, applying Caroline's makeup. "I'm almost done. Let me look in my purse. I think that I grabbed some extra lipstick samples at the cosmetic stand in the mall today." Caroline started laughing. "Girl, I'm serious. It's hard out here for a receptionist. Shoot, I got to get my freebies on wherever I can boo," Tangie said, pulling everything out of her purse, until she found the makeup samples.

After applying some of the free lipstick that Tangie got at the mall, she put both of her hands on her hips and said, "Ok, we are halfway there." Since Tangie's purse was actually the size of a gym bag, she put Caroline's suit jacket in her purse.

"Now, usually, I bring some shoes to dance in, because these stilettos be killing my feet," Tangie said, while looking down at the six inch spar- kling silver heels that she was wearing with her leather little black dress, which was very little, maybe two sizes too little.

"Oh, I could never walk in something that high," Caroline said, while admiring the fact that Tangie walked in heels like it was second nature. "I know. That's why we are going to start off small, and you are going to wear these three inch heels in my bag. I couldn't decide which ones I wanted to wear. The stilettos give me an extra lift in the back area, but I think that these are cute and classy," she said, holding the pair of heels up and admiring the falling jewels on the straps. "And what are you going to wear if your feet start to hurt?"

"My flip flops," Tangie said, reaching into her bag before pulling out her shoes and waving the Old Navy flip flops in the air. "I have all the colors at home. I got them on sale for a dollar each." Caroline tried on the heels, but her foot slipped, and she almost fell.

"Thanks, but no thanks to the heels. I'll just put back on the shoes I wore here." "Um, no ma'am, you will not," Tangie said before dropping Caroline's shoes in the trash. "Girl, what are you doing? Do you know how much these shoes cost or how long I've had those shoes, and they still look new." Caroline reached in the trash in an attempt to get the shoes, but just before she grabbed the shoes, she realized that they were sitting in someone's vomit.

"Ugh, Tangie, you owe me double time. What a waste, I could have at least donated those shoes to the good will or a homeless shelter." "Believe me, sista," Tangie said, while opening the bathroom door, "a homeless person would rather walk barefoot than be seen in those shoes." "That's not true," Caroline said, while trying to walk normal in the three inch heels that were only an inch higher than her work shoes. Before exit- ing the bathroom, Caroline caught a glimpse of herself in the mirror, and she couldn't believe how different she'd looked, but it was a good different.

"Wow, thank you, Tangie. I don't know what you did, but I look and feel amazing." "You're welcome girl. Thank you for coming. Now, loosen up and let's party," Tangie said, while walking and dancing to the table where her friends and the guys were seated.

"Everyone, this is Caroline. Caroline this is everybody." Tangie begin to introduce everyone to Caroline, one by one, while speaking loud, so that everyone could hear over the music. Hipnotiqa, who is one of Tangie's friends told Caroline that everyone in their circle has nicknames, and no one goes by their real name, so she gave Caroline the nickname Candy. "Thanks, but no thanks, just call me Caroline."

Tangie's friends burst into laughter, one almost spitting her drink out. "How old are you Caroline?" "Thirty-two, why?" Because Car-o-line sounds like a white girl's name, and an old white girl, at that." "Yeah well, my mother named me after my grand mom, who happens to be white." "Hence," Hypnotica chuckled.

"I'm sorry, but I'd rather have a name that sounds like an old white lady than to have the name Hipnotiqa. Hence," Caroline said, while looking at the girl's glass of Hipnotiq and looking back at the girl. Hypnotica got all in Caroline's face and looked her up and down and then burst into laughter and said, "Girl, I'm just playing with you. I just had to try you to see how you would respond, because we don't roll with punks." Caroline looked at Hipnotiqa, like she'd lost her mind.

"Girl, never mind Niq. She's crazy. That's you over there by the way," Tangie pointed to the guy, who was sitting on the end of the table, and you could barely see his face because of the dim lights. Just then, the man got up and straightened his blazer and walked towards Caroline. He looked ok from a distance, but when he came to greet Caroline, she knew exactly why he was single. His breath was kicking like a Taebo workout, and Caroline wanted to run for cover.

Caroline eyes started tearing up from the dude's tart breath, and she had to find a way to escape. First, she offered the guy a mint, and when he declined, she told him that she was going to go to the bar to get a drink. "I got you. What are you drinking, Ms. Lady?" Man, you can't smell that, Caroline thought to herself, Gees. "I'll have a bottled water please, thank you."

"A what?" The guy said, looking confused. "We have bottles of every brown and white liquor and some champagne at the table. Are you sure you don't want any of that?" "Nope, I'm good. I don't drink liquor." The guy motioned for the waiter to come, "Aye tell her what you want. She'll hook you up." Caroline almost wanted to throw up. The more he talked, the sicker she felt.

"Just a moment I forgot something," Caroline lied and excused herself outside, where she got a breath of fresh air. A few guys tried to converse with her, but she lied and said that she was with her boyfriend. God forgive me, I am becoming quite the liar lately, she thought. Just then, she looked up to head back inside, and she saw stank breath dancing with two other women who had him in a sandwich. She lifted her head towards heaven and put her hands together, "Thank you God."

Just then, Mike and a couple of other men walked by, headed to VIP near the section where Tangie and everyone else was. "Hey, what are the odds of seeing you here?" "Oh hi, Mike, I was meaning to give Michael this, but it must have slipped my mind." Caroline reached into her purse and handed Mike his license. "I like the curly fro look too," she smiled.

"Anyways, I'm pretty sure that you need that." "Yeah, oh you like that? I might have to grow the old fro back, then." Caroline shook her head no. "No?"

Mike laughed. "I mean it was cute on you back then, but I like the waves much better. "Thank you, well you know, I try," Mike turned his head to the side and rested his chin between his thumb and pointer finger, giving his best GQ pose. "I was wondering what happened to my license. I just went to get another copy, today, but thank you Caroline."

"You're welcome." Caroline and Mike stood for an awkward second, "Well, I better get back to my friends," she said, while heading to the table and almost slipping, trying to adjust to the heels. "Yeah, ok but it was nice seeing you again." "You as well," Caroline turned to Mike and nodded.

"Who was that cutie pie?" Tangie was looking Mike up and down, admiring his undeniably good looks and attire. "Oh, just my neighbor," Caroline smiled, blushing a little bit. "Neighbor my butt, you like him, don't you?" "Tangie, don't be ridiculous," Caroline said, looking at Mike out of the corner of her eye to catch a second glimpse.

Tangie and her friend's song came on, and they took Caroline by the hand and brought her to the dance floor. "This is my jam," Tangie said, singing to one of Nicki Minaj's latest records. Caroline stood there, looking like a lost puppy with its tail between its leg in the midst of Tangie and her two friends. They were pop locking, dropping, twerking, shaking, and everything else. Caroline was shocked at the way Tangie danced like a professional, especially when she hit the pole.

The crowd of people surrounding Tangie and her friends applauded and cheered Tangie on as she danced on the pole. A few people, both ladies and men, started throwing money at Tangie, and she happily picked it up off the dance floor. Tangie's friends ran up on stage, where Tangie was, when people started throwing money, and they dragged Caroline along. "Girl, you better dance," Hypnotica yelled over the music as she backed it up and dropped it to the floor. Caroline stood like a deer in the headlights for a couple of seconds and then she started two stepping. "What the hell are you doing, Caroline?" Tangie put her hand on her hip and leaned her head to the side and let out a smirk.

"Follow my lead before you make a fool out of me and you. This is a hip hop club. You ain't at a square dance party, honey." Tangie started rolling her body from top to bottom and swaying her hips side to side, while holding on to the pole, and Caroline followed suit.

"Oh my goodness, I can't believe that I'm actually doing this. I hope that I don't see anyone else that I know in this club." "Girl, relax, you are having a good time, aren't you?" The men were going crazy at Caroline's amateur moves. Caroline couldn't believe the attention that she was getting.

"I am actually, and before I met you, I would have never been even caught dead in a club like this." The club wasn't bad looking on the inside. Compared to the outside, it actually was bigger than it appeared to be. Caroline looked in the VIP section to where Mike was earlier, but he and the guys he was with were already gone. "Are you looking for your neighbor?" Tangie said sarcastically.

"He and his buddies left right after he spoke with you. Humph, they must not have liked the atmosphere too much." Beneath the disco balls that hung from the ceiling, people danced to the best of hip hop music, and everyone seemed to be having a good time. Caroline felt like she was trapped in a club from the seventies with the disco balls dazzling everywhere, yet she did have a good time. "I have really enjoyed myself Tangie, but I have to get going. I have church duty in the morning."

"Oh you're one of them super freaks, huh?" "Excuse me," Caroline said confusingly, as she and Tangie walked to their cars. "Y'all church girls be on a whole different level of freak. Don't try to play me, because I'm one too," Tangie said, poking out her butt as she bent over to stick her car key in her car door. "Girl, you are a mess. Anyways, since I did you a favor sister Tangie, won't you come and help me out at the homeless shelter tomorrow?" "Aw man, do I have to tomorrow, Caroline?" "Yes, because you tried to hook me up with Halitosis junior over there," Caroline said, while pointing to the guy, who was still getting his freak on with two women in the parking lot. "Look, I know that he is short, but he's your size, and you got to start somewhere. How else do you expect to get a man?"

Caroline interrupted Tangie, "It's not only his height; it's his breath." "Girl, I know," Tangie said, speaking low enough for only Caroline to hear. "Why do you think that he was the only one sitting on that end, and everyone else was over here?"

Caroline and Tangie burst out laughing. "See y'all wrong. Why hasn't anyone told that man his breath smells bad?" "Oh, believe me, we have. We all go out all the time, but he is the only one who always needs a date, because every girl that meets him ends up changing her number or making it known to him that they're not interested." "Dang poor thing, but it looks like those two girls like it." "Yulk," they both said at the same time before sharing a laugh.

"I know, right, but anyways, what were you saying about I owe you, because I do, but I am glad you came." "So am I, but be ready bright and early in the morning, because I need help in the a.m. at the homeless shelter." "No can do." "Why not?" "Girl, we probably going to the waffle house when we leave here, and I won't be home until about five a.m., so I'm sorry, but I'll have to decline, but maybe next month, though."

"Aw man, come on Tangie, please. I really need the extra hand seeing that two girls from the church already bailed on me, because they have a date." Tangie shook her head at Caroline. "See everybody got a man except for you. Why is that? You're like the perfect woman. You have a great job, you're cute, you have a booty that people will pay to have, you have the perfect skin, you like to help people, you're a Christian, and you're involved in the church. What more can a guy ask for?" "Girl, let me tell you, I'm far from perfect, but I'm working on it." "Yeah you're right, because you do have a slick mouth." They both start laughing.

"On the real, you are a cool chick, Caroline, thanks for coming." Tangie hugged Caroline, and Caroline returned the hug. "No, thank you, I really enjoyed myself, but I'm going to be looking for you bright and early in the morning." Caroline headed towards her car. "I told you we're going to the Waffle House and maybe an afterhours spot." Caroline turned around and said "You better get Waffle House to go, because I will be looking for you in the morning." "Well, at least, come to pick me up," Tangie shouted over the music she had blasting in her car. Caroline winked at Tangie, "Cool, text me your address." Caroline got home at two am. Tangie had called her to make sure that she'd made it and said that everyone was at the Waffle House. Caroline was exhausted. She set her alarm for seven a.m. and took off the heels that Tangie let her borrow and crashed in the bed.

3

wo years later, Caroline and Tangie had become best friends. They would take their lunch breaks together or meet up after work for a girl's night out. At least twice a month, outside of work, they'd go bowling, out to eat, the movies, or even a ladies' night in with take out and a movie. Tangie persuaded Caroline at least to start dating, which had not been successful, and yet, it had been fun. One evening, Tangie talked Caroline into coming over her house to play spades and have drinks with her and her two friends that Caroline met at the club.

"Come on, Caroline, one drink is not going to hurt you," Niq said, while scratching her blue weave and making her a cocktail. "No thank you, Niq, but the bottled water is cool. Tangie I do want some of those hot wings though, girl, and that spinach dip looks delicious." "Girl, go ahead and dig in. You know that I don't fix plates around here, so go ahead. The plastic plates are right over there," Tangie said while licking the hot wing sauce off her fingers from the plate of wings she was scoffing down. Caroline fixed her a small plate of wings and a plate full of fresh fruit and vegetables. "Girl, what are you going to do with three wings?" Niq said with her right hand on her thick hips. "See, that's why you don't have a man, now, because you're just skin and bones. No one wants to rub against a skeleton, honey," Niq sucked her teeth and rolled her eyes, and her trusted cosigner Pam frowned and said, "I know that's right." "Niq, leave my girl alone, and Pam stop dang on cosigning all the freaking' time, honey. Don't you have a mind of your own?"

Tangie always had Caroline's back when Niq tried to go in on her with her lame and envious comments. Caroline always had a comeback to whatever Niq threw her way and was far from intimidated by her remarks. "Look Niq, you are, what, five eleven? You have the best features that money could buy," Caroline put her plate of food on the dining room table. She looked Niq up and down, starting at her silicone boobs to her silicone butt.

"It's a shame that out of all the men you've tricked off with and all the money you've spent trying to better your appearance, you're still ugly as hell on the inside. While we're on the subject of men, where is your man, Niq? I've only known you two years, and I've met at least twenty of your so called male friends, but yet and still, you can't claim one of them as your man," Caroline said while standing with her right hand on her hip and looking at Niq up and down and waiting on her comeback. "Oh no she didn't, Tangie, you better get your lil friend, because she don't know me. I'm from Bank Head. I will whoop dat." Tangie interrupted Niq, "Hey, hey y'all calm down. There won't be no fighting going on up in my crib, so look, we came here to have our ladies' day in I've slaved over this hot stove, making all this food. Now, y'all sit down right now and play spades."

Everybody sat down at the table like children that had ticked their mother off and were cautious not to anger her any further. "Now, Caroline this is how you play spades." Tangie began to give Caroline the basic rules of spades, and they began the game. Niq rolled her eyes at Caroline every time Caroline won a trick. Caroline just smiled and winked at Niq, which made her angry, even more. "Caroline, girl, you got it going on over there. You're a fast learner," Pam said before Niq bowed her in the side and she put her head down. After Tangie and Caroline won 10 games in a row, Niq got salty and decided to leave.

"Come on Pam, I'm ready to go," she yelled. "But I'm having fun. I'm not ready." "Now!" Niq yelled.

Caroline and Tangie looked at each other, like have this trick lost her mind? "Look Pam, maybe you better go." Tangie grabbed Pam's purse off the coat rack and handed it to her. Niq stormed out of the house, and Caroline took the opportunity to give Pam some quick advice. "Look Pam, I know that you and Niq are best friends. You grew up together and all this and that, but you are thirty years old, and you are nothing more to her than her flunky. Don't you think it's time to evaluate your life and make your own decisions?"

"Nah, it's not like that. She's just hot about earlier, but she'll be alright. Look, it was fun, but I got to go. See y'all next week." Caroline walked Pam to the door and outside, Niq was talking to Tangie's boyfriend of six months. Tangie was in the kitchen making him a plate, because he works late, and he's always hungry when he gets home. "Well, your boo is here, so I guess that I'm out as well. I'll call you when I get to the house." "No you don't have to leave. Besides, I'm still waiting on Carmen to get here. She went out with some friends, and I always stay up to make sure that she makes it home safe." It was almost two o'clock, and Caroline was wondering why a sixteen-yearold was out at this time without calling and telling her mother where she was. "Is she on her way home?"

Caroline sat back down at the table and drank her bottled water.

"Caroline, I don't know where she is, but I trust her, and she will be home soon. Look, my parents were strict with me, and it just made me into a wild child. I try to be lenient with Carmen and let her have her space, so that she won't feel alone or go through a lot of the things that I've went through, like being a single mom and struggling to make ends meet. Tangie's boo didn't come into the house until twenty minutes after talking to Niq, but Tangie just rubbed it off as Niq and him being old friends, and that they're always talking about somebody or something going on in their old hood.

It was four a.m. when Caroline was on her way home from Tangie's house, and Carmen had not gotten home yet. Caroline was two miles down the road when she saw an ambulance and a three car accident in the middle of the street. One of the cars was flipped over down the hill.

Caroline slowed down, and she slammed on her brakes when she saw the paramedics putting Carmen in the ambulance. "Oh my God, oh my God, oh my God," Caroline hurried out of her car, which was in the middle of the street, and ran to the ambulance. The police officers tried to calm Caroline down and get her to move her car to the side of the road.

"Officer, I know this girl. She's the daughter of a friend of mine. The officer took down Caroline's information and told her about the accident. Caroline was hysterical. The police officer called Tangie and told her what was going on and that Carmen was in an ambulance on her way to the hospital.

Twenty-two days later, Carmen was still in the ICU. Every day after work, Caroline would sit with Tangie and try to comfort her and give her encouraging words. Tangie took all twenty-two days off of work to be with her daughter. This was a trying time for Tangie, but also for Caroline. According to the doctor, it was a less than two percent chance that Carmen would walk again, and if she did, it would take several years of therapy.

Caroline knew God and the power in believing in Jesus, but her faith was being tested. It was hard for her to be strong for Tangie, when in the physical, it looked as if Carmen would never walk again. "Why, God why did this have to happen to my baby?" Tangie sobbed.

"Carmen is a good girl. I just can't believe this. Why?" she plopped into the waiting room chair and wept.

Caroline looked at the bags under Tangie's eyes from days of no sleep and asked Tangie to call her boyfriend to come and get her, and she would stay with Carmen at least a day, until Tangie got some rest.

"He's cheating on me, Caroline." "What, are you sure?" Caroline said, while rubbing Tangie's hair as Tangie lay on Caroline's shoulder. "I'm more than sure, Caroline," Tangie lifted her head and grabbed some tissues off the table beside her and wiped her eyes.

Tangie stood up out of the waiting room chair and gave Caroline a straight face look. "Come on, Caroline. I know that you, of all people, know that he's cheating. Out of the twenty-two days that Carmen has been in the ICU, he hasn't come to see how she or I have been doing, not once. He's always claiming that he's working late. Besides, the signs have been there for a while, even before now. I should have listened to you when you warned me not to be so hasty in moving him into my house after three months of dating." Caroline did tell Tangie that, but thought that this was no time for should have, would have, or could have. "Tangie, I know what this must look like, but God is still in control," Caroline stood up to embrace her friend, who looked and sounded helpless. Tangie held her right hand up to stop Caroline from the embrace. Tangie shifted her weight to her left leg and crossed her arms.

"God?" Tangie sucked her teeth. "Please Caroline, now is not the time." Caroline jerked her head back and said, "What?" "Don't talk to me about God being in control, Caroline; that's what."

Tangie got a paper cup out of the waiting room and filled it with water out of the bottled water dispenser. Tangie took a sip of her water and looked at Caroline over the top of the cup, while Caroline stared back with a confused look. "You haven't experienced even half of what I've been through my whole life. You had it easy with a mayor for a dad and a prominent business attorney for a mother. You even had a nanny. You want to talk about God being in control? Well, let's just reevaluate a few things.

"I was raised in the projects with two hard working parents, who still lived pay check to pay check. I survived most of my life off fried bologna and Ramen noodles. I've watched friends lay in their own blood, dying from gunshot wounds; if they weren't dying, then they were going to jail, many of them still in prison. Carmen's daddy was gunned down at eighteen years old by some junkies, who robbed him. I've struggled since the day that I had Carmen to make ends meet.

"I've had to sell my food stamps to make sure that Carmen had clothes and shoes to wear. I was not only raised in the projects, but I've raised Carmen in the projects most of her life, because the struggle is real Caroline. Finally, was God in control when Carmen was in that accident, huh? Was he in control when the car flipped down the hill three times and damaged Carmen's c five vertebrae? If God is in control, why couldn't he control that car and save my baby?"

Caroline felt sorry for Tangie and went to embrace her a second time, but this time, Tangie threw the rest of the cup of water that she was drinking into Caroline's face.

"Get out, get out now!" Caroline just stood still for a few seconds, lost for words. Tears began to run down Caroline's face, blending with the splash of water that covered her face and her blouse. Caroline thought about what she was going to say next. She wanted to choose her words carefully, because this was a trying time for Tangie and her.

If she wasn't my friend, she would have been slapped right into this cement floor, Caroline thought. Jesus take the wheel and give me the right words to say, she said in her head.

"Look Tangie, it's been a trying three weeks, and there are even more trying times ahead. You're right. I have no idea what you have been through or what you are going through at this moment. I do love you and Carmen, like you are family and would give my last in a heartbeat to help you in any way, but there are some things I need to say before I leave, and you are going to stand here and listen to me, because you owe me at least that.

"A lot of decisions that we make, as humans, we make those decisions, not God. We make decisions without thinking about the consequences, but the bible said that we will reap what we sow. Instead of being so quick to blame God, let's just reevaluate some things, shall we, since you've given me a lecture on life. Carmen's father was a drug dealer and a thug who lived by the street code. Jesus doesn't call it the street code, but he did say if you live by the sword, you will die by the sword."

Tangie threw her hand at Caroline to wave her off, like an irritating insect. "I don't want to hear this, Caroline," Tangie sat in the chair. Caroline walked beside her and grabbed a few tissues off the table to wipe the water and tears off of her face and blouse. "No, you will listen." Tangie gave Caroline a disgusted look.

Tangie turned her head to the left, letting Caroline know that she wasn't paying any attention. Caroline continued to talk. "You made a decision to have sex, unprotected and out of wedlock, with Carmen's father. Your parents gave you the opportunity to continue living with them until you got on your feet, because they struggled and didn't want you in the same place that they were most of their lives. You decided that you wanted to move out of your parent's house, just so that you could get your own government apartment, when you had the option to stay with them and save money to buy a house and live better.

"Carmen was on her way home from a party that served alcohol to minors. This wasn't the first time that Carmen has stayed out all night, and she's only sixteen years old. Carmen knew that she was not supposed to be drinking, and that she doesn't have a valid driver's license, and third, she knew better than driving under the influence." "How dare you say this is Carmen's fault," Tangie stood up and got in Caroline's face.

"I am not judging you or Carmen, Tangie. I'm just letting you know that God is still in control. He is the great I AM. He protected you in the projects, when you lost many of your friends, that could have been you. He was there when your parents struggled to make ends meet, and now, your father owns the trucking company that he worked thirty years for, and your mother is regional manager at a hotel where she started off as a housekeeper. That's called a testimony, Tangie. God has been here for you and Carmen, all these years you've been club hopping and bringing all these men in your home with your daughter.

"God has covered Carmen, and not one man has ever laid a hand on her or touched her in any way. Do you know how many sickos are in these streets and what they could have done to her? Do you? Carmen could have lost her life in that car accident, Tangie, but God saw fit that she should live. He is still sitting high and looking low, and his grace and mercy has always and will always be there with you. This is not the time or the place to give up on him now." Caroline grabbed her purse out of the chair and placed it on her shoulder, straightened her blouse, and walked out of the hospital. Tangie sat in the waiting room chair, shaking her left leg and sobbing hysterically. A man asked her if she was ok, and she wiped her eyes with a few tissues and said "I'm not ok." Tangie got up and walked back to Carmen's room in the ICU and sat in the chair beside the bed and continued crying, with her head down on Carmen's bed. When Caroline got to her car, she broke down in tears and cried in the parking lot, sitting in her car for thirty minutes.

4

The next day was Sunday, and Caroline was already missing her best friend. Caroline decided to go to Tangie's church because she missed her so much. When it was time for alter call, Caroline asked the pastor to pray for Carmen and Tangie. On the way to Caroline's seat, she saw Mike and Michael praying with their heads bowed. Church ended after the offering and invitation to discipleship.

"Ms. Caroline," Michael ran up to Caroline as she was walking towards the doors. "Hi Michael, long time no see. How are you?" "I'm fine," he smiled. "Hi, how are you doing," Mike said, before going for a hug. It was awkward, because Caroline was going for a handshake, but Mike pulled her into his embrace.

"Hi, Mike I'm good. I was just telling Michael that it's been a while since I've seen him. Are you all members here? No we aren't members, but we are looking for a church home, and we've been here a few times. Are you a member here?"

"No, my best friend usually attends church here, and I usually visit with her from time to time, but she couldn't make it this week, so I came on her behalf." Mike nodded his head, like he understood, but not really. Michael interrupted their conversation.

"Hey Dad, can Ms. Caroline come to dinner with us, please Daddy, please." "I'm not sure about that, son. Ms. Caroline may have plans of her own, but if not, she's more than welcome." Caroline hit the unlock button on her Audi and prepared to get in. "No, I'm sorry, not this time Michael. I do have plans, but maybe another time." Caroline winked. Michael leaned up against her car with a pout. "You know they're not married anymore." "Alright Michael, that's enough. Leave Ms. Caroline alone, and let's go." Michael hesitated. Mike blew his truck horn and yelled, "Now Michael." Mike waved good bye to Caroline and mouthed the words, "I'm sorry." Caroline smiled and waved good bye. As Caroline and Mike were pulling out of the church driveway, they were side by side. He was going to the right and she was turning left. Mike rolled his window down and signaled for Caroline to do the same. "Are you sure that you don't want to take us up on that dinner offer?" Caroline smiled, "No I don't think that would be such a good idea." "Ms. Caroline," Michael yelled from the passenger seat. "Come on and have dinner with me. Forget about my dad."

Mike gently pushed Michael back into his seat and said, "Boy sit back." Mike shook his head at Michael. "Going once, going twice, Caroline?" Caroline was cheesing, but she still declined the offer. After a few cars were blowing their horns for Mike and Caroline to pull out of the driveway, Michael waved his hands sorry to the line of cars behind him and left.

Caroline decided to cook this Sunday. It was one of the few things Tangie taught her how to do over the past two years. Caroline cooked baked turkey wings, mixed greens, fried corn, and corn muffins.

Between cooking, she caught up on the latest season of Gangsta Files.

Caroline hadn't watched Gangsta files religiously like she used to, ever since befriending Tangie, which actually gave her a life.

Caroline was intrigued by these mobsters and the feds, money, and trifling women who played on the show. Tangie was right. Caroline did have it easy, compared to how Tangie grew up, but Caroline was no stranger to her own trials and tribulations. Bang bang bang bang, the TV sounded off with one of the mobsters lying on his back in a puddle of blood, while his pregnant wife screamed her lungs out. The mobster was betrayed by his own brother, who used a female to set him up to be robbed. As Caroline watched the guy on the screen laying in the puddle of blood, she thought about how Tangie must have felt, seeing her child's father die right before her eyes.

Caroline picked up her cell in an attempt to call Tangie to see how she was doing, but something said give her some time. She'll come around, so Caroline hung up her cell and continued to watch TV. Ding dong ding dong ding dong ding dong, Caroline's doorbell rang. Caroline rushed to the door, thinking it was Tangie. When Caroline tiptoed and looked into the peep hole, she saw Mike at the door, smiling with those darn pearly whites. Caroline opened the door slowly, but not all the way, remembering what happened last time she went over to help Mike. "What's going on, guys?"

"Sorry to bother you, Caroline," Mike said, while leaning forward with his hands in his pant pockets. "Someone has lost their key to their mother's house and was wondering if you found a Ninja Turtle wallet with a key chain attached to it in your yard.

The last time I brought him to visit his mom, he must have lost it while riding his bike through people's yard, although I've told him a thousand times not to." "Um no, I haven't seen it," Caroline said, putting her hair behind her ear on the right side of her face. "Well, looks like we're stuck outside until Mom gets home," Michael said.

"No sir, we are going home, and we will have to get up extra early and come to get your shoes in the morning." Mike whispered to Caroline, "He left his favorite shoes at his mother's house, and all he has is his church shoes and his gym shoes at the house, and he refuses to wear any other shoes, except those he so happened to leave over there." "Oh I see," Caroline said. Caroline scratched her head, hoping that she wasn't making a mistake with what she was about to say. "Well, you both can wait here if you'd like until your wife..."

Mike cut Caroline off in the middle of her sentence. "Ex." "Oh, yeah, ex-wife gets home." "Yeah," Michael yelled. "Dad, Ms. Caroline has the coolest house ever with a big entertainment room, a gym, and a guest room with a bathroom inside."

Michael was always thrilled to come over to Caroline's house because of all the amenities. He said it looked as if she was rich, but Caroline insisted that she was far from being rich, but she was proud of her home. Caroline has a four-bedroom home, including the guest room, entertainment room and gym. She also has two and a half bath rooms, a living room, dining room, breakfast area, and a glass outdoor patio with a built in fireplace. The home also has an acre of land in the backyard, with a pool, and only a couple minutes away from the lake. Caroline didn't think it was much, but it was perfect for her, and besides, she loved the view of the sunset overlooking the lake.

"Man, aw man, something sure does smell good up in here. I didn't know you cook Caroline," Mike smiled and turned to Caroline, who was locking the front door. "Dad, Ms. Caroline doesn't cook. She microwaves, like mom," Michael said as he plopped down on the couch.

"No son, you're wrong. Your daddy knows what a home cooked meal smells like, and that's some soul food." "That's right, Michael, you've been gone for a year now, and you left me all alone, so I had to find something productive to do with my time, so I learned how to cook."

Michael blushed at Caroline's words. "Yeah, well I'm here now, so you don't have to miss me anymore," Michael got up off the couch and hugged Caroline. "I'm just finishing up dinner. Would you all like some? I have plenty."

"Maybe later," Michael rubbed his stomach, which was poking out from the five plates of crab legs he'd demolished at the Seafood Buffet that he and Mike went to after church. "Yeah, me too," Mike said rubbing his stomach, "but we'll definitely take a couple of plates to go." "Oh, Ms. Caroline has the new Avengers movie. Can I watch it, Ms. Caroline?" "Yes you may go into the entertainment room. I know that you know how to work everything already."

"Yes," Michael said with excitement as he made a fist and jerked his elbow down and ran to the entertainment room. Michael yelled from the entertainment room, "Can I turn the surround sound up, Ms. Caroline?" "Sure, but not too loud, ok. I don't want to be responsible for you losing your hearing." "Go ahead. He'll use it as an excuse that he can't hear me when I tell him to clean his room," Mike joked. "Oh stop it," Caroline said opening up the refrigerator, to get a tomato out and cut for her greens. "I'm serious," Mike stood against the counter across from Caroline with his hands on the counter behind him. He noticed a cheesecake in the refrigerator and begin to walk towards the living room. "He has selective hearing, see watch this." Mike yelled to Michael in the entertainment room. "Michael clean up after you watch the movie."

There was a brief silence. "Now watch this," Mike yelled again, so that Michael could hear him, but pretended to be talking to Caroline. "What's that Caroline? You have cheesecake? You picked it up on your way home?" Michael flew into the kitchen. "Did somebody say cheesecake?" Mike and Caroline started laughing. "You heard that didn't you?" Mike rubbed the top of Michael's head.

"Where's the cheesecake, Ms. Caroline?" "It's in the refrigerator.

I actually got it from the bakery next to my job to take to work for my boss's birthday tomorrow, but you are welcome to some. I can always stop by there tomorrow on my lunch break, since its only walking distance." "No, he doesn't need it, besides," Mike turned to Michael, "you need to let everything you just ate at the buffet digest. You just had a brownie, a piece of cake, and two servings of ice cream with gummy bears. You have school tomorrow, and you're not going to have me up all night, because you have a belly ache, or you're too hyped up to go to sleep."

"Well, young man, looks like your daddy has spoken," Caroline turned to Michael making a half smile. Michael went back into the entertainment room with a sad face. "Aw, you're no fun. Mike you only get to be a child once. Won't you let him have a piece of cheesecake? It's really no problem. I only got it because I heard that it was just as good as the Cheesecake Factory's. I was thinking about cutting it anyway to try out, just in case it isn't that good. It's not in my diet plan, but I can beat the guilt by telling myself that I had company over, and he wanted cheesecake, and it would be rude to say no. Besides, friends don't let friends eat cheesecake alone," Caroline smiled and winked at Mike. "Why diet when you are perfect the way that you are?"

"It's not easy keeping up with my shape," Caroline smiled, looking at Mike up and down as she passed him with a slight twist on her way into the living room to sit down. Caroline couldn't believe that she was flirting with Mike. Here she was, feeling like a school age girl with a crush around him one minute, and then she was flirting like a well-experienced woman the next. "Well, whatever you're doing, you do it very well. No disrespect, but you look good," Mike smiled, and this time, Caroline could have sworn she saw a sparkle in his teeth this time. There were a few seconds of awkward silence and then Caroline cleared her throat.

"So, are you sure that you don't want anything?" Caroline was trying to break the tension in the room. "A soda, some water, juice?" "No I'm good." Ok. Caroline was rubbing her palms on her pants, which were sweating, because she was so nervous. The timer on the oven went off, which meant the turkey wings were done. "Thank God." "I'm sorry," Mike said, thinking that Caroline had asked him something. "Oh no, I'm starving. I was just thanking God that dinner was all done," she lied. She was really happy that the timer broke the tension. "Are you sure that you don't want anything? It's just me, you know, but I have more than enough." Mike stood up and walked into the kitchen. "And why is that?" Caroline turned around, halfway startled, because she hadn't realized that Mike was standing behind her. "I'm sorry?"

Caroline reached into the cabinet to get a glass out to pour some sparkling cider. Mike chuckled, because she is so short, she could barely reach the top cabinet. "Let me help you with that," Mike reached into the cabinet and got a glass, like it was nothing. "You make it look so easy," Caroline smiled. "So, are you going to answer my question?"

"I'm sorry what was the question, again?" "Why isn't there a mister Caroline," Mike winked at Caroline and then picked up an apple out of the fruit basket on the counter and bit into it. Caroline walked quickly to the dining room and tried to think of the right answer, but Mike was fast on her heels. "Well, for one, I am very busy with my work, and I really don't have time to date," she lied. Mike took another bite out of the apple.

"You know, Caroline, you don't lie so well." Caroline stared at Mike with her mouth open. "For your information, that is not a lie sir, well maybe kind of, a little; ok it's a lie," Caroline sighed. "I'm really not completely sure." Caroline bowed her head and closed her eyes to say her grace.

Just as Caroline was beginning to pray, Mike interrupted with his version of grace. "Lord, we thank you for this food that we are about to receive for the nourishment of our bodies in Jesus name, Amen." Caroline opened her eyes and was getting ready to dig in when Mike continued. "And Lord, please help Caroline to relax and let her know that you have her back, and that I don't bite, except for this delicious granny smith apple that she has allowed me to have. And one more thing Lord, forgive Caroline for lying, especially since she isn't very good at it, in Jesus name, amen."

"That was cute," Caroline said as she bit into the fork full of greens topped with fresh tomatoes. "I'm that bad at it, huh?" "Yeah you suck pretty badly at lying. It's not one of your strong suits." "Well, I sure didn't get it from my mother, because she's a very successful lawyer who was a professional liar in and out of the court room, but that's another story.

Ten minutes later Mike decided to ask Caroline why she was really single but she wouldn't give a straight answer. "So, Mike, why don't you tell me your story?"

"I like how you're avoiding my question, but that's ok. What would you like to know?" "Anything really, I mean I really don't know much about you, except you were married, and you have the cutest and smooth talking little boy." "Yeah, he gets it from his father." Caroline laughed out loud as she drinks the last of her cider and went to place her dishes into the dish washer. "I'm pretty sure he does, but I'll be the judge of that," Caroline winked at Mike. "Oh and let's not forget the scare you gave me and Michael on the night that we met. Did you ever go to the doctor?" "Yes madam, I did. Thank you for your consideration, but that's something that I've been dealing with since I was in college, during my baseball days."

"Oh really, you played baseball? I would have never guessed. You look more like a football type," Caroline said slick eye balling Mike's sculptured arms and chest through his dress shirt. "Well, I haven't always been a big guy," Michael said, making his heavy chest full of muscle jump. Although Mike is a big guy, he is a muscle machine, who is fit from head to toe. "I used to be tall and lanky, but I gained a lot of weight after the accident, because I wasn't moving like I did." Caroline gave Mike an interested look that made him feel compelled to tell her more. Caroline washed her hands and fixed Mike and Michael a plate to take home, and then she put it into the refrigerator, along with the remainder of leftovers.

5

ike was standing inside the patio, admiring the sunset's beauty, overlooking the lake that seemed to make the clear waters glisten, like sparkling diamonds. "It's beautiful, isn't it?" Mike almost jumped out of his skin. Caroline had caught him off guard and stuck in a trance of nature's beauty. "I remember when Angel and I would go down by the lake near my parent's house and take a blanket and a bottle of wine, and we would eat sushi, one of her favorites, and watch the sunset and just enjoy each other's company." Caroline could see the heartbreak in Mike's eyes as he reminisced about Angel, even though it has been a year since their divorce. Caroline sympathized with Michael, because she had her run in with love before, and she knew that love may come easy, but it was hard to get over. Caroline tapped Mike with bottled water she'd brought for him, breaking his thoughts of the past. She then quickly shifted the subject to Mike's baseball days, trying to lighten the mood. Caroline also figured this would be a good opportunity to learn more about who Mike was, exactly. "So Mr. Babe Ruth, come sit down and tell me about your baseball days."

Caroline motioned her hand for Mike to sit down, as she sat down in her Cradle lounge chair and snuggled up with the pillows, waiting for Mike to tell his story. Mike sat down on the high back love seat and took a sip of water and sat the bottle on the coffee table. "Well, I've always loved baseball, since I was knee high. My father was a professional baseball player, so I learned the game at the age of two.

"While other toddlers were busy playing in the toilet, I was on a roll outside, learning how to make home runs. I got my first baseball and bat at the age two. It was plastic, of course. My parents still have pictures of me in the yard, trying to play baseball on my own. My mom said that I loved it so much that when my dad was away, I used to throw the ball up and swing at it, and sometimes, I'd actually hit it, and then I would take off and run from base to base with my little arms up, yelling look mom home run. By the time I was thirteen, I had won five trophies in two years, with two of them as most home runs in a season.

"So anyway, I got a full Baseball scholarship to go to college, and that's where I met Michael's mom, Angel." Caroline shifted in her seat and gave Mike a strange look. Mike read the look of shock on Caroline's face that Angel attended college. "Angel didn't attend the same college as I did, but I met her through a mutual friend." Caroline started making a snoring sound imitating sleep to let Mike know that was enough talk about Angel.

Mike started laughing. "Ok, back to baseball. To make a long story short, I was great at what I did and would do anything for the win, and with years of diving, sliding and crashing head first, I guess it all caught up with me. One day, during the college world series, I slid and my helmet flew off, head first I hit the plate and blacked out. When I woke up in the hospital, the doctor said that I'd suffered a head injury, and that I would never be able to play baseball again. I suffered from seizures a lot during the first few months after the accident, and my vision became blurred, but everyone said that the way blood came rushing out of my head, I should have been dead."

Caroline nodded her head, understanding where the scar on Mike's head and the seizure came from the day that she and Mike officially met. "It has been over a decade, and my doctor said that, because of the damage to my skull, it's a good possibility that I could be dealing with seizures for the rest of my life. I just try to stay stress free and sleep well, and that usually helps. I haven't had a seizure in over a year, thank God. Instead of baseball, now I spend my free time playing laser tag or watching the latest super hero movie with my little man, and you know what? I wouldn't change it for the world. I tell you what though, it's a good thing that my dad always told me to have a backup plan, especially in the sports industry, because anything can happen."

"And what was your backup plan?" Caroline smiled. "Well, after the accident, I was out of college and work for seven months, but I did go back and finish school and received my Bachelors in Marketing. I am now a Retail Executive Distributor for Beauregard." "That would explain those nice suits that you wear," Caroline blushed.

"Well, thank you. You know, I try," Mike smiled, while straightening his black silk tie that matched perfectly with the onyx cuff links he was wearing. "Things haven't always been as good as they are for me. I would say in the last eighteen months, my life has made a total turnaround from where I was when you and I first met. During that time of my life, I had just gotten laid off at a distribution warehouse that I'd worked at for ten years, due to many of the stores closing. I was distribution manager, at that time, but I kept a good rapport with my manager and other top executives who would visit our facility, and one day, I got a call from Beauregard, saying that I was recommended for the position." "Wow, that is absolutely amazing. Somebody was looking out for you." "Yes, and I know exactly who he is," Mike pointed up. "I owe everything to him, because a lot of things that I've been through many people don't recover from or they just give up on life, but I've kept pushing and praying, and thanks to God, I am where I am now." Caroline was curious as to why Angel could let such a handsome, family oriented, and career focused man go. "She has to be crazy," Caroline blurted out before realizing she had spoken her thoughts out loud. "I mean that is crazy," Caroline cleared her throat, trying to change the subject.

Mike was on to Caroline. "Yes, she is pretty crazy, but I knew what I was getting into when I first met her. I guess that I was so infatuated with her beauty that I couldn't see past the gold digging. I started having money problems, and then came the marriage problems, and the ugly truth came out on both of our ends. The truth of the matter is, we were married ten years on paper, but our marriage ended a long time ago.

"I was young and naive when I met Angel, and my friends tried to warn me not to fall in love with her, because she was a so called fun girl. I played baseball well, and everyone knew who my father was, so I was popular with the ladies. Actually, I was a little player back in my high school and college days, but I guess it's always that one that makes you want to change your ways. You know, as men, we may think that we have game, but women invented the game." Caroline raised her eyebrows, "No, I think that any game we have, we learned it from men.

It's just that y'all can dish it out, but y'all can't take it like we can." "Oh no, I'm going to have to disagree with you on this one, Caroline," Mike stood up and walked towards the glass windows, where the African violets hang on the shelf above the Purple Calla Lilly. "See it all started in the Garden of Eden. You see, Eve is the creator of the game. You know how, you ladies, like to buy that little black dress that fit just right or wear those jeans that fit like skin that just makes a brother want to," Mike sealed his lips, but slapped his hand in the air one time, as if he was giving someone one good smack on the behind. "But no, Eve didn't do that. She went all out.

"She went to the crystal clear lake, and I can just hear her- oh I'm going to get him to try this fruit tonight; he's not going to be able to resist me, honey," Mike said in a girly voice. "She took a bath in the lake and got all clean, because before, she didn't care about being dirty. She used to roll around in the dirt with Adam and have mud fights and everything, but no, she had other things planned. She switched up on him and when he saw her hair blowing in the wind, and she was all oiled up from the olive tree and put a little strawberry on her lips, so that they were red. Then, she bit into the fruit all seductively and used her pointer finger to tell Adam to come here. He knew it was wrong, but she was looking so good and whispering sweet nothings in his ear, and he just fell for it."

Caroline was cracking up with the Mike version of what happened in the Garden of Eden. "You are something else. Anyway, it did not go down like that." Just then, Michael came to the patio. "Can I have a piece of cheesecake now?" "Sure baby, I could use a piece of cheesecake to go along with your father's hilarious entertainment." Caroline got up and rubbed the top of Michael's head as she headed to the kitchen with Michael fast on her steps. "Hey, save a piece for me," Mike said, before answering his ringing cell. "Sorry, every man for himself, Dad," Michael smiled as he continued to joyfully hurry to the kitchen. Mike headed to the kitchen after talking on the phone a couple of minutes. Caroline had cut Mike a piece of cheesecake, and sat it at the table with her and Michael.

"Oh this looks good," Mike said as he sat down at the dining table, rubbing his hands together. Michael had already finished his piece and was ready for another. "Dad, Ms. Caroline said that we can take the rest of the cheesecake home. You know how grandma loves cheesecake."

"Yes I do, she loves it almost as much as you," Mike said as he grabbed his fork and dug in. "By the way, your mom called and said that she dropped your shoes off at home, so we will have to leave in a bit."

"Aw man, can we stay just a little longer?" "No you have school tomorrow."

"Well, can I watch cartoons until you finish eating?" Mike shook his head, "Sure son, go ahead, but remember what I said." "Yes sir, I already know to clean up if I mess up anything."

Mike winked his eye at Caroline, "Good job son, now go ahead." "He is the cutest little boy," Caroline said, smiling at Michael. "Thank you, and he might be a little boy, but he eats like a grown man. I'm still trying to figure out where he puts it all." "Oh he's going to be tall like his father, that's all."

Caroline got up and took her plate to the kitchen and came back to the dining room table to sit with Mike. "You know; chocolate is my guilty pleasure. Sometimes, I'll drive to this little café not too far from my office and order a cup of Joe and a slice of rocky road chocolate mousse um um um," Mike said as he finished the cookies and cream cheesecake. "I can take that for you," Caroline reached for the plate and took it to the kitchen then she handed Mike dinner and the leftover cheesecake to take with him. "Here you go. I know it's getting late." "Are you trying to put me out, Ms. Caroline?" "Of course not. I've enjoying the company, but I know that Michael has school in the a.m., and I need my rest as well, because Monday mornings at the station can be hectic." Mike remembered that Caroline had told him that she worked for GPSG the night she drove him to his parent's. "Oh, I can definitely understand that," Mike said as he picked up the bags of food.

"So, about what I was asking you earlier." "I'm sorry?" Caroline was trying to avoid the question about why she was single by pretending that she didn't know what Mike was talking about. "No one is alone because they want to be alone. Everybody needs somebody, sometimes, for whatever the reason may be," he said staring down into Caroline's eyes.

"So I was wondering." Oh goodness, Caroline thought, I think he's about to ask me out. What do I do? What do I say?

"Mike, I don't think so," Caroline blurted out before Mike could finish his question.

"Well, I just thought, since Michael likes you so much, and I'm pretty confident that you won't try to run off with him that you would look out for him, while I am out of town on business next week. I just talked to his mom, and she's going to watch him for the week, but it would help to have someone that I can trust just to keep an extra pair of eyes on him. If it's too much for you to handle, don't worry about it." "No, I'm sorry," Caroline said scratching her head and thinking about how stupid she sounded, but also wondering why Michael's grandparents couldn't watch him. "Of course, I will keep an extra eye out for him. Don't be silly."

"Are you sure?" "Of course," Caroline smiled. "Great, my parents are going on a cruise that week to celebrate their fortieth wedding anniversary, and I didn't want to disrupt their plans, because they would have a fit if they knew that I was allowing Angel to keep him for a week. I would take him with me, but he'd miss school, and I would need a nanny, because I will be working long hours, and it will be too much. Can I give you my number, just in case you need to reach me?" "Sure," Caroline handed Mike her cell.

"You can put your number in my cell. I'm going to get Michael and let him know that you're ready," Caroline hurried off, still feeling silly about thinking that Mike was going to ask her out. "Michael, your dad is all set and ready to go." Caroline had to gently shake Michael a few times to wake him, because he'd dozed off and fell asleep that fast. Caroline turned off the TV and helped Michael up, because he was still trying to shake off his sleep. "Hey lil man, I see that you fell asleep and on time, for a change, during a school night."

It was a little after ten p.m. when the guys left, but not before thanking Caroline for her hospitality, and she returned the thanks for their company. Caroline smiled as she waved them off, and all of a sudden, her phone vibrated. "Now who could this be?" Caroline thought maybe it was Tangie, but it wasn't. Caroline opened her text message, and the name in her in box was one for the reason with a question mark in the message box.

The next day, Caroline was swamped at work, but still managed to go and pick up another cheesecake that was already paid for by an anonymous person. Caroline smiled, because she already knew that it had to be Mike. The surprise office party for Caroline's boss was a success. After work, everyone gathered in the conference room, and the catering company that was hired by the top executives served cocktail style foods, and there was an open bar as well. Caroline couldn't take her mind off Mike and how sweet that was of him to replace the cheesecake that he and Michael had taken home the night before.

Caroline decided to text Mike a simple thank you, and a few seconds later, his reply was a simple, you're welcome. "I enjoyed doing it. It was my pleasure," another text message said in Caroline's cell.

"You really didn't have to, but thank you so much for buying the cheesecake. My boss is taking it home to share with his wife and kids," she replied. "Cheesecake?"

6

Caroline was confused. If Mike didn't buy the cheesecake, who had? Caroline decided to call and see if there had been a mistake and to see who this mystery person was. The hostess said that it was an employee. Caroline thought that it was weird that one of the employees knew that she was coming to buy another cheesecake and insisted on paying the employee.

Caroline went by the restaurant on the way home from the office party, and when the hostess went to get the employee, who had paid for Caroline's cheesecake, she couldn't believe her eyes when she saw who it was. It had been seventeen years, since she'd seen his face, but he looked the same as he did when they were teenagers, tall, dark, and handsome. Only, he'd grown dreads, and he wore a beard guard to cover his goatee.

"Stacy, hi, how are you? I can't believe it's you. What are you doing here? It's been what seventeen eighteen years?" "Actually, it's been seventeen years two months, fifteen days, three hours and," he took his cell out of his pocket and checked the time, "thirty-eight minutes." "How long have you been back? I mean, it's been a long time. How's Mrs. Annie doing?"

Stacy smiled down on Caroline affectionately and put a strand of her hair behind her ear. "How about we catch up over dinner, because right now, I'm needed in the kitchen," he said, pointing with his head to his manager, who was staring at him in the door way of the kitchen. "But how will..." "Shhh," Stacy said interrupting Caroline mid-sentence and placing his finger over Caroline's mouth. "You know where to find me now," and with that said, he winked at her and went back into the kitchen.

Caroline was in a daze after seeing Stacy. She bumped against people on the way out, because her mind was taken back to her teenage years, when she and Stacy were in love. Caroline met Stacy when his mother, Ms. Annie, was her nanny. Caroline grew up in Buckhead, the upper class area of Atlanta, and Ms. Annie was from Bankhead, an area known for its projects, street hustlers, and most famous rappers. Caroline's parents hired Ms. Annie, when Caroline was only two weeks old, to look after her and cook and clean their home, because they were very busy people.

Stacy is a year older than Caroline, but they quickly became best friends from toddlers to teens. Stacy was Caroline's first everything, first friend, first love, and the first to make love to her. When Stacy was about sixteen, Caroline's mother started to see them becoming a little too close for her comfort, so she told Ms. Annie that he was no longer welcome to her home.

Ms. Annie continued to work for Caroline's family for another two years, in which time she knew that Caroline was secretly seeing Stacy.

Stacy and Caroline's relationship was only dating the first year, but on her seventeenth birthday, Caroline decided to give in to her raging desires and make Stacy her first.

On the drive home, Caroline thought about how she would disguise herself and ride the bus and train to Stacy's side of town. On a few occasions, Ms. Annie would tell her that she had to stop seeing Stacy, because the money that she made from Caroline's parents was all she had, and she couldn't afford to lose her job. Ms. Annie became pregnant with Stacy in her late forties, during the time when she'd just sent her oldest son off to college and wasn't expecting any more children. As Caroline pulled into her driveway, she could still hear Ms. Annie telling her, "Honey, nobody's going to hire a woman at the age of sixty-six or pay me good money like what I make from your mama and daddy. You have got to stop coming over here, before I lose my job, and you lose your life, because that's what's going to happen if your parents find out that you are coming over here almost every day." "Ma Ann," the affectionate name Caroline called Ms. Annie, who was more like a second mom to her.

"Don't worry. I won't get caught. Besides, my parents work so much, they don't know if I'm going or coming." "You are still their child, and I just don't feel right about you being over here. Now, I know that you and Stacy think you are in love, but you both are young, and you both have a bright future ahead of you.

"You have your whole life to be grown, and when you get grown, you'll see it's not all it's cracked up to be, either. Y'all are in puppy love. That's all that is now. Stacy's father and I was in love up until the day that he died." Ms. Annie would tell Caroline the story of how Stacy was her blessing in the storm, because she'd lost her husband to heart disease five months before realizing she was pregnant. "God took my husband, but he gave me life, as well, when he blessed me with Stacy.

He blessed me with a son during a time that I thought that my child bearing days were over, just to show me that he can do anything."

That night, as Caroline lay in the bed, she thought of Stacy and the vivid thoughts left her tossing and turning all night. The next day, Caroline was restless. Normally, she wasn't a coffee drinker, but she found herself stopping by the café near her job to grab a cup of Joe. It was a medium crowd, coming to get their dose of caffeine before starting their work day. The manager was out on the floor, today, assisting customers.

Caroline remembered her from last night and the way she was eye balling Stacy, as in he needed to get back to work. The manager of the café is a tall, slender woman, with bedroom type hair that looked as if she could be a Victoria Secret model. "And here you are, Caroline, small mocha latte," the beautiful manager said in her slight Spanish accent as she turned on her heels and sashayed back to the beverage station to help assist customers. Caroline admired her for working in heels all day. Two years ago, Caroline couldn't stand in even a two-inch heel for more than two minutes, but Tangie had her trained well now, and she could run in heels if need be.

As Caroline left the café, she wondered if Stacy was working, or if he worked the later shift. She thought that it was odd that he didn't bother giving her his phone number, but then again, she thought maybe he didn't give her his number, because he was busy working. The thought of Stacy gave Caroline some hope about her love life, which for most of her life, had been pretty boring. At work, Caroline was smiling more than usual, and a few times, her manager caught her in a daze. Even the two supermodel rejects that are part of the hair and makeup team couldn't get under Caroline's skin, today, with their whispering and smart remarks about Caroline's messy hair bun.

During the week that Mike was out of town, he and Caroline talked every night. To Caroline's surprise, Angel was at home with Michael, and when she wasn't, she'd already asked Caroline if she'd mind watching him. Caroline thought Angel had made a total turnaround from two years ago. The judge had declared Angel unfit, due to negligence, based on evidence from neighbors. Maybe Angel had learned from her mistakes, but one thing was for sure; she did love Michael and was trying to make up for her mistakes.

On several nights, Michael asked Caroline if he could stay at her house, because he didn't want to go over his mom's house. "I don't really know her like that, Ms. Caroline," he plopped down on the living room couch and sat his book bag on the floor beside him. "What do you mean you don't know her? She's your mom. You've lived with her and your father most of your life. How can you not know her?"

"You can live with a person your whole life, Ms. Caroline, and not know who they are." Michael's comment shook Caroline to her core. Here she was, talking to an eleven-year-old about reconciling with his mom, and she hadn't had a decent relationship with her own mother. Caroline knew exactly how Michael felt, but decided to point out the good in Angel. "No one is perfect Michael. Angel has made a lot of mistakes, but who hasn't. You have to learn to forgive and move on, or the pain and hurt can turn into anger, and it will haunt you for the rest of your life." "I do forgive her, and I love my mama. I just don't know her like that, and it feels awkward when she tries to watch TV with me or play the game." "Give her a chance, Michael. She does love you. I can tell how she smiles when she comes to pick you up or how she hugs and kisses you on the cheek." "Yuck, that's another thing that I have to talk to my mama about, because she did that in front of my friends at school, and they were calling me a baby and a mama's boy. "It don't help with the ladies either, if you know what I mean." Caroline laughed, "Michael, you are a trip. Besides, you don't need to worry about impressing anyone at your age. You have more important things to worry about, like finishing up that home work," Caroline motioned her head towards Michael's back pack. "See now, you're sounding like her. I think she's rubbing off on you, Ms. Caroline." "Your mom isn't a bad person. She was just going through a bad point in her life; give her a chance."

Give her a chance was echoing in Caroline's head so much that she didn't hear Angel ringing the doorbell. "Ms. Caroline, are you going to open the door?" "Oh yes," Caroline hurried to the door. "Hi Angel. I'm sorry I didn't hear the doorbell. Were you out here long?" "No maybe a minute, but not too long. Hey, my little man," Angel ran to Michael, careful not to fall in her heels with her arms open wide. Angel gave Michael a big hug and kissed him on his left cheek and got red lipstick on his face. Michael eye balled Caroline, and Caroline smiled and winked at him. "Caroline, thanks so much for helping me out this week. Is there anything that I can do for you?"

"No way girl, don't be silly," Caroline said, helping Michael put on his backpack. "It was my pleasure." "Well, I feel like I owe you, so lunch on me this weekend, and you can't say no." "I'm sorry, Angel, but I have plans this weekend," Caroline had made plans for lunch with Mike and was still uneasy about being buddies with Angel, although it did seem as if she'd changed. "Are you sure?" "Absolutely," Caroline smiled.

"Okay, well see you later and thanks again." Caroline waved Michael and Angel off as they walked out of her driveway and a few feet down the street, next door to Angel's house. It is funny how God speaks through people. Here, Caroline was thinking that she was helping

Michael reconcile his relationship with his mother, when all along, God was speaking through her about what she had avoided her whole life. Caroline decided to make that call that she had been on the fence about for years.

"Hi Daddy," Caroline said as she went outside to watch the stars that seemed as if they were within hands' reach at night. Caroline loved how the moonlight hit the lake and made it sparkle.

She'd hoped tonight would go as beautiful as her surroundings. "Hey Caroline, baby, how are you? Your mother and I were just talking about you. I was looking at some of these baby pictures in the photo album."

"My my my where does the time go?" Caroline thought she could answer her Dad's question really quick with sarcasm, but she opted not to. After all, tonight was her night to be the bigger person and forgive and forget. "So, what do I owe the pleasure of this phone call, baby girl?

Is everything alright, do you need anything?"

"I don't need anything, Dad, but I would like to speak with mother." "Just a minute, baby girl." There was a brief silence before Caroline's dad returned to the phone. "Baby, your mother is getting ready for the American Lawyer Awards. She's going to be receiving the Lifetime achievement award tonight. Isn't that great," Caroline's father said with enthusiasm. "Yes, that's great Dad, but this can't wait. Can you tell her that it will only take a minute of her time?

"I promise to let her get back to what has always been her first priority in life." There was a brief silence, and Caroline's father returned to the phone. "Baby she'll give you a call back on the way to the show tonight." "What, I can't believe her. Dad, I mean come on? She asked you to take a message, like I am a client of hers? No, not even a client. She will give them even more attention than her own daughter. You know what, Dad, never mind. I don't even know why I called." "Honey, wait a minute I'm here. What is it? Talk to me." Caroline's father pleaded with her, but all he could hear was a click and then silence. Caroline's father tried to call her back, but Caroline was busy, crying her eyes out. "God I am really trying to do the right thing here, but she makes it so hard. I just want her to be my mom and listen for a change."

Caroline curled up in an infant position, hugging her pillow tight as she cried herself to sleep. The week flew by, and Caroline was ready for the weekend. Caroline had plans for lunch with Mike and was looking forward to the date. She didn't officially call it a date, but Mike wanted to thank Caroline for keeping an extra eye on Michael while he was away. Caroline happily obliged, although she turned down Angel's lunch offer.

Caroline started her day off early, with a six a.m. salon appointment to get her naturally curly hair straightened. After three hours at the salon, she decided to go get a French manicure and pedicure. Caroline had numerous clothes and shoes in her walk-in closet that was the size of a small room. She'd really missed Tangie and her eye for flair and style. Over the course of their friendship, Tangie had helped Caroline upgrade her wardrobe from fashion geek to classy chic.

Caroline decided to wear a purple floral print maxi dress and black leather lace up heels that added five inches to her height. Caroline added light mascara to her naturally long lashes and a natural shade of lip gloss, and she was on her merry way. Caroline and Mike met up downtown Atlanta at an upscale fusion café that was famous for its Asian and Mediterranean cuisine. After lunch, they decided to catch a movie at Atlantic Station and then a carriage ride in late afternoon. They both were really enjoying each other's company, and although Caroline had only planned for a nice lunch outing with a friend, it had turned into a romantic and memorable first date.

Neither Mike nor Caroline wanted the date to end, so by evening, they found themselves walking through the park, talking about their dreams, goals, family, and even making a few jokes with each other.

Caroline was proud that she'd mastered the art of walking in heels and all day, for that matter. "I love your hair this way. Why don't you ever wear it down?" Mike stroked Caroline's hair back into place, as a breeze blew it and left a single strand on her lip, which he gently removed and looked deeply into her eyes, while cupping her face with his right hand, and he gave her a soft kiss.

Caroline blushed, and they held hands and continued walking through the park. It was a little after seven when they parted ways, and

Caroline promised to give Mike a call to let him know that she made it home safely. That night, Caroline and Mike talked on the phone from ten at night until four in the morning. "I really enjoyed myself, Mike. Thanks again for a wonderful date." "Oh so it was a date?" Mike was smiling from ear to ear on the other end of the phone.

"Yes, it was and a much needed one at that. I haven't had that much fun in a long time, so thank you." "You're very welcome. I told you that you would enjoy yourself. You just have to loosen up and don't be afraid to take a chance once in a while."

When Monday rolled around, Caroline was busy as usual. One of Caroline's tasks for the day was to meet with her boss and committee chairs to discuss the company's summer fund raising campaign. When the COO stuck his head in Caroline's office door to say good morning, he didn't recognize her at first. "Hello, where's Caroline?" Caroline had her back turned towards him as she filed paperwork in the filing cabinet.

"Good morning, sir," Caroline closed the file cabinet drawer and smiled. "Well, well, well, Caroline is that you in there?" Her boss was being sarcastic, but very much impressed by Caroline's long silky tresses, her knee length skirt suit, and three inch heels. Caroline smiled and said, "Yes, sir, it's me, the new and improved version. Come on in and have a seat. I need to brief you on the fund raising campaign."

Caroline had been working on the fund raising campaign for four months, and the summer campaign was now two months away. Caroline briefed her boss on investors, potential investors, and their background, as well as the location, volunteers, themes, caterers, and budgets. "As always, good job Caroline, but we still need one more investor, just in case someone decides to back out." "I am on it, sir, and I'm waiting to hear back from them as we speak. I should have an answer before our meeting this morning."

"Ok, sounds good. See you in a few. Oh and I like this new you, but don't change too much. I like the old Caroline just as much," Caroline's boss winked and closed the door behind him as he left. Caroline smiled and nodded her head, "Yes sir." Just as Caroline was about to take a seat at her desk, a delivery guy from the local florist arrived with eleven red roses and a single purple rose. After Caroline signed for the flowers, she read the note card, and it said I've missed you. I need to see you. Come to the café after you get off work. —Stacy.

Caroline's heart fluttered as she smiled a big Kool-Aid smile. "Oh my, did I come at a bad time?" One of the makeup assistants said as she peeked in Caroline's office door. Caroline wanted to tell the Victoria Secret reject that her secret was out, seeing that her double D's were spilling out of her blouse, but the roses had brightened Caroline's day. "What can I help you with Ru Paul, I mean, Raul, I'm sorry, Ramona," Caroline said, squinting her eyes pretending to make out the lady's name on her badge although she knows who the lady is. Caroline placed the vase of roses on her desk.

"Yeah you may have jokes, but just remember that I'm in charge of your makeup today for the fund raiser at the art gallery." "The fund raiser may be at noon, but you're not doing my makeup. I have my own makeup team, stank you very much," Caroline said, fanning her nose from the loud perfume Ramona was wearing and thinking to herself that if need be, she'd phone Niq before letting Ramona lay a finger on her face. "Well, I was told that I am in charge of makeup for the executive team today, so if you have an issue, I suggest you speak with the COO." Just as Ramona finished speaking, her Supermodel friend from the makeup team informed her that she no longer needed to do Caroline's hair and makeup.

Ramona rolled her eyes and twisted her narrow behind out of Caroline's office. "I guess he really does like the new look." For the past two years that Ramona has been in charge of hair and makeup, Caroline avoided the camera. Her worst nightmare is getting on TV, looking like something out of a horror movie. After waiting, but still no answer from the potential investor, Caroline had to leave her office and head to the conference room for the meeting.

7

The meeting was a success, even with the potential investor still in limbo about whether he would invest in GPSG. The Art Gallery fundraiser was also a success, putting GPSG exactly where they needed to be, budget wise, to kick off the big summer fundraising campaign.

"Caroline, great job putting all of this together. I am still counting on you to use your charm to help persuade Mr. Lavado to come on over. We need his money. I mean, if he decides to invest in GPSG, then we wouldn't have to worry about having one fundraiser to cover the next fundraiser. We receive enough donations to keep GPSG on air and to cover salaries and expenses, but it's time to take GPSG to another level.

We are talking about expanding beyond Georgia into South Carolina, North Carolina, and Florida. We are well on our way. We just need to persuade Lavado, and that will give us the funds we need at least to start to expand in Florida." Caroline had confidence that she could persuade Mr. Lavado. It was only a matter of time. "Oh, and by the way," Caroline's boss said as he sipped from his glass of Merlot. "Let me introduce you to the man who has raised most of the money to help support GPSG this evening." Caroline's boss walked towards the man, who was busy signing autographs and talking to other business colleagues and executives. He had long dreads tied in the back, and he wore a navy blue suit that was tailor made with Gucci loafers. When he turned to the side and smiled, Caroline couldn't believe her eyes.

Caroline hurried and took a sip of the bottled water in her hand, and she almost choked when Stacy extended his hand and said, "Nice to meet you, Caroline." "Caroline, you and SAG will be working closely together for the next few months, because we are thinking about having another art fundraiser at the Atlanta Art Museum this fall, which is where SAG will be showcasing his art work. He has agreed to donate twenty percent of all proceeds to GPSG. Isn't that great?" Caroline's boss said with enthusiasm as he patted Stacy on the back and took another sip of Merlot. "Yes, I will be," Stacy said, nodding at Caroline's boss, "but please, call me Stacy. All my friends call me by my first name." "Well, Stacy, welcome aboard GPSG. Caroline will be in touch with you, so that we can get going on our fall fundraiser."

"Yes, excuse us for a minute. Sir, may I have a brief word with you?" Caroline motioned for her boss to come speak with her. After Caroline's boss excused himself from Stacy and other executives, he came over. "Nice fella, huh," Caroline's boss said as he turned and looked at Stacy and held his glass of wine towards him before turning back to face Caroline. "Yes, I'm sure that he is, but sir, we already have the Walk the Runway fundraiser scheduled this fall for our Back to School campaign, remember.

"I have many volunteers, boutique owners, and department stores that have agreed to allow the models to use their merchandise. Remember, this is usually one of the ways that we rake in hundreds of thousands of dollars?" "Yes, I remember, and that's why we're going to continue with the Walk the Runway this fall, but we are also doing an Art Gallery fundraiser. Caroline, I need your assistance with this, because if anybody can pull this off, then it is you." Caroline was starting to feel like more than an executive secretary and more like Mr.

Taylor's personal assistant.

Caroline felt as if she needed an assistant to assist her. There wasn't any money in the budget to get Caroline an assistant, and she knew that. She would just have to buckle down and make it work, like always. Besides, she loved what she did, because it was always exciting, and she always dreamed of being a part of making a difference in people's lives and being in the television industry. At times, when Caroline would get frustrated with work overload, she remembered the thousands of kids throughout Georgia that GPSG was helping to read, write, learn basic math skills, and core values with educational programs that were broadcast on their station.

"Caroline, I know that it seems like a lot, but I am here to assist you with anything that you need, and trust me that it will all pay off in the end." Mr. Taylor was starting to sound like it was all about money. Caroline understood that money was a major factor, but it seemed like that was all Mr. Taylor was focused on lately. Maybe, she was just frustrated with the work overload. "Yes, sir well,"

Caroline paused for a moment and thought it over, "We will get right on the Art project then."

"That's my girl," Mr. Taylor gently patted Caroline on the back, and they walked back towards Stacy, who was, again, conversing with fans and investors, who loved his art work. Caroline gave Stacy her card and told him to give her a call tomorrow, so that they could start on the fundraiser. Caroline excused herself and headed home, because this was now three projects that she needed to work, all while working on potential investors and doing payroll, along with the gazillion other things that she had to do. As Caroline was getting ready to pull out of the parking lot, her phone buzzed, and it was a text from Stacy, asking her if they were still on to meet up at the café tonight. "Sure, meet you there in a few," she texted back and then pulled out of the driveway to head to A la mode café.

The café had a medium crowd, and Caroline was seated quickly as she browsed the menu of a la carte items that were a fusion of American and Cuban cuisine. There were also numerous desserts that were all served a la mode with ice cream that the chefs made in-house. Everything on the menu was fresh and made in the kitchen. Caroline heard people, dining near her, talking about how good the food was and how the desserts were even better. The manager was walking around, asking how everything was and getting customer feedback.

After about ten minutes, Caroline was starting to wonder where Stacy was, so she decided to send him an I'm waiting text. Stacy immediately replied and said that he was parking, and he would be inside shortly. A supervisor of A la mode came in and apologized to the manager for being late. The manager told her that it was ok and asked the supervisor if everything was alright. After a couple of minutes, the manager looked at her phone and said goodnight to her employees and left.

The supervisor noticed Caroline sitting at the table with no food or drink and asked her if a waiter had been by to take her order. Caroline said yes, but she was waiting on someone. "How does she do it?" Caroline's remark caught the supervisor off guard as she was getting ready to head to the kitchen. "Your manager," Caroline nodded her head towards the front door that the manager had just exited.

"Every time I see her, she's here, and she has on heels all day, and her hair and makeup is always on point. I see her working just as hard, if not harder, than some people here, but she doesn't break a sweat. How does she stay so intact?" Caroline looked up at the supervisor as she smiled and nodded. "Well, she does more than a lot of restaurant owners that I've worked for." "Owner?"

"Yes, she's the owner and manager of the restaurant. She started off small, but as word of mouth traveled, business picked up. Not to mention that her parents know people, being that they are two of the wealthiest people in Atlanta. She really doesn't have to work a day in her life, but she loves what she does, and it shows. I guess, when you love what you do for a living, you can walk around with that certain glow that draws people to you. I know, if my father owned several banks through Georgia, I wouldn't work if I didn't have to, but she said cooking is her passion, and she loves people, so here she is." Caroline nodded her head, understanding and respecting that the café owner would rather do something that she loved than have everything handed to her. Caroline was the same way. Her mother and father are wealthy, as well, but she decided to pursue her dream rather than to have money handed to her without earning it.

"If Mr. Lavado was my father, I can't say that I'd be working at a café."

"Wait, did you say that Mr. Lavado is her father? The Mr. Lavado?" "Yes, he and Mrs. Lavado comes here to dine with their daughter every now and then and don't say anything, but they are thinking about opening several other A la mode cafés throughout the Atlanta area." "Wow that is amazing," Caroline said, while gathering her thoughts on how she could possibly get in good with the café owner through Stacy and possibly get Mr. Lavado to invest in GPSG.

"Anyway, you didn't hear this from me," the waiter smiled and winked at Caroline, and Caroline nodded ok.

Stacy, finally, made it inside, after keeping Caroline waiting another ten minutes after their text. Caroline wasn't bothered by the time, though, because she was working out a plan on how to get in good with the Lavado's. During dinner, Stacy and Caroline caught each other up on their lives over the past seventeen years. They picked up without a beat, just like it had been only a few hours since they'd seen each other. They laughed and joked and sat at the table a couple of hours, until the café closed.

As they left, a few of Stacy's coworkers waved goodbye and congratulated him on his new job at the Art Museum. Caroline was so full, she told Stacy that she had to walk off some of those calories before heading home, so they agreed to walk to the park nearby and walk the trail. "So, your art work brought you back to Atlanta, huh?" Caroline said looking up at Stacy. "Yes and no," Stacy said, ready to give Caroline the answer that she was looking for.

"Ok, you can't have a yes and no answer, so which one is it?" Caroline waited for Stacy's answer as they slowly paced the trail. "Well, I could have stayed at the Art Gallery in DC, but I decided to come here, because I was offered more money, and I feel like I have a better opportunity to expand as an artist here, and not to mention, I have unfinished business to take care of. "Unfinished business?" Caroline looked at Stacy confusingly.

They both stopped walking, and Stacy grabbed Caroline's hands.

"Caroline, I can't lie. I have loved you since we were kids, and leaving like that, without getting to tell you just how much I loved you or without telling you goodbye, must have been one of the hardest things that I've ever done in my life. I hated that me and ma had to leave like that. I love you, Caroline. I've always loved you, and I have been trying to find you forever, it seems. So, when I saw you the first time, I panicked, because I couldn't believe it was you, but then, my suspicion was confirmed when I read your name and your business address on the receipt for the cheesecake." "So the cheesecake gave me away, huh?" "Well, you have always loved cheesecake." "I was wondering how you knew where I worked. You've been stalking me?

That's kind of creepy, but yet, I'm turned on at the same time." "I've missed you, Caroline," Stacy kissed Caroline lips and she returned the favor. Each stroke of their tongue met with more passion than the stroke before. "I've missed you too, Stacy. I love you so much," Caroline said between the kisses. Stacy's phone rang, and he held up his pointer finger and told Caroline to hold on. It was his job calling. After a few seconds, Stacy said that he had to leave, but not before apologizing and stealing more kisses from Caroline as they walked back to their cars from the park. "This supervisor is always late or forgetting something, so she called me to use my keys to lock up, because she couldn't get in touch with Amanda." When Stacy said Amanda, Lavado popped back into her mind, and she decided to try to get more info about her from Stacy.

"So, are you going to continue to work at the cafe?" "Yes, at least, until my work at the museum takes off. I don't see a point in leaving yet; besides, the café money is what's paying the bills, right now. I have talked to Amanda, though, and she supports me one hundred percent, although she is going to hate losing her head cook. She loves art, though, so I promised that when my career takes off at the art gallery, I would make sure that she had tickets to every event."

Oh, she likes art, does she? Caroline pondered in her head. This may be easier than I thought. "So, what do you think about Amanda catering the Art Fundraiser this fall? I'm thinking something upscale and elegant. It would be a great opportunity for more exposure to the café, and she gets a firsthand look at some of your art work. Hey, she might even decide to buy a piece or two, or she may even decide to bring her parents and that could be very profitable." Caroline tilted her head to the side, "What do you think?" Stacy smiled, "You just might be on to something. I will call you in the morning, and we can discuss this further." Stacy kissed Caroline goodnight as she got into her car and left, and Stacy went into the restaurant to close and lock up. Caroline couldn't believe that everything was all coming together and maybe quicker than she thought.

The Lavado deal was in motion, and Stacy was back in Caroline's life, and the best part about all of this was that they get to work together. On the way home, Caroline's cell rang, and it was Tangie. She sounded hysterical and asked Caroline if she could come over immediately. "No problem, sweetie. I will be right there," Caroline said as she made a U turn to get onto I-85 to head to Tangie's house. There was a lot of noise in the background, like glass was being broken and heavy objects hitting the floor, while Tangie screamed, "I hate you, I hate you," in the background.

8

Caroline pulled up to Tangie's house, so fast, you could hear and smell the rubber burn from screeching the pavement. Caroline hurried out of her car and ran into the house. Carmen was in her wheelchair, watching TV, and shaking her head. "Hey Auntie Caroline, Mama's on the back porch, barbecuing. Caroline hurried to the back porch to see what was going on, and Tangie was barbecuing all of her boyfriend's clothes and shoes.

It smelled awful outside, like charcoal and leather rubber and way too much lighter fluid. "Tangie, what on earth? What is going on? What are you doing?" Tangie didn't say anything; she was too busy piling a closet full of True Religion, Gucci, and other clothes into the grill. Caroline grabbed Tangie's arm, trying to get Tangie to talk to her.

"Tangie, what is going on? Did he hit you? Talk to me." "No, I wish he would have so that they could lock his good for nothing ass up. I should go to the cops on his trifling ass and tell them about all the dope."

"Dope what dope? Was he selling drugs out of your house, Tangie?" "No he isn't that stupid. He played a good game for a minute, and he had me thinking that he worked overnight at a warehouse. He wasn't working at a warehouse. He was working at a trap house. I should have known, though," Tangie shook her head. "The jokes on me, Caroline. I should have been kicked him out when he wasn't there for me or Carmen after the accident. He always had to work," Tangie held up quotation mark signs as she said work. "I thought that he was just having a hard time coping with seeing me sad every day or he couldn't handle seeing Carmen the way that she is. I made up every single excuse in the book to make it work with him, and come to find out, this sorry excuse of a man is married." "What?"

Caroline took a step back with an expression of disbelief on her face. "Are you serious, Tangie?" "As a heart attack, Caroline, and that's not all. The wife is pregnant with their fifth child." "What," Caroline said again, not believing how trifling this dude was.

"Oh, but that's not it either. Just wait until you hear about the icing that tops the cake. He has another baby on the way." Caroline could have died. "What?" Caroline yelled this time.

Caroline began to help Tangie burn the rest of this trifling dude's clothes. They both ran into the room to get the rest of his clothes and went back outside and kept piling clothes on the grill, until there was no more room left on the grill. The grill was so full of clothes that it couldn't close, and this was a pretty big grill. Between Tangie and Caroline running back and forth with clothes and the serious look on Caroline's face as she tossed the clothes onto the grill, Tangie began to laugh. Tears were still falling from her eyes, but the sad had turned into laughter. "What?" "Caroline, you are funny, honey," Tangie let out another laugh. Tangie sat on her lounge chair on the porch to catch her breath from running back and forth, and Caroline took a seat in a chair beside her.

"Girl, you should have seen the look on your face as you were running back and forth with those clothes. You were serious." "Yeah, well, he deserved this and a lot worse," Caroline said as she leaned back into the chair and watched the clothes burn.

After a few minutes, Tangie started to speak. She wasn't crying or yelling. She talked calmly as if watching his clothes burn was some sort of therapy to her. "The worst part of all this was that I was betrayed by two of who I thought were my best friends. Niq knew that he was married, and he gave her cocaine not to tell me, and the pregnant lady is..." Caroline looked at Tangie with a look of shock. "Oh no, please tell me that Pam isn't the baby momma?" "Well, she is," Tangie rubbed her eyes to stop the tears that may have tried to escape her eyes. She took a deep breath as if she was done with the whole trifling situation. When she exhaled, she went inside to check on Carmen, and she came back out with a wine cooler for her and bottled water for Caroline. "Thanks," Caroline said as she took the top off the water and took a big gulp. "You're welcome. That was like a workout, huh?"

Caroline laughed, "Yes ma'am," as she finished off the water. "Do you want another, because I have a freezer full?" Caroline loved that Tangie kept water in the freezer, and they always seemed to be just the way that Caroline liked them, almost slush like. While Tangie went back inside to get Caroline another water, Caroline thought of what it must feel like for Tangie to be betrayed, not only by someone she thought was her man, but also both of her childhood friends. Tangie had gone through all this, but yet and still, she had her sense of humor.

When Tangie came back, she handed Caroline her bottled water and sat back in the lounge chair. "Caroline, I'm sorry." "For what?" Caroline tilted her head to the side and held Tangie's hand. "I wasn't thinking clearly that day at the hospital and..."

"Shh," Caroline interrupted Tangie. "You don't have to apologize to me. I'm sorry for not being more understanding." Tangie smiled, "It's funny how you can think that you know some people for so long, you put your trust in them, and they become like family, only to find out that they never had your best interest at heart, and that they were just waiting to stab you in the back all along. Anyway, after some time of not having anyone to turn to, I did a lot of thinking.

"I made amends with my parents, who always loved and supported me and only had my best interest at heart. I was being stubborn for a long time, and I wanted to live my life the way that I wanted, without their help. You have to be careful what bridges you burn in life, though, because there will come a time when you will need someone, and you will definitely need that bridge. I just thank God for you being there for me, and I am sorry for pushing you away. We've only been friends for two years, but I love you like a sister. Thank you, Caroline." They held hands tighter and then Caroline hugged Tangie. Caroline walked away with her left hand massaging the left side of her forehead, in deep thought. "Oh ohh, I know that look," Tangie said. "What's the matter?"

Caroline put a strand of hair behind her ear and took a deep breath. "I'm seeing someone. Not only am I seeing him, but we almost got it on in the park." Tangie laughed, "You, getting it on in the park?" She laughed again.

"People get it on at the park all the time, that's not hard to believe. I haven't gotten it on at the park since I was sixteen. But you? I don't believe it. With who?" "Stacy."

"Your one and only true love, Stacy, who your mom paid to go to Timbuktu and to never return, Stacy?" Caroline laughed, "The one and only." "Shut the front door, are you serious? When did he get back? I mean, how did y'all find each other again, wow?" "Well, he has been looking for me and come to find out, we will be working together." "Get out," Tangie said, not believing what she was hearing. "So this is what you've been praying for, right? For Stacy to come back into your life and whisk you off your feet?" "I think so, but the way that things are falling into place so perfectly, it's kind of scary, you know? It's almost like it's too good to be true." "Well, if something seems too good to be true, then it probably is. Just be careful. You have dedicated yourself to God for seventeen years, and to just throw that away in one night, in the park, you might want to rethink homeboy's motives. You know, it's not God, because God will not tempt you with evil, and sin is sin, Caroline. You know, God has no respect of person. I mean, I know that I am far from perfect, and I sin. I was even angry at God and Carmen's dad for a long time, and that's why I was so rebellious. I went to church, but my heart wasn't there, but God has a way of getting your attention, and when you belong to him, he will break you down, so that you won't have a choice, but to look up, and that's where I am now. I am, finally, making the choice to live right and be the mother that Carmen needs me to be, and I am forgiving and forgetting everything as soon as these clothes finish burning." Caroline started laughing, "See, Tangie, I can't take you seriously." Tangie laughed, "No, on the real though, I meant everything that I just said. To be honest, Caroline, you helped me realize my mistakes and helped me turn to God. All the times that you were quoting scriptures to me, and I acted as if I wasn't listening, I heard every word you said and took it to heart. It's just that, sometimes, we, as Christians, try to make the bible conform to our lives, instead of living by the word. Now, I know that I'm not perfect, and I have a long way to go, but I'll get there eventually.

"I'm saying all of this to say that I love you, and I am happy that your long lost love has come back in your life, but before you just put your all into this man, I think that you should take the time to get to know him all over again. After dating him for some time, and you feel that he's the one for you, then that's your choice, but don't be so easy as to throw all these years away that you've dedicated your life to God and believing him for a husband on an old flame, especially when you're not sure where the relationship is heading." Caroline nodded in agreement, but at the same time, she felt like Tangie had rained on her parade. It was something how Tangie and Caroline's friendship worked. When one person was down, the other one always knew what to say, and when one was going through any kind of life crisis, the other one always directed the person in crisis to God.

Carmen rolled her wheelchair to the patio and tapped on the door with the Waiting to Exhale DVD. "Hey mama, hey auntie, I think this might be a waiting to exhale moment. I have some popcorn in the microwave popping. Do y'all want to watch it?" "Sure baby," Tangie said, getting out of her seat and coming into the kitchen with Caroline following behind.

"Caroline, do you want water or some fruit or something? I have some grapes in the freezer." "Sure you can bring the grapes." Frozen grapes were another favorite that Tangie had turned Caroline on to.

While Carmen and Tangie were in the kitchen, Caroline thought about what Tangie said, but she couldn't help but think, what if Stacy coming back into her life was an act of God? Keeping her legs closed was a battle of the flesh, but why was she so quick to give up seventeen years of celibacy for one night of passion?

The next day, Caroline and Stacy worked on the Art fundraiser project for the fall. Caroline tried to be strong and remember what Tangie said, but her vagina seemed to have a mind of its own. This man was intoxicating. All Caroline could think about was grabbing his dreads and screaming his name, amongst other things. Mike texted Caroline several times to see if she could get away for lunch, but she ignored the messages.

"So, it is lunch time, Caroline, and I have a few errands to run, but I will meet you back here at the office in, say an hour?" Caroline shook her head out of the daze and said, "Sure wait, I was thinking that maybe we could grab a bite to eat together. You name the place, and I will treat." Stacy smiled, "I would love to, but I have a business meeting that I have to get to in about twenty minutes at the Art Museum. The Art Director wants to start showcasing my art immediately." "Oh that's great, Stacy, go ahead," Caroline waved her hand for Stacy to go ahead.

Stacy peeped his head back into the door, "Tell me where you are going to be, and I'll try to make it there before lunch is over."

"I'm just getting some take out from this Korean restaurant up the street, but don't be silly. Go ahead to your meeting before you are late. I can bring you something back to the office." "Beef bulgogi?" Stacy said, peeping into the door, "and I like it spicy." He winked at Caroline and she smiled. "If only you knew just how spicy it was," Caroline said, fanning herself with a manila folder.

Caroline didn't find herself pulling away from her desk until twenty minutes till one o'clock. She looked at her Michael Kor's watch, "Gees, my break is almost over." She looked in her desk drawer for the menu to the Korean restaurant to try to order delivery, but she couldn't find it, so she hurried onto the elevator and downstairs, so that she could quickly order lunch. On the way from the Korean restaurant, Caroline saw Stacy speaking with Amanda Lavado and thought that maybe he was telling her about the Art Fundraiser and seeing if she was interested in catering. Caroline stepped onto the elevator, with Stacy fast on her heels.

"Let me guess; you worked your whole break?" "So did you, I see," Caroline turned towards Stacy with the bag of food. "Oh, let me get that for you." He grabbed the bag of food and when the elevator stopped, he motioned his hand for her to get off first. "Ladies first," he said as he watched Caroline strut out of the elevator.

"So, how did the meeting go?" "It went well, but I had to speak with Amanda to let her know that I would begin work at the Art Museum sooner than I thought." "And when is that?" Caroline said as she took the food out of the brown paper bag and placed it on the round table in her office. "Well, he has several potential buyers, already that were interested in my work, so he wants me to start tomorrow."

"So where will that leave you as far as the café?" "I told Amanda, and she said that she will work around my schedule at the art gallery." "And how are we going to finish the plans for the fundraiser?" "I will make time. Don't worry, Caroline." "I'm not worried. I just don't want you to work yourself to death. It seems like you're going to have a lot going on."

The weekend couldn't have come fast enough. Caroline and Mike had made plans for a movie date, and later on, they would have dinner at an upscale diner in Midtown.

The whole evening, Caroline's mind was in another place. "Caroline what's wrong? You haven't said much all evening."

"Oh, nothing is wrong. I just have a lot going on at work and am really feeling the pressure." "Well," Mike said as he got out of his truck and went around to the passenger side to open Caroline's door.

"Tonight, you should forget about work." Caroline gave Mike a 'yeah right' look.

"At least for a few hours, try to forget about work and concentrate on what makes Caroline happy. You owe yourself at least that after all the hard work that you've put in all week." What made Caroline happy was a hard question to ponder at the moment. Here she was, with this wonderful man, who loves God and is very interested in her. He is a great single father, he's very handsome, any woman would love to be on his arm, and he is a top executive at his job. "You're right; tonight I need to forget about work and have a good time, and that's exactly what I'm going to do."

As Caroline and Mike were about to enter the movie theater, Caroline's phone ring. It was Stacy. "I'm sorry, Mike, its work," she lied, "Let me take this phone call right quick, and I will meet you inside." Mike shook his head and motioned his mouth to say "Hang up, tell them no, you have plans." Caroline smiled and held up one finger and motioned her mouth to say give me one minute. "One minute," Mike said as he turned to open the door and go inside the movie theater. "Hey Stacy, what's up," Caroline said, smiling from ear to ear. "Hey, Caroline, I had some free time and was wondering if you'd like to meet me at the W hotel downtown, so that we can work on the art fundraiser?" "Um, well, I'm kind of busy at the moment, Stacy, but I could probably meet you after church tomorrow? Why are you at the W anyway?"

"Well, there's an art convention here, today, and I thought that it would be a good place for me to get my work out there and to let people know about the art fundraiser this fall. It's a lot of money walking around here, Caroline, and I'm sure that we could rake in some major cash for GPSG. I've talked to some people already, and they are interested in my art and investing in GPSG, but they would like to know more about the company." The phone went silent on both ends. "That is where you come in, Caroline." Mike came back outside and motioned for Caroline to come inside.

Caroline threw up her pointer finger again and motioned her mouth, "I'm sorry, one more minute." Mike stood outside the movie entrance patiently waiting on Caroline as women from all races and walks of life flirted with him as he opened the door for them. "He is a cutie pie" one older black lady said, "If he would have caught me about thirty years ago, I would have..." The young lady with the old lady cut the old lady off. "Grandma, stop."

The old lady fanned herself and winked at Mike and motioned the words "call me" as she slipped a card in his hand. The card read Private Investigator with the name Mary written on the back. Surely, the old lady wasn't a private eye, but maybe her granddaughter was. Without thinking much of the card, Mike placed the card in his pants pocket and continued to hold the door for the other ladies. "Thank you papi," one Spanish girl in her early twenties said, as she gave Mike a seductive eye and put an extra twist in her walk.

One white lady, who was very attractive in her late thirties to early forties, flirted with Mike. "Hi, handsome, I'm here now you don't have to wait any longer." Mike smiled, "Thank you, but I'm actually here with someone." "Well, where is she? She must be crazy to keep a man like you waiting," the lady said as she turned on her stilettos then she and her two friends walked inside the theater.

"Mike, I am so sorry, but I have to cancel." "What? Aw Caroline don't do this. You deserve at least the weekend to get your mind off of work." "Mike, I am so sorry, but can you drop me off at the Art Convention held downtown at the W? "My boss is there with some potential investors," she lied. "He needs my assistance. I am so sorry. I promise I will make it up to you." Mike scratched the back of his neck, "Yeah, you have some major making up to do, come on." "Oh thank you so much, Mike. If you like, af- ter church tomorrow, you can come over, and I will cook dinner, whatever you like." Mike looked at her and smiled, "Whatever I like, huh?"

"Sure, just name it, and I will go to the grocery store tonight, and I will cook it for you tomorrow, and we can stay in and have dinner and a movie." When Mike pulled up to the hotel, Caroline hurried out of the truck, without realizing she'd left her purse.

"Hey, wait up. You sure are anxious to get to work; you almost left your purse." Mike handed Caroline her purse. "Thanks and thank you for understanding. I just don't want to miss this opportunity; you know?"

"Don't worry about it. You will be in the kitchen, making it up to- morrow, so just make sure that you are well rested, because I have a big appetite. See you tomorrow." "See you tomorrow," Caroline smiled and waved as Mike pulled off. When Caroline arrived at the W, she spotted Stacy standing near the entrance of the meeting room. "Why didn't we know about this event?"

"Well, it's a private convention, but it just so happens that one of the artists from the museum got me in. I told him about the art fundraiser, and he said that I should come through, because I could meet a lot of people who are not only interested in art, but could also be potential investors. If they invest in me, they are, ultimately, investing in GPSG." Caroline knew that Stacy was right. He got his job at the museum, because the Art Director at the museum and Mr. Taylor are best buddies, and hiring Stacy at the museum was a win win for both of them.

Caroline and Stacy met a lot of people and exchanged business cards, and several people even agreed to come to check out the fall art fundraiser. By eight p.m., Caroline's stomach was growling, because she hadn't eaten since nine am. Stacy laughed at the loud growl from Caroline's stomach. "Yeah, me too," he said to Caroline, who was now holding her stomach, hoping the noise would stop.

"Let's grab a bite to eat before we get to work," Stacy said, walking towards the W restaurant BLT Steak. "Can we work while we eat, because it's already eight, and by the time I get home, it will be nine thirty or even ten o clock?" "Oh don't worry about the time, Caroline. I rented a room, so that we can work in peace, and if you do get tired, then you can spend the night." "No I don't think that's such a good idea," Caroline said, shaking her head, trying to shake the thoughts of what would actually be going down if she went in a room alone with Stacy. "Well, it's your choice, but I got the room anyway, because my best art work comes when I'm in random places."

"It may be hard to believe, but I can concentrate more when I'm not at home." Caroline gave Stacy a 'yeah right' look. "I'm serious I have a painting that I've just completed upstairs if you don't believe me.

You don't have to stay upstairs with me, but I need another person's opinion of it, so after dinner, if you would just let me know what you think, and I will gladly take you home, and we can meet Monday afternoon to continue the plans for the fundraiser." Caroline agreed.

Stacy decided to check out the raw bar, and he tried to persuade Caroline to try it as well. Caroline gagged when she saw Stacy suck the raw oysters down. "Ewe, that looks so nasty." "You should try it; it's really good. Here, try some lemon juice and tabasco on it."

"No sir, I don't think so." "Suit yourself," Stacy said as he kept downing the oysters, like shots of vodka. Caroline frowned and shook her head. "Do you remember when we were kids and we use to play truth or dare?" Caroline smiled, "Yes, I remember."

"I would always go for truth, and you would always go for the dare," Stacy took a sip of his beer. "Like that time I dared you to go shoot craps with the guys on the block and you did. I couldn't believe you actually did that." "Yes I did and I won all their money too." "Yep and every time you would come to the hood, the guys would try to get you to shoot craps with them."

"Yes that was crazy, and sometimes, I would. I was like a little tomboy back in those days. I was on the court, shooting basketball with the fellas, and remember climbing trees?" "I do, especially our tree. It was the tallest tree in the projects, and we would go up there and sit and look at the stars and think about our future, together," Stacy gently rubbed Caroline's hand and looked into her eyes.

Caroline could have sworn that she felt the same feeling that she'd felt all those years ago. It was something about, when they touched, it was like a shock of passion and life and love all in one. All Caroline could hear was Tangie's words. If something seemed too good to be true, then it probably was. She could also hear her telling her to take her time and don't be so quick to throw away seventeen years of celibacy for one night. Stacy could see that Caroline was a bit uncomfortable, so he tried to lighten the mood. "Truth or dare?" Caroline almost chocked on the sip of water she'd just taken. She wiped her mouth off with a napkin. "Excuse me?" "You heard me," Stacy said, "Truth or dare?"

"Stacy, we are not teenagers, anymore. You can't think that you can just dare me to do something and I will." "Ah ha," Stacy said. "I knew that you couldn't pass up a good dare. I know you too well, Caroline. Look, I will even go first if you are uncomfortable, so let's hear your best truth question, but you have to promise to go along with whatever I dare you to do." Caroline tilted her head to the side and took a deep swallow and agreed, "Alright."

"Is it true what they say about oysters? Are they an aphrodisiac?" Stacy said, "No, now it's my turn." Caroline was nervous. She hadn't been dared to do anything since she was in eleventh grade, and now, here she is, thirty-four, playing truth or dare. Stacy took an oyster and squeezed lemon juice and shook Tabasco sauce on it twice and said, "I dare you to eat this oyster." Caroline made a disgusted face and motioned her hand for Stacy to give her the oyster. "Fine, give it to me," Caroline looked at the oyster in disgust as if it was a snail on the sidewalk. "Bon appetite," Stacy said as he gulped down another oyster. Caroline opened her mouth and the oyster slid in. She was about to chew it, but Stacy said, "No don't chew it; just swallow it."

Caroline swallowed the oyster and hurried to take a sip of water. "So, what did you think?" Stacy laughed. "It actually wasn't that bad, but I don't think that I can wolf them down, like you." "See I told you.

"Do you feel any hornier?" Caroline ignored that question and decided to keep going with the game. When the steak arrived, they ate and continued to talk, while keeping the game of truth or dare going. They talked and laughed, especially when Stacy dared Caroline to pretend that they couldn't afford their dinner and volunteered to wash dishes to pay their bill. Although Caroline and Stacy thought that it was a good joke, the waiter did not think that it was funny and was relieved to know that they were paying guests and that she had a big tip.

When Caroline and Stacy got up to the room, it was already nine thirty. When Stacy opened the room door and Caroline saw the painting, her heart melted. Caroline knew this painting, because it was a place that she and Stacy visited often. It was their special tree. Tall as ever with the greenest leaves.

"It's our tree," Caroline turned around to face Stacy with her right hand over her heart. Caroline turned back to face the painting as she examined every part of the tree, and before she knew it, she was lost in a time when it seemed like all that mattered was their love for each other, and life was so simple. As Caroline lost herself in her thoughts, her hand touched the painting in the most loving and gentle way. "You see it, then," Stacy said, not realizing that Caroline was lost in time. Caroline heard Stacy talking, but in her mind, it was replaying another moment in time.

"You see it then," Stacy asked Caroline, who had once again left her home, against her parents' orders to go see her boyfriend, Stacy.

Stacy had carved a picture of him and Caroline into their favorite tree with the words forever at the bottom. "Yes, I see it, baby. This is beautiful. How long did it take you to do this?" "Two weeks, the last time I saw you, I knew that it would be a while before I would get to see you again, ever since your parents found out about us, but I knew that, one day, I'd have you back in my arms, because our love is forever, girl."

Caroline blushed, it was like Stacy was all she needed. He saw her, when no one else did, or when people just saw her as the daughter of two Atlanta Moguls. Stacy knew Caroline and understood her. The guys in the hood walked to the basketball court and teased Stacy about being in love, but he didn't care. "Y'all just jealous, man. Baby, you want to go beat these guys in a game of hoops, right quick? We can come up on at least twenty dollars. I don't know about you, but I can use an extra dub." "Let's get 'em, baby," Caroline agreed. "Hey guys, wait up. Y'all got all that mouth. How about y'all put your money where your mouth is?" The guys laughed at Caroline's question.

"Stacy, you better get Ms. Pretty, before she be heading back to Buckhead or wherever she comes from barefoot, because if we win, I want them J's off her feet," one of the guys replied. The other guys laughed. "Man, you heard my lady. Let's do it and what are you going to do with her little J's anyway, Big Foot?" "If we win, all y'all owe me and my girl ten dollars each, and it's five of y'all, so are y'all ready to drop that Grant?" "Yeah man, whatever," the guy replied, "Let's do it, then."

"Let's go, I'm ready, when you ready. Baby, this is going to be easy money," Stacy licked his lips and smiled then winked at Caroline. Caroline tied her hair into a ponytail, smiled at Stacy, and got into position. Hanging around Stacy all those years had taught Caroline how to keep up with the guys in any sport or recreational activity, even illegal ones, like shooting craps. "Do you see it?" Caroline heard Stacy calling her as she slowly came out of her daydream.

"Caroline you see it, right?" Caroline studied the tree and wasn't sure what Stacy was talking about, until she moved her hand, and it was amazing. When Caroline moved her hand off the part of the tree where the leaves and branches were, she saw the word forever in the branches and leaves. Caroline was amazed, because she hadn't seen it before. "Wow, it's beautiful, Stacy."

Stacy wasn't certain that Caroline had actually seen what he really wanted her to see. Stacy moved to Caroline's side and folded his arms.

"So, what do you think?" "Well I love it, of course. This tree brings back a lot of memories," Caroline turned her head to the right to face Stacy. "Forever," Stacy said after a brief moment of silence as he and Caroline admired the painting.

"Yes, I think that is brilliant how you put those words in the branches and leaves. It took me a minute, but this painting is outstanding, Stacy." "Thank you," Stacy replied with a slight smile then he scratched the side of his head. Forever is the name of the painting. Stacy used Impressionism art style in most of his work, so the painting may look like an unfinished painting of a tree to some, but if you look closely, you see that it's complete, and you also see the words forever.

Stacy knew that Caroline didn't see what Stacy wanted her to see, but that only meant that the painting was exactly the way that he meant for it to be, Impressionism with a touch of optical illusion. "Forever will be on display at the museum, and I don't know, but I have a feeling that a lot of people will like it." "Well, they should, because it's a wonderful painting," Caroline said in slow motion as she exhaled, and Stacy moved her hair to the side and softly kissed her on the neck. He smelled so good. Caroline closed her eyes and embraced his kisses.

Caroline missed church the next day, and she had three text messages and two missed calls from Mike. The first text message from Mike read: Just making sure that you made it home ok. That text was sent at eleven p.m. the night before. He called at twelve midnight Sunday, and Caroline did not answer. "Oh my goodness," Caroline shook her head, not believing that she'd slept until noon.

The next text read, see you at church, and that was at ten am. Caroline had just missed Mike's phone call at eleven fifty-three a.m., saying that he was on his way and asking Caroline if she needed anything. Caroline couldn't really remember what happened last night and was unsure of how she got home. Then it hit her that Stacy drove her home and that he was asleep downstairs on her sofa, while Mike was on his way over.

"Oh no, no, no, no, no," Caroline said as she tied her robe and ran down the stairs to tell Stacy that he had to leave and, hopefully, to confirm that she hadn't done anything that she would possibly regret. When Caroline ran downstairs, Stacy had opened the door for Mike, and Mike stood in the doorway with a bouquet of purple roses and a bottle of Caroline's favorite cider. "Mike," Caroline said, gasping for air, because her heart was racing a hundred miles a minute as her mind tried to come up with an explanation. "Caroline," Mike said with a fake smile. "These are for you," he handed her the roses and cider and turned around and headed back to his truck. Caroline gave the roses and cider to Stacy, without thinking about what she was doing, and ran after Mike as he was getting into his truck. "Mike please wait a minute," Caroline pleaded. "Well, at least, I know now why you haven't been answering my phone calls or texts and why you're so busy working. You had me for a minute, though, Caroline. I thought that you were different." Mike put his truck into gear to back out of the driveway. "I am different, Mike, please wait. Allow me to explain."

"Is everything alright, Caroline?" Stacy yelled from the door way. "Everything is fine, Stacy; just please give me a minute." Mike eyes widened, "Stacy, Stacy? Your first love Stacy? The man that has had your heart since you were a kid?" Caroline nodded her head yes. "Wow, at least I know the reason to the question that I asked you that Sunday that Michael and I came over." "What are you talking about, Mike?" "Nothing, you have a minute to explain everything, because I have something to do."

Caroline backed up from the truck and put her hand on her hip. She was frustrated that Mike wasn't truly trying to hear her side of the story, and even more frustrated that he pretended that he had to be somewhere. "Well," Mike said impatiently. "That's exactly what I thought; goodbye, Caroline." A tear fell down Caroline's cheek as she tried to get her thoughts together on exactly what to say, but the words never came.

Mike sped away in his truck, and as the truck faded away, Caroline said to herself, "Goodbye Mike," and slowly walked back into her house. "Do you mind telling me exactly what happened between us last night, Stacy, and why I can't remember anything?" "Calm down, Caroline. Nothing happened that you didn't want to happen and what happened last night is that I gave you a little something to help you relax. You had been going on and on about work, and we were up until three a.m. working on the fundraiser, and no matter how much I begged you to just stay the night, you wouldn't, so I drove you back here, and I told you that I was tired and asked if I could stay the night, because I was too sleepy to drive back to the hotel or home and you agreed. Even after we got here, you tried to stay up, and by five a.m. you still weren't sleep, so I put a sleeping pill in your water, so that you could get some rest.

"Look, I'm sorry for giving you the pill, but I was looking out for your best interest. You are going to overwork yourself. You also made it very clear that I wasn't getting any, even though I tried multiple times, so I respect that, and like a gentleman, I slept on the couch. Look, the guy was ringing your door bell, and out of habit, I just got up to open the door. I'm sorry."

"You know what, Stacy? I can't do this; just go please, and the next time you think that you have my best interest at heart, please inform me, so that I can make a conscious decision about exactly what my best interest is."

Caroline tried to ponder exactly how Stacy put a sleeping pill in her water at her house. It wasn't at her house. It was at the hotel when he kept telling her that she should relax and get some rest and that he would take her home first thing in the morning. Caroline drank some of a bottled water that Stacy had given her, but did not finish it. Then, she thought, hey, I saw him get the water out of the refrigerator, so he couldn't have put it in then, unless it was already in the water before I got to the room. Then she thought about their stop at the gas station, on the way to her house. Stacy bought her another bottled water, and she didn't go into the store with him, so maybe he went into the restroom and put something in the water then.

Was the top sealed or not? She couldn't remember. Too much talking, reminiscing, and having a good time, and not enough paying attention. Caroline felt sick to her stomach and, immediately, ran to her bathroom to throw up. Caroline felt uneasy about exactly what really went on at the hotel and at her house. She really didn't know what to think, but two things were for certain. She didn't trust Stacy, and she had to make things right with Mike.

9

The next day, Stacy had the local florist to fill Caroline's office with an array of roses of all kinds and colors. There was a cute teddy bear sitting on her office couch with the words, I'm Sorry, in its chest inside a big heart. "Ooo, well little Ms. Prixie has got somebody's attention," Ramona said as she tried to enter Caroline's office behind her to be nosy, but Caroline smiled and closed the door, leaving Ramona outside, looking through the glass. Everyone was looking towards Caroline's office to see what was going on, so Caroline smiled, waved with one hand, and quickly closed her blinds. Caroline was still upset about yesterday, but the bear was cute, and she'd hoped it was from Mike, but it was from Stacy.

Caroline was very upset with Stacy, but she would have to work with him, so she decided to put yesterday behind them, forgive Stacy, and she didn't allow her personal feelings to interfere with business. Caroline received several phone calls and texts from Stacy, and every time her phone vibrated, she hoped that at least one time it was Mike, replying to her messages that she'd left on voicemail or text. Maybe Mike needed time to think, so after several failed call attempts and no response, Caroline decided to let Mike be for a while. Caroline decided to respond to Stacy, but only via text, so she texted him and said, I forgive you, but

I think it's best that, from now on, we only see each other on business terms. Stacy agreed and then apologized again for what seemed like the hundredth time.

Months went by and before Caroline knew it, the Fashion Show was over and done with, and so was the Art Fundraiser. Caroline was working with Stacy almost every day, mostly via email or phone, but at least twice a week, in person due to his contract with the museum. Part of his proceeds was for the benefit of not only the Art gallery, but GPSG, as well. It was Caroline's job to get Stacy as much exposure as possible as a new artist, so many times, she would book events for him and introduce him to famous artists and people who were interested in investing in an artist. Although Caroline decided to keep the relationship between her and Stacy strictly business, it was very hard.

Why does this guy have to smell so freaking good, and why do his teeth have to be so white and perfectly aligned, and why, Lord, why does he have to look so freaking good? Caroline sipped on a cup of hot chocolate at her desk and looked at Stacy, conversing with the hair and makeup crew, as a few girls peeked from behind their cubicles to get a view of the tall, dark, and handsome masterpiece. Despite Caroline's daily attempts to keep everything strictly business between them, Stacy still tried to get in where he once fit in. He would buy Caroline lunch and have it delivered, because he knew that she often worked through her breaks. He also sent her to Hawaii for her birthday, although he bought a ticket for himself, too, but after Caroline declined, he gave her both tickets, and she decided to take Tangie with her. Caroline didn't notice her boss staring at her from her office door. Mr. Taylor cleared his throat, and Caroline quickly came out of her trance of admiration for Stacy. "Mr. Taylor, Hi I'm sorry. I didn't see you standing there." "Well I did knock but your attention seemed to be focused elsewhere," he tilted his head towards Stacy and welcomed himself into Caroline's office and closed the door behind him. "Caroline, may I speak with you for a minute?"

"Sure, of course, have a seat please, Mr. Taylor. Would you like something to drink?" Mr. Taylor waved his hand no and said, "I'm good, but let's talk about you. Caroline, I've noticed that over the past several months, there has been a change in you. Now, forgive me if I'm wrong, but it started when you and Stacy began to work together. Is there something going on here that I should know about? If so, I can easily get someone else to work with Stacy if you feel uncomfortable or if he's a distraction. Our last fundraiser of the year is coming up, and I cannot pull it off alone. I need you to be focused. I feel like this fundraiser is what will close the deal with Mr. Lavado, and we can proceed with expanding GPSG and, hopefully, get you that assistant that you've been asking for." Caroline smiled and put her hand on the side of her chin.

"There is no need for that, Mr. Taylor. I have just been a bit overwhelmed with work, trying to juggle payroll for the company, being an event coordinator, a personal assistant, along with all the other tasks that I'm responsible for that, sometimes, it may appear that my focus is off of one thing, because I'm concentrating on another, but I guarantee you that I'm ok, and everything will be ok. Once this last fundraiser of the year is over, I'm going to take a long vacation and come back refreshed and ready to take on the world."

"I totally understand, and I don't want you to think that I don't appreciate everything that you do, Caroline. I know that over the years, as we've expanded, your job duties have also expanded, and you have been doing an awesome job juggling everything, but I have a feeling that if you stay focused and keep doing an awesome job, the hard work will most definitely pay off." "I agree sir," Caroline smiled. "He is a rather striking young man, and I just don't want him to throw you off of your game. Besides, I don't think his fiancée will like that too much, although they appear to have an open relationship." Caroline almost chocked on her hot chocolate. "I'm sorry, but did you say fiancée?"

"Yes, how do you think that I found out about this young man?"

Caroline looked even more confusingly at Mr. Taylor. "I'm sorry, Mr. Taylor, but I don't understand." "Mr. Lavado?" Mr. Taylor said, hoping Caroline would realize what he was talking about. Just then, Stacy knocked on the door, apologized for interrupting, and opened Caroline's office door, and asked Caroline if she was ready to continue work. Mr. Taylor could tell that Caroline had no idea about Stacy being engaged, so he stood up and straightened his suit jacket and said, "Hey, Stacy, no worries. Caroline and I were just finishing up a quick meeting, but Caroline, Google it and tell me what you think." Caroline made a slight frown and then she thought about it. "Oh yes, yes I will do that, and I will get with you first thing tomorrow and let you know what I think." Caroline walked Mr. Taylor to the door and closed the door after he left.

Fiancée? Caroline pondered in her head. How could Stacy have a fiancée, and not only that, why hasn't he told me? Then she thought, okay, well maybe it happened a couple of months ago, when they decided to work as business partners only. Then again, he sent her on a vacation a month ago, and he is always buying her lunch.

Caroline never paid any attention to all the things that Stacy was doing for her, until now. She thought that he knew, since that last incident, that there was nothing personal ever going to happen between them, yet he was persistent. But now, she was second guessing herself. Clearly, she had made up in her mind that Stacy could not be trusted, and with this bit of information, it was confirmation. But now that she knew that he had someone else in the picture, she felt threatened, like someone was taking what was hers, although before, she'd made up her mind that the past was the past and that chapter of her life was over.

Caroline started second guessing herself. Did she make the right decision about not giving Stacy and her a second chance in life? She thought to herself, surely everyone makes mistakes, and she began reasoning with the way that Stacy thinks. I do tend to overwork myself, she thought, and maybe he did put the sleep medicine in my water so that I could rest. He didn't rape me or try anything, because despite his word, I went to the doctor the next morning, and there was no evidence of penetration or bodily fluids. Caroline told Stacy that she was going to call it a day early and that she wasn't feeling well. She decided to leave the office for the day two hours before her usual time and decided to go home and do her research. Caroline couldn't believe how much she'd fallen off her game. Mr. Taylor was right. She had been distracted. Caroline knew every investor profile along with other business partners and even the employees who worked for GPSG. But why didn't she look Stacy up on the internet to see what he'd been up to all these years. "I guess that I was naive," Caroline shook her head as she stopped at a red light. A young lady waved for Caroline to roll her window down, and then she asked Caroline how she was doing and then she introduced herself as a hostess of Soulful Jazz Restaurant, and she asked Caroline what was her name and if she liked Soul Food? "My name is Caroline, and um, of course, I love soul food," Caroline smiled. "Do you like Jazz?" The young lady asked as she wrapped her red hair that had fallen out of place back into a bun with one hand.

"Yes... I like Jazz," Caroline said. "One more question, do you like poetry?" "It's pretty cool, I mean, I couldn't write poetry to save my life, but it's cool to read." "Well," the light skinned, freckled face young lady said, "it's even cooler to listen to. Want to come out tonight and check us out? We have the best soul food ever. We are fairly new, so if you bring a friend, that would be great. I promise you that you won't be disappointed. We also have amateur poets' night tonight, so I know that you don't do poetry yourself, but perhaps, your friend does? It's really a lot of fun, even if you don't have a talent for it. We usually have a fair crowd, and everyone seem to enjoy themselves, so if you aren't busy, it would be a great place to kick back, relax, and enjoy the evening." Caroline smiled. "Great, I will think about it." "Beep." The car behind Caroline honked as loud as it could possibly honk. Caroline was holding up traffic in the turning lane.

"Oops my bad," the young lady said as she backed up and waved bye. "Come check us out, Caroline. It will be a lot of fun. After sitting in Atlanta traffic for what seemed like forever, Caroline pulled up to her home and her stomach growled. "That soul food sure does sound good, right about now," Caroline read the flyer that the young lady had given her.

The flyer read "Come in for some comfort food for your body and soothing jazz for your soul." A couple of famous poets' pictures were displayed on the flyer, as well. Caroline thought it would be a good idea for her and Tangie to go, since they both agreed, no more clubbing. It had been a stressful week, and from what Caroline found out about Stacy, she felt some soothing jazz would help her get her mind right. Caroline hurried inside her house ready to surf the net to see what she could find out about Stacy.

Her cell rang. It was Tangie. "Dang it, not now, Tangie." She ignored her cell as she typed in SAG, the name Stacy was known by. Caroline's home phone ring. It was Tangie's cell number on the caller id. "Lord, what does this child want," Caroline said before answering the office phone.

"Hey, girl, what's going on?" Tangie asked anxiously on the other end of the phone. "Not too much, girl, just got off work. What's up with you? You sound excited about something." "I am, Caroline. Brother Robertson asked me out on a date tonight." "What, the guy that always tells you how nice you look at church?" "Yes, well, he didn't officially ask me on a date, but he asked me to come check him out at poetry night tonight at his sister's new restaurant, Soulful Jazz." "What, I was going to see if you wanted to go and check that place out with me tonight." "I was going to ask you the same, because I didn't want to show up by myself, but since you answered my question, I'm on the way."

Caroline knew that, unlike a lot of brothers and sisters she knew, when Tangie said that she was on her way, that meant she was outside of your door. Caroline quickly got up to go open the door, and there Tangie was. Caroline burst out laughing, and so did Tangie. "Girl, you know me like a book, huh?" "Unfortunately, yes," Caroline shook her head.

When Caroline and Tangie arrived at the restaurant, it was packed. They had to park across the street and put money in the meter, because all of the restaurant parking was taken. Caroline and Tangie hurried across the street as fast as they could, without breaking a heel on their stilettos. Traffic was on going in both directions with many people coming to the restaurant. "Wow, this place is packed," Caroline said as she entered the building.

All of the tables were full, and there weren't any seats available. The bar and the booths were filled as well. There were a few people standing and socializing, while having drinks. "How long is the wait?" Tangie asked one of the hostess, who was busy taking people's names and the number of their party. "Right now, its fifty minutes for a table, but a lot of people are staying for poetry night, so to be honest, it could be even longer to get a table."

The guy who was the front door host gave Caroline a buzzer and told her when it vibrates that their table would be ready. Although Caroline had mastered the art of walking in stilettos, she did not feel like standing in them for who knows how long, especially after a long day at work. Tangie was busy trying to see if she could find her church crush, and right when she gave up, he tapped her on the back. "Hey, I've been looking for you," he said as he smiled and looked Tangie up and down in a pleased way. "You look very nice, as usual, sister Tangie," he said as he came in for a hug, and Tangie returned the favor with a nice pat on the back church hug.

Tangie liked Brother Robertson, but she was playing as if this visit to hear him perform at poetry night was just a church friend supporting another church friend and nothing more. Brother Robertson told Tangie and Caroline that he already had a table reserved for them, and they didn't need to wait on a table. As Tangie and Caroline followed Brother Robertson to the table, they found out that they weren't the only friends from church that Brother Robertson had invited. Ladies from the praise team, dance team, bible study teachers, and everyone else were there. Brother Robertson was looking like a gigolo, until Caroline and Tangie fully came around the corner, and saw other people from church, like the youth pastor and several other men who attended Tangie's church.

Everyone was drinking water or sweet tea. Tangie did not want either. She wanted her normal glass of Moscato, but she didn't want to be the only wine drinker, so she sipped her sweet tea. As the food was brought out, everyone socialized and ate, while the sweet sounds of soft jazz played in the background by a live band. The restaurant appeared small on the outside, but it was bigger on the inside than what the outside appeared to be. There was a deck where some guests enjoyed their meal outside with the view of downtown Atlanta.

While Tangie and her man crush, Brother Robertson, flirted and other single church women with the other single guys that attended the church, Caroline was busy on the Internet, taking up all the info on Mr. Lavado, who Caroline knew was the café owner's father, but she also found out that Stacy wasn't just her employee, but her soon to be husband. A hot flash flew over Caroline from her feet to her head, and she started to sweat on her forehead. She began to fan herself with the dessert menu. "Caroline, are you ok?"

Tangie asked with a concerned look on her face. "You look as if you just saw a ghost or something." "I'm fine, Tangie. It's just a little hot in here. I'm going to go outside and get some air." Caroline made her way through the packed restaurant to the patio and leaned on the balcony, feeling sick. "Why am I letting him get to me like this?"

"I don't know, but you're too fine to let anyone stress you out, baby," an older guy in his late fifties said to Caroline as he came and stood beside her, holding a bottle of beer in his hand. He took a swig and asked Caroline if he could buy her something to drink? "No, thank you. I don't drink." The older guy started rambling about who knows what, as Caroline continued to scroll down her smart phone and read all the Internet had to offer on Stacy. Every now and then, the older guy would ask Caroline, "You know what I mean?" and she would pretend that she had heard whatever he was talking about and nod her head.

"Excuse me please," Caroline said to the older guy as she made her way back into the restaurant, where the owner, Brother Robertson's sister, was at the table socializing with her brother and his friends from church. Tangie told Caroline as she sat down that they were starting a single committee, and that they all were going to be going different places together, and she asked Caroline if she wanted to join. "No, thank you. I have my obligations to my church." Everyone understood, but still welcomed Caroline, because she was a frequent visitor to Tangie's church, and Tangie always spoke well of her. Poetry night started off with one of the famous poets.

There was soft music in the background as he began to speak. The music and his words were one, and it spoke to everyone, because everybody was fully engaged by moving their shoulders to the beat or bobbing their heads, and you could hear an occasional "alright now." After the famous poet, there were several amateurs before brother Robertson, and we learned that the second famous poet was a fairly new author, but he was very good, and he would finish poetry night with a couple of poems.

When it was Brother Robertson's time to enter the stage, he brought his guitar with him. Brother Robertson is a tall, caramel skin colored brother, with deep dimples like L.L. Cool J. He was raised in the country, where they still made their own milk and butter and raised their own farm animals. He came to Atlanta in pursuit of his career when he received two full scholarships, one for football and the other was an academic scholarship. Brother Robertson played for Georgia State University, and although he loved football, he was equally a computer geek and built his first computer when he was fourteen.

He decided to pursue his love for computers and became a computer engineer. Brother Robertson took a seat on the stool on stage and, with one hand, fixed his wide brim hat on his head, and then he licked his lips and smiled, showing off those dimples. This one is called, "She is," and he looked at Tangie and winked, and she smiled back, ready to see if Brother Robertson really had poetry skills, another gift that would be added to his athletic abilities and his smarts. Tangie was smiling the whole time as Brother Robertson played his guitar and made rhythmic analogies. He was pretty good, and a few groupies stood and cheered him on, as he went into detail about how he admired whoever "She is." When Brother Robertson finished his poem, everyone clapped, and all the single women stood, and a few even tried to make conversation with him as he made his way back to the table.

Later that night, Caroline tossed and turned in her bed, because her head was full of thoughts of Stacy, Amanda, and her, and this unexpected love triangle. Twenty-four hours ago, she had dismissed any thoughts of ever being with Stacy, but now that she saw someone else on his arm, she could not stand it, and she felt as if that should be her.

She scrolled down her smart phone of all the pictures of Amanda and Stacy, and she said, "That should be me. That will be me." After hours of laying down in her thoughts, she finally went to sleep.

It seemed like Caroline had just shut her eyes when her alarm went off. Today, she had to help out at the women's shelter, and it seemed as if it was night a few minutes ago, but now, the sun was shining bright. Caroline rubbed the sleep out of her eyes and got out of bed and into the shower. After breakfast, Caroline called Tangie to see if she wanted to go help out at the shelter, because Caroline wasn't feeling being around Mother Thomas and her smart remarks. Mother Thomas has always said whatever thoughts came to her mind, but no one ever really appreciated it.

Caroline didn't feel like getting fancy today, so she threw on a jumpsuit and some sneakers and grabbed her bag and headed to the shelter. She and all the other ladies arrived at the same time. Mother Thomas had her oversized bag on her left arm and the leash to the poodle in her right hand. She wore an oversized hat to compliment her oversized bags, no matter what day of the week it was. Everyone greeted each other, and Mother Thomas greeted everyone with her nose in the air.

No one ever really paid Mother Thomas any mind, because they knew that it was the way she was, and you had to have thick skin to deal with her. "Caroline, you look a hot mess today. Why didn't you put your hair up in a bun or something? My goodness." Mother Thomas looked at Caroline from head to toe.

"Well, at least, you don't have on those Jezebel heels today." She rolled her eyes and reached into her purse and gave Caroline a barrette to put her hair into a ponytail. "Leave Caroline alone," Mother Brooke said to Mother Thomas. "Caroline, my dear, you look fine, but you could use a comb in the back." Caroline hated having curly hair because of times like this. She had combed through her hair before she left home, but it somehow got matted together in the back.

"Maybe, she's right. I need to just brush it up into a bun or something, because it is just going to get frizzy," Caroline said to Mother Brooke. Mother Brooke is seventy-seven years old, but don't look a day over fifty. She is one of those older women who makes it a daily routine to walk the mall early in the a.m. with some of the other Mothers at the church. Mother Thomas looks every bit of her age, but the only thing anyone notices is the costume jewelry, hair dye, and expensive dress suits, hats, and bags that she wears. Mother Thomas held the barrette up, and Caroline took it and put up her hair.

10

fter helping to serve the women breakfast and passing out some clothing, the Mothers prayed for women who wanted it, and Caroline found herself counseling a young lady, like she so often did when visiting the shelter. Caroline isn't certified in any kind of therapy or counseling, but she did have a God given gift to help others along the way, when they needed advice. Caroline wished that she could take her own God given advice, and she could before Stacy came back into her life, and now, she is the one who needs prayer and counseling. "I wish I had all the answers," Caroline said to a young mother of three at the women's shelter, who left a physically abusive relationship and came to the shelter. Caroline looked at the three young kids, who ranged in age from one to four.

The three kids all seemed so happy, without a care in the world, as they sat on the floor in the playroom and played with toys. "You don't have to have all the answers, Caroline, just one. The right one." The battered lady smiled and pointed up to the ceiling, and Caroline looked up and smiled. The woman was right.

The right answer is to look to God, and Caroline knew Psalm 121:2 all too well, but these days, her vision was blurry. "Pray for me, sister," Caroline said to the young lady. "And you for me, Caroline," the young woman said as Caroline and the Mothers left the shelter. "It's something different about you, Caroline. I can see it all over you, Caroline, and it's not a good different. Ever since you started wearing those stilettos, it's like you grew into a totally different person, but I come to serve those demons, warning that they have to go," Mother Thomas said as she opened up her holy oil that she always had handy and started to throw it on Caroline.

Mother Thomas was throwing the oil and yanking her dog leash, without even knowing it. Caroline held up her hands and tried to run, and Mother Thomas was right behind her. The poodle got tired of being yanked around and bit Mother Thomas on the ankle.

She screamed and told the poodle, "Bad pooch; no treats for you this afternoon." She limped her way to her BMW and put her poodle in and then she got in and drove off. Everyone smiled and waved her off, but felt relieved that she had left. "Caroline, are you ok?" Mother Brooke said as she gave Caroline some tissues out of her purse, so that she could wipe the oil off of her face and clothes. "I'm fine, thanks, Mother Brooke." "Lord give us the strength to deal with that woman," Mother Brooke said as she watched Mother Thomas ride down the street until she was out of view.

"Are you sure that you're ok, Caroline?" Caroline nodded and said "yes ma'am." "Look at me, Caroline. I'm not talking about are you ok with what just happened with Thomas. I'm talking about are you ok in life? You know we could always talk. I may not be your Ma Ann, but she was my best friend, and I promised her that I would look after you when she moved so many years ago. I know when something is bothering you, and its ok that you don't want to talk about it, but just know that I am here for you, and yet praying for you and your family every day." "I know, Mother Brooke, and I thank you so much, but really, I'm fine." "Ok," Mother Brooke said as she opened her arms and hugged Caroline.

"I love you just as much as I love my own kids, and if you ever need me, you know my number, and you know where I live, and you are always welcome." Caroline smiled, "Thank you, Mother Brooke, and I love you too." They said their goodbyes and agreed to see each other bright and early for Sunday school tomorrow morning. On the way home, Caroline called Tangie via Bluetooth and told her about Mother Thomas.

"That old bag," Tangie said. "See, you are good, Caroline, because there are some things that I haven't been delivered from yet, and beating up people is one of them." "Girl, I don't pay her any attention. She is an old miserable woman, who has been widowed for five years now, and she's really harmless," Caroline said as she turned into her driveway and noticed Mike's truck parked at his ex-wife's house. "Anyway, I would go to church with you tomorrow and give her a piece of my mind, but Brother Robertson is coming over for dinner after church, so I won't be able to come, and not only that, but my mama did teach me to respect my elders, but if she tries something, I'm just a phone call away." Caroline laughed, "Girl, you are a trip, but I think that I can handle Mother Thomas, but if I can't, you will be the first person that I call.

Look I have to go, but I will call you back in a few."

"Wait, what? Already? We just started talking like five minutes ago, and you didn't ever tell me what was so important that you were on your phone all last night." "Look, Tangie, I will call you back, but right now, something just came up, and I have to go." Tangie was still talking when Caroline hung up the phone. "Rude," Tangie said to the cell phone, as if Caroline was still on the other end. Besides an occasional text, Caroline and Mike hadn't talked for months. Caroline was really happy to see his truck parked next door and hoped that he would stop by to say hello. Caroline decided that she would not let Mike leave without seeing him. She opened her living room curtains, so that she could see if he was leaving, and she decided that if he tried to leave without coming to see her then she would go outside and make him talk to her.

She hadn't figured out just how she would make him talk to her, but she was working on it. Caroline sat on the love seat in front of the window and occasionally looked to see if Mike was still there. She thought about going over to Angel's house and asking him if they could talk. Caroline thought that it was odd that Michael hadn't come to say hi, and she hadn't seen him outside or riding his bike. Caroline started to wonder if Michael was even over there.

After a couple of hours, Angel came out and headed to Mike's truck and then Mike came from behind her. Caroline peeked out the window, so that they couldn't see her. Mike opened the passenger door for Angel, and she got in and then he went to the driver's side and got in and they pulled off. "So, Michael isn't with them. I wonder what this is all about. Maybe she needed a ride somewhere. It's probably nothing. If she needed a ride, why didn't she drive? She has a car," Caroline said out loud, but to herself. A couple of hours later, Caroline was taking out the trash, and Angel and Stacy pulled up. Caroline had taken her hair out of the bun she had earlier, and her hair was wild like a mad woman. Angel waited for Mike to open her door, and she got out of the car. Mike picked up some bags that looked like take out from somewhere, but Caroline couldn't really tell. She smiled and walked fast back to her house, trying to hide how awkward she felt seeing them look so happy. Mike didn't notice Caroline outside, but Angel did, and when she noticed Caroline, she kissed Mike on the cheek and grabbed his hand. Mike told Angel something in her ear and she smiled then looked back at Caroline and rolled her eyes as the two of them went into the house.

Caroline was sure that they must be back together. She felt terrible. Caroline closed her curtains and decided to get her pint of ice cream out of the freezer and eat it, while she felt sorry for herself. Although she'd closed her living room curtains, every now and then, she would take a peek outside, and Mike's truck was still parked next door.

At nine p.m., Caroline took one last look outside, and she was startled, because there was Mike coming towards her door. Caroline couldn't believe that he was actually coming over after spending all day with Angel. She felt some type of way about that, but she told herself that she wouldn't jump to conclusions about Mike and Angel. She would give him the benefit of the doubt, because if she didn't, it would turn into another conflict, due to miscommunication. Her doorbell rang, and she threw a baseball cap on her head and grabbed a book, pretending that she had been reading before she opened the door.

"Mike hi, what a nice surprise." "Hey, Caroline I hope that you're not too busy. I just wanted to talk with you, because I feel like the last time that we saw each other, there was some miscommunication on both of our ends, mainly because I did not want to listen, at the time, but I wasn't completely honest with you, as well, and I don't want you to be in the dark or mislead, so I came over to confess something to you." This was it, Caroline felt like she was going to die. She imagined the next words that came out of Mike's mouth were that he and Angel were getting back together. Caroline could not take two heartbreaks in two days. As Mike begin to talk, Caroline quickly forgot about giving him the benefit of the doubt, and she said, "Look Mike, you don't have to explain. I know that you and Angel are back together, and I may not like it, but I respect you for coming over to let me know, instead of keeping me in the dark."

"What?" Mike said confusingly. "Haven't you heard a word that I just said?" "No, but I saw the two of you earlier looking like high school sweethearts, and I saw her kiss you, and you whispering in her ear." Mike laughed.

"I'm sorry that I don't find any of that amusing, so if you'll excuse me, I have a book to finish reading." Mike shook his head. "I took Angel to get her wisdom teeth pulled, so she can't drive for one. Two, I guess the medicine has her feeling all jittery, because she hasn't kissed me in years, and I wasn't whispering sweet nothings in her ear. I was asking her if she was sure that she was ok.

"Look, I took her to her appointment and then to the pharmacy to pick up her meds and a few other items that she needed from the drug store, but that was it. The dentist said that she was going to be a little groggy, and I've been over here to help her out, but nothing else is going on between Angel and me." Caroline was upset and she felt jealous that Mike was taking care of Angel like she was still his wife. Then she remembered that Angel really didn't have anyone else to look out for her like Mike.

"What happened to Angel's boyfriend? Why couldn't he take her?" "Look, Caroline, I don't get into her business, just like I don't want her in mine, but I have told her that I didn't want her to get the wrong idea about her and me. I am doing what I feel is right for my son's mother, because I want him to grow up and respect women. I'm not going to treat her any kind of way because of our past. I am still going to respect her, because she is the mother of my child." Caroline looked at Mike dumbfounded, but she understood and respected Mike for setting a good example.

She didn't know what to think. "Where is Michael?" "He should be here any minute. He went to a birthday party at the skating rink with his friends up the street, and the friend's mother is dropping him off here soon." "Ok, so what about what you have to confess to me? If nothing is going on with you and Angel, then what do you have to tell me?" Mike paused for a minute. "I have to tell you that, first and foremost, I am sorry for the way I acted that day. I should have given you a chance to explain, but I was hurt and then pride was in the way, because I didn't want another man to think that I was some kind of sucker or something by staying there in my feelings, so I left. I know that we occasionally text each other, but I think about you every day, and I just didn't know how to go about telling you the truth." "And what is the truth, Mike?"

Mike took a deep breath in and a deep breath out. "I love you, Caroline." "What? Are you sure that you haven't taken any of Angel's meds?"

"I'm sure, but even more sure about my love for you. People speak of love at first sight all the time, and even though I had seen you before, when I saw you that night that I had that seizure, I knew that I loved you, and it was your face that I want to see every time I wake up for as long as you let me. Now, I know it was wrong to think that way back then when I was still married, and I've repented, and God and I have moved past that, but I know, without a shadow of a doubt, that I love you, and if you give me a chance, I will prove it to you every day, but I need for you to be honest with me about your feelings. How do you feel about me?" Caroline swallowed hard. She knew, without a shadow of a doubt, that she cared for Mike, but did she love him?

She weighed Mike and Stacy on a love scale in her mind, and when she added it all up, she and Stacy had history and their love ended due to time and circumstance. Caroline did not want to lose Stacy to Amanda, when

Stacy was undoubtedly the only man that Caroline was a hundred percent sure that she loved. Mike, on the other hand, is a pure gentleman; he is smart, handsome, funny, an awesome father, and most importantly, he seeks God. Stacy's mother raised him in the church, but Stacy hasn't been to church in years. Caroline was confused, but when she looked up at Mike and into his eyes, she knew that he was the better choice.

Her heart was tied to Stacy, but her mind told her to go with Mike.

"All I want is for you to be honest, Caroline. I will never pressure you in any way, and if you aren't ready for a relationship, then let me know. Even if you're not ready now, I know in my heart and mind that you are the woman for me." Caroline took a deep breath and stroked the bottom of her face as she thought about what to say.

Time seemed to be going in slow motion, but she knew that she was running out of time, and if she kept stringing Mike along, then sooner or later, all ties would be broken, and she'd lose him forever. "Mike, I'm…" Before Caroline could finish her sentence, Michael ran up to Caroline's house and knocked on the door. Caroline was sitting on the couch so Mike opened the door. "Hi, dad!" "What's up son? How was the skating rink?"

"It was fun. Hi Ms. Caroline." "Well hello Michael, you are getting tall. Every time I see you, it's like you've grown a foot. You're taller than me now."

"Michael, go say goodbye to your mom, and make sure that you get everything that you brought over, because I'm not coming back for any shoes, games, iPod, or whatever you leave behind." Mike rubbed Michael on the top of his head, messing up Michael's baseball cap.

"Dad, you messed up my fitted." Michael fixed his cap back the way he had it and smiled at Caroline. "Is my hat on right, Ms. Caroline?" "It's perfect, Michael, just the way you had it." "Thanks, because Dad be trying to mess up my mojo, sometimes. I keep telling him that I'm a young man, now. He can't be rubbing me on the top of the head like I'm still in elementary. I'm in middle school now." "That's right you are; my oh my, how time flies," Caroline said as she went over and gave Michael a hug.

"You are a young man now, aren't you?" Michael popped his shirt collar. "See, I told you, Dad." Mike and Caroline looked at each other and smiled. Mike shook his head.

"Ok, young man that's enough. Go ahead and say goodbye to your mother and see if she needs anything before we leave." "Yes sir," Michael said as he left out the front door and walked to his mother's house next door.

"What's that new walk that he has now?"

Caroline was looking at Michael, who walked to his mother's house with a slight limp in his walk. "Yeah, he got that from a friend of his at school, and that's their "swag walk." Caroline burst out laughing. "They use to call that the pimp walk, when we were growing up, remember?" "Yeah, I know, but you know, there's nothing new under the sun. People just find new names for it."

"That's very true," Caroline said. Mike looked down into Caroline big brown eyes and caressed her right cheek. "You had a little something smeared on your face." "Oh thanks," Caroline said, but thinking all this time she's been talking to Mike with ice cream stuck on her face. "How embarrassing," she said as she wiped the side of her cheek.

"Is it still there?" "No, I think that I got it the first time." Caroline let out a small chuckle, "Thanks." "I got you, you should know that by now." "I do," Caroline said, knowing that Mike wasn't leaving until he got the answer that he needed.

"Mike um, this is very hard for me to say, but," she paused for a few seconds. "I'm sorry, but I just can't," she paused again. Mike looked into her eyes, longing for an answer. "You can't what? Caroline, talk to me. I'm right here, and I'm not running away this time. Tell me, I can take it."

"I can't express my feelings easily, and how does a person know when they are truly in love? I mean, I was a child the first time that I fell in love, and now I am a grown woman, and I don't expect love to happen the same way, but when it does, I feel like a person will know without a shadow of a doubt. I'm not sure that I even know what love is, Mike, but I do feel something for you, and I am willing to explore exactly what that is if you give me a chance. Maybe you can teach me exactly what love is, and how to love, because I don't think that I fully understand what it is. Can we take our time? I am willing to give us a try if you can be patient with me."

Mike kissed Caroline on her forehead. "Baby, when I say that I love you, I really do. And when a person falls in love, it usually doesn't happen the same way twice. I know what you've been through in life and how you felt abandoned by your parents, because they worked all the time, and never really spent quality time with you. "I know how you feel like your first love abandoned you when you felt as if you had no one else in the world to turn to or understand you. You told me how you were closer to his mother than your own, and how you felt lost without them in your life. But in your lost, you also found God, the one who loves you more than you'll ever know. The one who died on a cross for you and knows you better than you know yourself. "You found comfort and love in him, and you became so close to him, and that's one thing that I admire about you, and it's one thing that made me want to get my life in order. Seeing how strong you are in the midst of everything life has thrown at you motivated me. I would not even approach you if I felt like my life wasn't in order, but for the first time in a long time, I feel like I am heading in the right direction, and it's you that I have to thank for helping me get there. Now, we may not be perfect, and I don't have all of the answers, right now, and I may never, but when I say I love you, believe me; it's real. So are we going to give us a chance?

"If it's only for the reason that I love you, do you think that we could make it work and will you allow me to show you what it's truly like when a man loves a woman?" Tears were in Caroline eyes as she nodded her head yes, "Yes, I am willing to give us a try." They hugged, and when they did, both of their hearts felt like one, and they both could feel the warmth and the genuineness of each other. "I'm ready, Dad," Michael said as he approached the front door to Caroline's house.

Mike wiped Caroline's eyes of the few tears that had rolled down her face. "Ok son, I'm coming. Go ahead and put your things in the truck, and I'm right behind you." "Yes sir. Bye Ms. Caroline."

"Bye baby." Michael turned around and gave Caroline a funny look. "Oh I'm sorry you're not a baby anymore. You're a young man. Bye, Michael, I will see you soon ok." "Ok, it's about time," Michael said as he waved.

"Good job, Dad." Mike shook his head, "That boy, excuse me, young man, is something else. He is almost twelve and he thinks he's almost twenty-one." "Yeah, but he means well." "I know, and he reminds me so much of me when I was younger. That's the funny part."

Mike grabbed Caroline's hands and kissed them. "I will call you when I get home." Caroline smiled and went in for another hug. It is something about Mike's hugs; she felt safe when she was in his arms. "I love you," Caroline said as she came out of their embrace.

Mike smiled, "I know, and I love you too." Caroline walked Mike to the door and waved him and Michael off. After they were out of view, she closed the door behind her and stood with her back against the door, and her head to the ceiling as she smiled. The words I love you just came out, without Caroline having to think about it. When she told Mike that she loved him, she surprised herself.

"I love him," she said, still staring up at the ceiling. "I really do love him," she said again as she turned around to lock the door and headed to her bedroom. That night, Caroline and Mike talked on the phone from eleven at night until five the next morning. Mike had to go to work on a Sunday for inventory at one of his company's major distributor's location, and Caroline tried to get two hours of sleep before getting up for bible study, but she could not fall asleep. Caroline was too busy thinking about her newfound love for Mike and all the possibilities that love could have in store for them. Today, the pastor preached about strongholds and spiritual bonds, mostly known as soul ties. The pastor used as an analogy, how people sleep with one person, but when they sleep with that one person, they also unknowingly are having sex with everyone that the person they slept with, had sex with. He also said that when people fornicate or commit adultery, that they are picking up, not only people, but demonic forces, and they are allowing those demons into their life. The things that the pastor was preaching on were making a few people uncomfortable, but he said that the Holy Spirit had been pressing on him to discuss that issue. Caroline had learned a thing or two and was sure that she was definitely done with Stacy for good. After all, God was calling her out. Caroline understood why all these years she still loved Stacy and felt a bond with him that no one could break. It was an ungodly soul tie. Caroline had heard of people being soul mates, and she thought that maybe Stacy was hers, but she quickly found out that a soul tie and a soul mate can be very confusing, if you don't understand what each of them mean. A soul tie keeps a person in bondage after a relationship has ended. A soul mate is God instituted, better known as marriage.

Ephesians 5:31 says, "For this reason a man shall leave his father and mother and hold fast to his wife, and the two shall become one flesh." Caroline had a better understanding of why she was feeling the things that she was feeling for Stacy after seventeen years. It was a stronghold, not love, and that soul tie had to be broken. Caroline went to the alter and asked her pastor to pray for her and for that soul tie to be broken off her life and for God's will to be done in her life. Mother Thomas came up to pray for Caroline, and she started pretending to be speaking in tongues and shouting, while she threw her holy oil all over Caroline and some splashed on the pastor.

The pastor was about fed up with Mother Thomas and her behavior and had only tolerated her for so long, because he felt sympathy for her, since she'd lost Deacon Thomas, but today, he was tired. "Satan, you are a liar, and the truth is not in you," the pastor yelled. "I rebuke you in the holy unmatched name of Jesus Christ, come out of our sister, right now! You have no control over her life. She has been washed in the blood of Jesus, and no weapon formed against her shall prosper. You cannot have her mind; neither can you have her soul. Anger, I bind you up in the name of Jesus, and I loose peace that surpasses all understanding that only comes from our Lord and savior Jesus Christ. Bitterness, hatred and pride, I cast you back to hell from which you came, and Lord, I ask you free our sister's mind and fill her with your love, meekness, and holy spirit, so that she can forgive whomever for whatever and walk fully in your light. In the precious name of our Lord and Savior Jesus Christ, and the church say." Everyone said, "Amen, Amen and Amen." Now, Caroline had cried her eyes out and felt free after the pastor had prayed over her, but when she had opened her eyes, it was Mother Thomas who was on the floor, passed out.

God had cast all kinds of demons that had been holding Mother Thomas hostage for years. The ushers were fanning Mother Thomas, and some of the Deacons came to help her up. Mother Thomas cried and threw a hand up in the air, without a saying one word. This was highly unlikely for Mother Thomas, because she always had something to say. She sat down in her seat, without saying anything to anyone for the rest of the church service, and at the end of the service, she did her usual fellowship, but only by saying nice to see you, goodbye, shaking hands, or hugging.

She didn't make one rude comment, and her nose wasn't so far in the air anymore, like she was better than everyone else. She had a level head as she walked to her car a free woman. The pastor came from behind Caroline and touched her shoulder as Caroline watched Mother Thomas get into her car and leave quietly. "She'll be fine, Caroline. You know she wasn't always like that. I remember when she was so happy, but then her and Deacon Thomas started going through some things that I counseled them through. She said that she'd forgiven him for whatever he'd done, but I could tell that her forgiveness had a cost. He spent the rest of his life trying to make up for his mistake by buying her all kinds of diamonds and pearls, a huge house that they really didn't need, and all sorts of other things. He died before she could really truly forgive him, and the way she acted before today was a result of anger, bitterness, and pride that has been a stronghold in her life. I should have called it like it was a long time ago, but there's a season for everything." The pastor began to walk away from Caroline and then he turned around and faced her and said, "Oh, and you'll be alright too," then he smiled and walked away to greet other members of the church.

Caroline smiled and said to herself, I will be alright. Then she started singing a song that she used to sing in the choir when she would visit the same church with Ma Ann. "I got a fee-ling, everything's going to be al-right. Jesus told me, everything's going to be al-right." Caroline smiled and sang her way home.

11

"Everything will not be alright!" Mr. Taylor shouted over the phone to one of his business colleagues, who was trying to persuade him that everything was going to work out for the good at GPSG. It was now another year, and Mr. Lavado still hadn't been persuaded to invest in GPSG, but due to Stacy and other artists at the museum, proceeds were coming in heavily, and Caroline was able to get an assistant. Mr. Taylor wanted to begin work and expand sister stations in the south eastern region of the U.S. Mr. Taylor had given up hope that this major banker would ever invest in his company, and having part of Stacy's earnings going to the proceeds of GPSG did not help in the matter. Mr. Lavado did not like Stacy, but he does love his daughter, Amanda. Getting Stacy major exposure and helping him to create clientele and a job at the largest art museum in Atlanta wasn't a big deal to Mr. Lavado, but Amanda was proud of her man. Mr. Taylor knew the best way to get to Mr. Lavado was through his daughter, who was head over heels for Stacy. Amanda and Stacy weren't the typical good girl and bad guy couple, because Amanda was worth millions, and her parents were billionaires. Stacy was born and raised in the ghetto and was rough around the edges, but he never sought out the easy way to get rich; instead, he worked on his art and created a portfolio and would go to different museums and galleries, trying to get exposure.

Knock, knock, knock, Caroline tapped on Mr. Taylor's office door, which was not completely closed all the way. "Come in, Caroline. I was just finishing up a phone call with a colleague. Please tell me that you have some kind of good news, because we're already eight months behind on expanding GPSG, and at this point, I'm starting to lose hope. I was sure that Stacy would have had his soon to be "wifey," Mr. Taylor said, putting up quotation marks with his fingers, "to persuade her dad that his money would be of good use." Caroline and Mike had been happily dating for months now, but somehow, it still bothered her when she heard anything about Stacy and Amanda.

Working with Stacy, mostly every day, and being responsible for him gaining exposure as an artist and setting up jobs at fundraisers and other benefits for GPSG did not help. Stacy felt like he owed his success to Caroline and would grace her with roses, lunch, or expensive gifts every chance that he could get. Caroline would tell Stacy that his gifts weren't necessary, and that she was only doing her job, but he insisted on her receiving the gifts as a token of how thankful he was. Caroline never told Mike about all the gifts Stacy would buy her, like the diamond studded bracelet, necklace, or Michael Kors handbag. He even bought her a dress and some red bottom heels for the art fundraiser last fall. Caroline never told Mike about the gifts, because she knew that Mike would never understand why Caroline would take gifts from Stacy.

"Caroline," Mr. Taylor said as he scratched the side of his head, right where his grey hair was beginning to come in.

"Yes, Mr. Taylor." "I have some good news, and I have some bad news, depending on how you take it, but first, give me the morning briefing." Caroline had no idea what she'd walked into this morning, but hoped with the good news of new investors that it would ease whatever bad news Mr. Taylor had.

If it was one thing that took him from a bad mood to a great mood, it was the smell of new investors, aka the smell of money. After the briefing, Mr. Taylor's mood did lighten up, but he was still hesitant on how he should tell Caroline the good/bad news. "Ok Caroline, I'm going to be straight forward and not beat around the bush. Would you like the good news or the bad news, first?" Caroline had become really concerned, at this point, and knew that her bonus was cut this year to recruit her an assistant.

The funds for the sister stations were slow, but steady, and GPSG was only making money to break even. Some people had to take a cut in pay, and some people left the job voluntarily. Maybe Mr. Taylor was thinking about getting rid of Caroline and leaving the assistant on, since the assistant was only paid half of Caroline's salary. Before Caroline could say whether she'd like to hear the good or bad news first, Mr. Taylor continued to speak. "Ok, I'll start with the good news. We have an investor in Florida, where we are trying to expand, and he would like to meet with us to discuss expanding GPSG. We already have a building set with all the equipment that's needed. We just need to make sure that we have enough money to begin broadcast and, of course, we need to recruit employees. Now, if everything goes well, we would oversee the new non-profit television station, and I would need for someone that I can trust to manage that location." Caroline was getting excited about the news of the new location, but she was trying to keep her composure, because Mr. Taylor hadn't yet told her the bad news.

"Mr. Taylor, this is very good news. We are starting to reap the results of hard labor. I knew that our new Florida investors were about business when we met with them last month." "Yes, but before you get too excited, let me give you the bad news." Dang way to mess up a good moment, Mr. Taylor, Caroline thought. "I need for you and Stacy to fly to South Beach and meet with the investor and a few of his colleagues and make a good impression on GPSG."

"That's it, that's the bad news? Mr. Taylor, I could use a little sunshine in my life, besides, in case you haven't noticed, the weather has been in the mid-forties for the past week." "Oh so you are ok with this?" Mr. Taylor said with relief. "Of course," Caroline stood with excitement. "Well, I was hesitant, because I know that working with Stacy

ONE FOR THE REASON OF LOVE

hasn't been the most comfortable situation for you, especially with the past history that you told me that you all shared. I just want you to be comfortable, because you are a valuable asset to this company, and we really couldn't have accomplished half of what we have without you."
"Thank you Mr. Taylor," Caroline said modestly. "I really appreciate that, but I could definitely use a little warm weather, and as you know, charming investors is what I do best. I am concerned about, why Stacy, though? My assistant would be a greater help if she could come along."

"Well, your assistant may be a lot of help to you, but Stacy would be a lot of help to the company, because our Florida investor has asked to meet with Stacy, and he has an offer for Stacy that will benefit not only us, here, but also in Florida." Caroline was curious as to what the museum director in Atlanta would think about Stacy leaving to work in Florida. "And he doesn't have anything to worry about as far as his current position at the museum here. I have already worked that out, and although we will be sad to see him go, if he accepts the job offer, then it would mean more money for him and a healthy percentage going towards our Florida location. It's not banker money, but every percentage helps, and who knows? Maybe his soon to be father in law will see his ambition and want to invest in the future. After all, whether he likes it or not, this man will be his daughter's husband, and I know that he will do anything for his daughter."

Mr. Taylor was still trying to bank on Mr. Lavado's money by using Stacy to persuade Amanda to get Mr. Lavado to invest in GPSG. It hadn't worked for a year, and things weren't looking too good, but Mr. Taylor was sure that his plan would work. He was sure that, in due time, everything would fall into place. Caroline did not like the fact that Mr. Taylor was using Stacy as his "come up" in a sense but when she discussed her thoughts with Mr. Taylor, he told her that it was all just business, and that he was not using Stacy, but helping him to help GPSG.

Caroline was excited about the business trip to South Beach, and maybe, she could get Mike to tag along with her. "I am so excited about this vacation," Caroline said before realizing what she'd said. She cleared her throat, "I mean business trip. I'm excited and privileged to step in for you, Mr. Taylor, and I will not let you down. You don't mind if Mike comes with us, do you? I can't wait to tell him about it. Oh, how long do we have before we leave, a month, two weeks?" "Slow down, Caroline. Remember, this is a business trip, and Mike can come along, but at his own expense, and as long as it doesn't interfere with you doing your job; however, you don't leave in a month or even two weeks." "Ok great, that means that I have even more time to work on notes for the meeting and to browse hotels. Mr. Taylor, I am so excited. I haven't been away from Georgia, since I went to visit my parent's years ago in D.C."

"Caroline, now just wait one minute before you get all excited about planning and whatever else," Mr. Taylor said with a hesitant look on his face. "What is it, Mr. Taylor, I know that look like the back of my hands. You have more bad news, don't you?"

"Well, Caroline, I don't know if it will be bad news or not, depending on how you take it, but you have less time than you think." "Ok," Caroline said, holding up her hands as in waiting for Mr. Taylor to give her a date. "You leave tonight, Caroline." "What!" "I know, I know, look Caroline, calm down," Mr. Taylor said as he peeked out his blinds to see if anyone had heard Caroline yell. Everyone was working as usual, faxing, looking over paperwork, or working on a project in their cubicle.

"Thank God for sound proof walls," he said with relief. "Now Caroline, I know it's a lot to ask, but I was going with Stacy, but my plans got canceled, because I have to meet with one of the major investors in what, hopefully, will be our South Carolina location." "What, we're looking to expand to South Carolina already?" "Well hopefully," Mr. Taylor said, scratching the side of his head. Caroline was starting to believe that Mr. Taylor's grey hair was a sign of stress on the side of his head, where he would scratch when he was under pressure or stressed.

If it was a sign of getting old, then the grey hair missed that memo about ten years ago, because Mr. Taylor was in his fifties with only a few streaks of grey hair on the side of his head. Now, Caroline saw why Mr. Taylor was stressed when she first walked into his office. "Look, Caroline, I know it's a lot, and I had mentioned this to Stacy months ago that he and I were taking a business trip to South Beach, but I wasn't sure exactly when. Both of these were a spur of the moment kind of thing, and everything is already booked and paid for. I got an email confirmation this morning from the investor's secretary, and she said it was to confirm the business meeting that she emailed me about a couple of weeks ago, but I never got the email. I called her this morning, and she said that tomorrow morning is the only time that he had to meet with someone from our company, and that he is a very busy man, who thrives on first impressions, so I couldn't reschedule, because how would that make us look?"

Caroline understood what Mr. Taylor was saying. "Ok, but I have a lot of work to do, today, Mr. Taylor and then I have to go home and pack, and I don't even have everything I need to try to fill your shoes."

"Caroline, calm down. I have total confidence in you. Here," Mr. Taylor gave Caroline a thick folder with the Florida location business plans, GPSG portfolio, and everything else that Mr. Taylor could think of that the investor may ask to see. "Now, I have already told your assistant that you are going on a business trip, today, so she has already started on whatever you normally do when you come in, but you will have to quickly brief her on whatever else that you need done.

"I called Stacy after I read the email this morning and told him about everything, so he is aware. After you do whatever you need to do here, I suggest you go home and talk with Mike and pack, because your flight leaves tonight at 9:55, and you have to meet with the investor at 8:00 am sharp." Gees, Caroline thought. Talk about pressure. But she was happy to be able to leave Georgia, even for a few days.

The thought of Mike being by her side made the unplanned business trip even more bearable. On Caroline's way to her car, she phoned Mike via Bluetooth. "Hey beautiful, I was just thinking about you," Mike said as he looked at a photo of Caroline that he had on his office desk, next to a photo of him and Michael. "I was just looking at your photo." Caroline put the palm of her hand on her forehead, "Oh my goodness that old photo.   Baby, are you forgetting that's a photo when I graduated college in my early twenties." "I know, but you don't look a day older than when you took this photo." "Aww thank you, baby," Caroline said blushing over the phone. Mike took a sip of coffee out of his tall coffee mug, "So what's up, baby?" "Baby, I wanted to know if you wanted to take a trip with me to South Beach?" "Of course, so when do we leave?" "Great, we leave tonight." "Tonight?" Mike laughed. "Caroline why so soon baby? I know a vacation is much needed on both of our ends, but tonight?" Caroline told Mike everything that Mr. Taylor told her. Mike sighed, "Baby I would love to go, but I have a lot of work that I have to catch up on this week, and I wish that I could just up and leave but Michael's nanny has a life of her own and I won't just up and leave him with her. It's not fair to either of them. My parents just had him this past weekend, so that you and I could spend some QT together, so I won't ask them to watch him again. It's for how many days, now?" "I will be back Friday," Caroline said sadly. "Stacy has to accompany me on this business trip as well." Mike didn't like it but he understood, after all, its just business. "So you will be there four days?"

"Yeah," Caroline said again with disappointment in her voice. "Baby, don't sound so disappointed. Look, I promise that I will plan a vacation for us real soon. You just caught me at a bad time, baby, and nothing would please me more than to be down there with you, especially since old boy is going." "Baby you know that you don't have anything to worry about as far as Stacy and me."

"Yes, I know, and I trust you one hundred percent, but I don't put anything past him." "Baby, don't worry about that. I can handle Stacy. I will miss you though." "I will miss you too." Knock, knock, knock, Mike's friend and business colleague knocked on his office door.

"Mike the meeting is about to start." Mike held up his pointer finger and mouthed to his friend, "one minute." "Look my love, I have to go, but don't stress about anything and try to enjoy yourself. I love you." "I love you too, Mike. Mwah," Caroline kissed through the phone. "Mwah right back at ya," Mike kissed back and they both ended the call. "Mwah," Mike friend teased him. "Man, go head on with all of that,"

Mike laughed. "But for real," Mike friend said. "I'm just glad to see you happy, my friend. She's good for you." "She is, isn't she?" Mike said as he smiled, and he and his friend headed to the business meeting. Caroline went home and packed and went over the itinerary. They were flying first class and staying in a five-star resort on the beach. Caroline surfed the web to look for places to dine and things to do. She was determined that this trip would not only be business, but pleasurable as well.

When Caroline got to the airport, Stacy was already checked in and sitting with his linen short suit on and his loafers. Some people were looking at him like he was crazy, because it was forty-eight degrees outside. Stacy smiled with confidence and was looking forward to the temperatures in the mid-seventies. Stacy and Caroline went over questions and answers to prep themselves for anything the investor might ask. That night, Caroline went to sleep immediately after checking into the hotel room, while Stacy signed autographs and took pictures with people on the beach and at the hotel.

12

"**Y**ou are going to need a security guard soon," Caroline joked because of all the female attention and women asking to take pictures with the artist, who had taken to fame so suddenly. Not too many men were asking for Stacy's autograph, but they would shake his hand, give him dap, or tell him how he is inspiring our youth to never give up on their dreams. Stacy was big on not forgetting where you come from and was known for going from the projects to pursuing his lifelong dream and being successful at it.

The next day a woman from a local newspaper caught Stacy and Caroline heading to their rental car and asked Stacy if he had time for a quick question or two, and that it would make the kids at the local high school so happy. A few of the kids were applying for the SAG Art grant that were proceeds from GPSG from a percentage of Stacy's earnings through the museum and art fundraisers.

"Well, what can I say; Stacy love the kids," Stacy said as he stood ready to answer a few quick questions from the reporter. After asking two questions, Caroline nudged Stacy in the arm, "Come on, Stacy, we can't be late for this." "Ok one more question," the reporter said. "SAG, is it true that on this road to success, you have accomplished everything that you ever wanted?"

Stacy looked over at Caroline, "I wouldn't say everything, but it's only a matter of time. You can accomplish anything in life if you believe in yourself, stay persistent, and when it seems like nothing is working in your favor, don't give up, but be patient. In due time, everything will work out for the best." Stacy winked at Caroline and chills went down her spine. Why is this man doing this in public? She thought to herself.

"Alright, Stacy, let's go," she said as she opened the back seat door and put her hand bag on the seat and went to open the driver's door, but Stacy rushed over and opened it for her. She felt awkward, but told him thanks, anyway. Stacy never opened the door for her, and Caroline figured it must be an act for the paper or whomever else was watching. On the drive to meet the investor, Caroline was upset. "Look Stacy, let's get one thing straight.

I have a boyfriend, and I love him. Not only that, but you are engaged, and I don't appreciate that stunt that you tried to pull back there." "Caroline stop lying to yourself," Stacy replied. "Yes, I have a fiancée, and you have a boyfriend and you may even love him, but you love me too." "It's not the same," Caroline said quickly.

"But you aren't denying the fact that you do love me?" "I do, Stacy, but I'm no longer in love with you." Stacy laughed, "Caroline, you've never been good at lying." Caroline swallowed hard, Stacy was starting to get on her last nerve, and it wasn't even noon yet.

"Caroline, don't you think that, after all these years, we ended up working for the same company for a reason?" Caroline thought to herself, if you only knew the real reason Mr. Taylor has you on board, you wouldn't be too thrilled. Stacy continued to talk, "I also know that, in the beginning, Mr. Taylor was trying to get to me to get Amanda to persuade her father to invest in GPSG." Caroline slowed the car down and pulled over to the side of the road.

"What?"

Caroline could not believe that Stacy knew. "Don't look so shocked, Caroline. You know me, baby; I'm from the streets. It doesn't matter what position you play; the game remains the same, baby. Mr. Taylor knows plenty of wealthy people. He could pursue any of them, but he chose me. Why? Because he thought that he was playing the game smart, but I already knew that he was using me to get to Mr. Lavado.

"I had been working at a gallery in D.C and wasn't making much at the time, so I thought that it would be a great opportunity. I met Amanda at the Art Gallery in D.C. and she approached me. Don't get me wrong; she is fine, but a woman like that don't usually go for a guy like me. I had nothing at the time and have never asked Amanda or her father for a handout. You even saw that I worked for her before I'd ever ask her for money.

"I believe, if a man doesn't work, he doesn't eat. My mama worked into her sixties and only stopped to take care of my grandmother; you know this. Mr. Taylor has never come directly out and asked if I could get Amanda to persuade her father to invest in GPSG, but he throws hints every now and then, and when he does, it goes in one ear and out of the other. I would rather earn my respect than be somebody's made man. I know that Amanda loves me and would do anything for me in a heartbeat.

She even came at me with a business proposal when we first met, but I saw that she was only doing it because she wanted a relationship with me. I guess, after spending so much time with her, I did fall for her, because she has been down for me when I didn't have nothing to offer. I still only have chump change compared to what she has, but I'm proud of what I've accomplished. I guess I'm telling you all of this, because well, let me put it to you this way. Amanda knows who you are, I told her about us a long time ago.

"She trusts me and sees something in me that I'm not even sure I see in myself. I do love her, but I love you too. I can't lie about it any longer, Caroline, and I've even talked to Amanda about this. Why do you think that we haven't gotten married yet? I refuse to marry her until I know for certain that there is no chance of us.

"I wish that I could explain how I could be in love with two women at the same time, but I can't. It's crazy, because I love both of you for the same reasons; you both are so much alike." "But we aren't the same Stacy," Caroline cut Stacy off. "I know that, Caroline, and I know that it would be easier for you to hear that I love you, but I am in love with Amanda, but that's not true. "I'm in love with the both of you. I just don't know what to do anymore, Caroline, but let's make the most of this business trip, and if at the end, you still feel the same way that you say you feel about me, now, then I will respect your wishes, and you won't ever have to worry about me ever again. Ok?" Stacy looked over at Caroline, who was still taking in everything Stacy had told her.

Stacy reached over and grabbed her hand. "Ok?" Stacy asked again, waiting for Caroline to reply. "Ok." Caroline drove a block down to meet with the Florida investor before they were late. It was five minutes till nine.

The investor had already made up his mind, and everything was in place for the new television station. The meeting was merely a refresher and to see what kind of impression Caroline and Stacy would make. After the meeting and touring the facility, they toured the museum where Stacy would work if he accepted the position. The museum was private and wasn't opened to the general public, except by reservation or invitation. Mostly celebrities or wealthy people would visit the museum and purchase art. The museum has a five-star restaurant, located inside, where people could dine, and there was an open bar, located in the gallery, where art of all kinds hung on the wall. Stacy liked what he saw and thought that it would be a great opportunity to expand his work. He also liked the nice weather year round. An older woman, who was in the gallery viewing paintings, approached Stacy. "Young man, are you SAG?"

"I am," Stacy replied. "Oh, I just love your work. You truly have a gift." The older lady looked over at Caroline. "You, I know you." Caroline thought maybe the lady was mistaken or maybe someone looked like Caroline, but Caroline was sure that she did not know this woman. Caroline stood awkwardly, hoping the older woman would stop looking into her eyes, like a creep. "I'm sorry ma'am, but maybe you have mistaken me for someone?" "Yes," the old lady said slowly. "Maybe I am, but I could have sworn."

The old lady's husband came over to grab her by the arm. He was six foot two, and she was as short as Caroline. "Sorry about that, folks, but my wife will talk you to death if you let her," the old man said, while walking off with his wife. The old lady quickly turned around as she and her husband were walking. She held up her pointer finger, "I got it, I know who you are. You are forever," the old woman said, waving her finger like she had a wand in her hand. "Oh Kay," Caroline said, thinking that maybe the lady was crazy or something. They continued their tour, and Caroline and Stacy decided to have lunch at their hotel on the beach. "What was up with that lady at the museum?" Caroline sipped a glass of water and cut into her steak.

Stacy bit into his shrimp and took a swig of his beer. "I'm not sure," Stacy said as he continued to down the shrimp cocktail, one by one, until nothing was left, and then he asked the waiter to bring him more. "Are you ok, you've been kind of quiet ever since the old lady at the museum spoke to us?" "Oh yes, Caroline, I'm fine. I just have a lot to think about as far as this new job opportunity, you know?"

"This is true," Caroline said. They sat and dined and talked about the pros and cons of the new job opportunity. Stacy tried to persuade Caroline to go snorkeling with him, since they had the rest of the day. Caroline declined and decided to stay in her room and talk on the phone to Mike, instead. The next few days, they would meet with other business partners at the Florida location and meet with contractors.

Wednesday, Caroline finally gave in and decided to have a little fun. Mike had told her that she should get out and enjoy the weather and stop staying locked up in her hotel room. Caroline decided to go shopping, and she even bought a bathing suit and decided to head to the beach. "Hey, I've been calling you," Stacy said with his dreads tied back and his swim trunks on with no shirt. Caroline pretending that the sun was blocking her view, but really, she was trying to block Stacy's six pack that stood in her face. "Oh yeah, I'm sorry. I left my phone in my hotel room on the charger. What's up?"

Stacy held up snorkeling gear. "Well, I had a partner that I was going snorkeling with, but at the last minute, she declined," Stacy pointed his head over to the old woman who was the same lady from the museum on Tuesday. The old lady and her husband waved. "She forgot that she had a previous engagement with her husband, so she had to back out." The old lady mouthed "I'm sorry." "It's ok," Stacy mouthed and smiled back. "So, what's it going to be, Caroline? You want to try it or are you too chicken?" Stacy started clucking around like a chicken and making chicken noises, and Caroline laughed.

"Stacy, we are grown now; that doesn't work anymore." "Hum," Stacy said. "I dare you to go snorkeling; matter of fact, I double dare you. I don't think you have the balls." Caroline laughed again, "You're right, I don't have balls, but like I said, daring me to do something doesn't work anymore. How old are you twelve?"

"Ok, little chicken, stay here then, and I will tell you how fun it was when I get back. When we get back to Atlanta, don't be all salty, because you didn't get to do anything fun." Stacy begin to walk off. Caroline thought about her conversation with Mike, and he wanted her to do something fun.

He would probably have a fit if he knew I was doing something fun with Stacy, she thought. I better not. It would just lead to confusion. Caroline held her hand over her eyes to block the sun as she saw Stacy walking. I haven't had any real fun, besides shopping, she thought to herself. I don't see what this could hurt; besides, Stacy knows how I feel, and at least, I can say that I got to do something fun.

Caroline breathed in and exhaled. "Stacy, wait up," she said as she ran towards him. The old man held up his thumb at Stacy, and the old lady winked her eye at Stacy. Caroline looked at Stacy and smiled.

"You aren't slick. I see what the three of y'all got going on. Did he put the both of you up to this?" The old lady zipped her lips with her finger and the old man folded his newspaper and pretended that he had been reading it all along.

Snorkeling was great. Swimming with all the underwater creatures and seeing the colorful beauty under water was amazing.

As Caroline and Stacy came back to shore, there were photographers flashing lights and many people all around. Stacy was smiling for the camera, as always, and his groupies were nearby, yelling his name, like always. Stacy tried to grab Caroline's hand, and she snatched it away.

Caroline looked Stacy up and down. "Did you set this up?" She asked under her breath.

"Of course not, Caroline, don't be ridiculous. The word must have gotten out that I was here, and this is what happened." Caroline shook her head and ran off to the hotel. Stacy ran behind her.

"Caroline, wait a minute. Can you just talk to me for a minute?" "Stacy, there is nothing to talk about. Our picture will be all over the paper and maybe even the news, and there's no telling what they're going to say.

Why were you trying to grab my hand back there?"

"Caroline, I was trying to grab your hand to let you know that it's ok. I knew you would think what you are thinking now, and that was my way of assuring you not to worry about anything. Why can't you just trust me, Caroline? I would never do anything to hurt you, ever. I love you." "Well, I don't love you, Stacy," Caroline said sternly. "Look, this thing that you have for me has got to end today, right now, and when we get back to Atlanta, my assistant will work with you from now on, because I can't do this anymore. I am done." "Done with what, Caroline? You haven't even given us a chance. Caroline, please," Stacy pulled her close and kissed her on her lips. A camera flashed from behind the bushes.

Caroline released herself out of Stacy's embrace and cried, "I hate you. Stay away from me, Stacy," she yelled as she ran towards the hotel. Stacy called and texted Caroline all night. Caroline turned her phone on silent. How am I going to explain this to Mike? She asked herself.

Caroline tried to call Mike several times, but he did not pick up the phone.

Caroline left a message on Mike's cell. "Baby, please give me a call as soon as possible. Something has happened, and I need to speak with you. It's urgent, so please give me a call as soon as possible." Mike called Caroline the next day, right when the plane was getting ready for take-off, and she could not talk. The plane ride back to Atlanta was short, but it seemed like it took forever.

Caroline braced herself for whatever was to come. Mike met Caroline at the airport, and she was excited to see him, so she ran to him and they hugged. "Baby, it's only been four days," Mike said. "I know, but it seems like forever," Caroline said. Mike got Caroline's luggage off the baggage claim belt and took them to her car for her.

"Baby, I want you to come back to my place. Michael and I have something to show you." "Okay," Caroline said nervously, not sure what Mike had to show her. When Caroline arrived at Mike's house, he and Michael had decorated the house with welcome back decorations and barbecue ribs with all the fixings, and for dessert, of course, a cheesecake. "Aww, thank you guys. Baby, this is really nice of you. Did you two do this all by yourself?" "Well, Maria might have helped out a little." Maria, who is Michael's sitter and the housekeeper, put her hand on her chubby hip.

"Ok, Maria helped out a lot." Maria gave Mike a look like, "really."

"Ok baby, Maria did all the cooking, but we decorated." A piece of the welcome back ribbon fell on the floor. They all laughed. "Welcome back, Caroline," Maria said. "Let me take your coat."

That evening, Caroline could not find the right time to tell Mike what had happened in Florida. They were too busy talking about other things, and then they had family time with Michael, and they all watched a movie. Caroline didn't want to spoil the night with the bad news, so she felt like maybe it could wait. I'll tell him first thing in the morning, she thought. That night, when Caroline went home, she thought about how the conversation would play out, over and over in her head.

Maybe he will understand, she thought. I do have the tendency to overreact, sometimes. It's not that bad. Caroline could not sleep at all that night, so she turned on her T.V and watched episodes of Gangsta Files. When morning rolled around, Caroline's eyes looked like a cartoon characters when they have red veins in their eyes from being restless. Caroline was just about to doze off when her cell rang and scared her. She jumped, because the ringer caught her off guard. It was Mike. Good, now I can tell him, she thought before picking up the phone. "Hey baby what's going on," Caroline said in an exhausted voice. "You tell me, Caroline." Caroline sat up in her bed. "Mike, what's going on?" "Again, you tell me, Caroline, because I'm looking at an article with a picture of you and Stacy kissing, and a portrait of you on the side that says, Ms. Forever at the bottom, so again, Caroline, I ask you. Tell me what's going on." Mike was speaking calmly, but Caroline knew that he was upset.

"Ms. Forever, baby, I have no idea what you are talking about. Baby, look I called you the night that this happened, and I tried to tell you." "Tell me what, Caroline? Was it really a business vacation or was it a way for the both of you to get away without any questions?" "Mike, please don't do this; just listen." "I am listening, Caroline, but you aren't saying much." "Give me a chance to talk," Caroline yelled. Mike became quiet. "I don't know what this Forever thing is that everyone is talking about, but Stacy tried to kiss me, and I ran away. I told him that I love you, and that he and I are over. I tried to call you when all of this happened, but you didn't pick up the phone, and you didn't call me back until I was on the plane the next day."

"Caroline, I didn't check my voicemail until this morning. I was at the hospital with my dad until Thursday evening, we talked about this at the barbeque. I drove my mom over to my parent's house and on the way I charged my phone, and that's when I saw all of your missed calls and texts. Look, I'm sorry that I didn't answer, but I didn't know what was going on with my father, and I guess, I just got busy, going back and forth from the hospital to take my mom there and back. It's just a shame that I had to find out like this. I mean, are we doing the right thing, Caroline? Do you truly love me?" "Yes, of course, Mike, you know that." "Do you still love him?" Caroline was silent. "I guess that I have my answer," Mike sighed. "Mike, it's not the same, and I'm in love with you. I'm not in love with him." "But you do love him?" Caroline sighed, "Yes, as a friend. The same way that you will always love Angel."

Mike and Caroline both remained silent. "Caroline, I put up with a lot of things, because I love you, but we can't continue if you keep hiding things from me. I know that he buys you gifts, because the things that he buys are not exactly your taste. That's why they sit in your closet or you give them to Tangie. I know that, sometimes, when I call you on your lunch break and you cut our conversation short, it's because he's right there with you. I won't continue to compete for your love. You have to make up your mind, right here and right now. If you want to be with me, then you need to speak with your boss, and you need to find a way, so that you and Stacy won't have to work so closely. If you can't stop working with him, then I think its best that we..." Caroline cut Mike off mid-sentence.

"We what, Mike? Take some time off? Go our separate ways? You know what, Mike? I had already had plans to stop working with Stacy, but for you to just be willing to walk away just like that, because of a news-paper with Lord knows what's inside? Maybe we should take some time apart." "Fine," Mike said nonchalantly.

"Fine," Caroline said and then she hung up the phone. Caroline had the tendency to speak, without thinking about what she was saying. She regretted breaking up with Mike, already. She curled up in a fetal position and cried until she felt sick.

13

Saturday afternoon, Caroline found herself at Tangie's house for brunch. It had been a couple of weeks since they'd seen each other, and they both were in need of some girl talk. "So," Tangie said, while scrambling eggs over the stove, and in another pan, she was frying some bologna in a cast iron skillet. "I saw Mike at the church this morning after choir rehearsal. He told me that you broke up with him. What's that all about?"

"Really, Tangie, he told you that we broke up, like we're kids or something?" "Well, he said there was some miscommunication on both of your parts, but he was willing to forget about it, but you snapped and told him that maybe you should take some time apart. What's that all about?" Tangie sat the pan of eggs to the side and took the fried bologna off the stove that had the perfect slightly burned edges around it. Tangie picked up the bowl of grits and plate of pancakes and set them on the breakfast table. Caroline got up and grabbed the syrup, butter, and jam and put them on the table. Tangie grabbed the bologna and eggs, and then she went to get the pitcher of freshly squeezed orange juice out of the refrigerator. It was almost one in the afternoon, but neither of them had eaten earlier, and Tangie could go for breakfast anytime of the day. "Fried bologna, eww," Caroline frowned as Tangie put a couple of pieces on her plate. "Girl, you haven't tried fried bologna before? Now, I know that you grew up all uppity, but you can't tell me that your Ma Ann never made you a fried bologna sandwich with mustard as a kid?" "Ah no," Caroline said while frowning again.

"Who does that," Caroline said, while putting two pancakes on her plate with a serving of scrambled eggs.

"Um, all black people, that's who does that, Caroline," Tangie said, while looking at Caroline, like she was from another planet or something. "No, not all black people eat fried bologna, Tangie," Caroline shook her head, before saying her grace and getting ready to eat. "Well, all the black people from the hood do, Caroline. Shoot, I grew up on fried bologna, fried green tomatoes, and fried grit patties."

"Hold up, fried grit patties?" Caroline said, not sure how you could fry grits. "Girl yes," Tangie said. "You take the grits that were left over from the day before, because I don't know about you, but we didn't believe in throwing any food away, and I still don't. But anyway, you just mix it with a little milk an egg and some flour and cornmeal or breadcrumbs." The smell of breakfast woke Carmen, and she came into the kitchen and greeted Tangie and Caroline with sleep still in one eye.

Carmen was always a late sleeper, but the smell of breakfast could wake her anytime. After Caroline said her grace, she opened her eyes, and Tangie was still saying her grace. Caroline noticed something huge, and she was about to speak out of shock, but Tangie was still saying grace, so she didn't want to be disrespectful. Caroline started choking from saliva going down the wrong windpipe. Tangie finished saying her grace. "My God, Caroline, are you ok?" Tangie began to pat Caroline. Caroline nodded her head yes. "I'm fine," she said in a half voice.

"Here drink some water."

Tangie grabbed a bottled water out of her refrigerator and opened it, and Caroline drank a bit. Caroline cough stopped. She wiped her watery eyes with a napkin. "Girl, what is that?" Tangie jumped up and grabbed a broom. She refused to look back, because maybe it was a spider or a bug or, God forbid, a frog, because she lived near a pond, and she would see them outside all the time.

"Caroline, don't tell me that I spend hundreds of dollars a year on an exterminator, and I have a bug or something in my home." Caroline laughed. "Girl, put that broom down, and if you did, how are you going to kill it with a broom facing me." "I don't know, but I would have figured it out," Tangie said, putting the broom back against the wall. Caroline shook her head.

"Girl, I'm talking about that big rock on your finger. Are you and Brother Robertson engaged?" Tangie held up her left hand and waved her fingers and started running in place with excitement.

"Yes, girl he proposed to me last night." "What?" "Yes, honey. I can't believe that it took you this long to see it," Tangie admired the huge rock on her finger, before going to the sink to wash her hands. "Girl, it is huge, but I guess that I couldn't see it, because you were over there cooking, and I wasn't paying any attention to your hands. My goodness, I am so happy for you. What happened?"

Tangie explained that, last night, she was at Brother Robertson's house, having movie night, and that she was cuddled against Brother Robertson. "He must have felt uncomfortable, because I was purposely trying to put my booty up against him, but he wasn't with it. He told me that he was going to make some popcorn, and he asked me if I wanted a soda or something, and I said sure. I felt bad, because I know that he is a good Christian brother, and he is trying to live right, but why did God have to make him so fine, though."

Caroline shook her head, "Girl, you are crazy. So what else happened?" "Well," Tangie continued to explain.

"When he got back, I told him that I had to ask him something, and he had to promise me that he wouldn't get mad.

He agreed, and I just came out and asked him." "No, you didn't, Tangie."

"Yes, I did." Caroline shook her head again. "I asked him if he was attracted to women. He said, of course, but he told me that he only had eyes for me. I told him ok, and then I said are you attracted to... But before I could finish, he said, 'Tangie let me be clear. I am not gay, bisexual, down low, or any of that. I like women, trust me, but I am in love with you.' He continued to tell me how I have captured his heart and soul and how he wanted to spend the rest of his life making me happy. Girl, at that moment, my mouth was hung open, and I reached into the popcorn bucket to grab some popcorn, so that I could close my mouth for once and think about what he was trying to say or do. Girl, when I reached my hand in a second time, I grabbed the ring box out of the popcorn. Girl, I couldn't believe it. Tears filled my eyes, and I asked him, while opening the box, 'What's this?' He took the ring from me, while still down on one knee, and he said, 'Tangie I have been trying to find the right time to ask you this, but I feel like the time is here. I want you to be my wife, I want us to continue this path of life together and see where it leads. As long as we are together, I know that it will lead to joy, peace, and most of all, an everlasting love. I adore you. You see, when I tell you no or get up and walk away when I feel things are getting too heated, it's not because I'm not attracted to you. It's because I've done it my way in the past, and I don't want to go down that same road again. I am trying to live God's way, and if I'm going to be the man that you want me to be, first I need to be the man that God needs me to be, with him as the head, so that I can lead my family.' He paused and said, 'that's if you'll have me."

Caroline and Tangie both had tears in their eyes. "Girl, I could have died and went to heaven, right then and there. It was so romantic. After a few seconds of trying to compose myself, I told him yes, with the biggest smile on my face. We both stood up, and we hugged, and he must have kissed me a thousand times all over my face, and then he told me that I have made him the happiest man ever. Caroline, it was like a dream come true. I was smiling the rest of the night, and he looked over at me and said, 'See that's one of the things that I love about you. Your smile. When I see you smile, it reminds me that there is sunshine after the rain, and that I can do anything. That's the smile that I want to wake up to every morning.' "Girl, Brother Robertson better go ahead with his bad self- Mr. Poetry man." Tangie laughed. "I know right. Girl, he is a really good man, and I can't wait to take his last name." Tangie started grinding as she said Mrs. Robertson, admiring the sound of her future last name. "You so nasty," Caroline said. "Sit your behind down before your breakfast gets cold." "Yes ma'am," Tangie said.

"Not to kill the moment, but back to you and Mike. As I was saying, he was at the church today, doing his usual upkeep of the lawn or whatever, and he waved for me to come over as I was leaving choir rehearsal, and we chatted for a minute. Caroline, don't make the mistake that I have for so long by being stubborn. Stubbornness and pride will have you all alone in the end. Trust me; I know."

Tangie and Caroline continued to talk and eat, and after they discussed the situation with Mike, they went to a much lighter subject, the wedding plans. Tangie, Carmen, and Caroline spent the day together looking at wedding dresses at different stores, and they also surfed the web for the location and even honeymoon vacations. Caroline got home late that night, but she called Tangie, as usual, to let her know that she'd made it home. "Won't you come to church with me and Carmen tomorrow, Caroline? The both of you need to talk."

Caroline said no, at first, and then she agreed to come. Caroline laid in her bed that night, happy that her friend's life had taken a turn for the good, and Caroline even daydreamed about her and Mike getting over their current test and trials and becoming Mike's wife. Caroline thought about their church situation, because Mike is a member of the church that Tangie attends, which is a big church with about twelve thousand members, and Caroline attended a smaller church, with a total of about two hundred members and most of them where older. Sleep found her easily, and she woke up Sunday morning, feeling refreshed. "Today is going to be a good day," Caroline said as she opened her bedroom curtains to let the sunshine in, and then she began to iron her clothes for church.

14

$\mathcal{T}$angie and Caroline arrived at church five minutes before morning worship service. The church was already packed, as usual. Brother Robertson sat near the front, and Tangie would sit next to him, until the choir would come up and sing praise and worship. Caroline spotted Mike and Michael sitting to the right of Brother Robertson. "Tangie, let's not sit so close to the front. Can we sit in the back, please?"

Tangie looked at the front isle to see why Caroline was acting strange, and sure enough, there was Mike. "Caroline," Tangie whispered. "Look, the two of you are going to have to face each other, sooner or later, so stop acting like you are in second grade and come on." Tangie yanked Caroline's arm as if Caroline was a child who had worked her mother's last nerve. Caroline yanked her arm back and said, "No," in a soft, but aggressive tone.

Caroline and Tangie drew a few members' attention that were seated nearby. Michael went to the restroom, and as he was coming from the restroom, he saw Caroline sitting on the end, several rows down from where he sat. Michael waved at Caroline, and she waved back. Caroline was seated next to members of the church, but she didn't know them.

Tangie had left Caroline behind to spend a few minutes with her fiancée before she had to enter the stage to sing.

Caroline saw Mike lean in to hear whatever Michael was telling him. Please don't tell your dad that I'm here, she thought. Please don't tell your dad that I'm here, she thought again. Mike turned around and looked Caroline dead in the face. Caroline froze. Michael was waving for Caroline to come sit with them. He waved his hand to say come on, and that drew even more attention. "Thank you, God," Caroline said, being saved by the keyboard player on stage, who began playing a soft melody as Tangie and the rest of the choir came on stage. A few moments later, an attractive lady, who looked as if she was in her early twenties, came and sat near Mike and Michael. The young lady had a pretty little girl with her who looked about Michael's age.

The lady and Michael hugged, and then she hugged Mike and kissed him on the side of his face. "Was that a blush," Caroline said out loud. "Shhh," some of the members said to Caroline. They were trying to get their praise on, because the choir had begun to sing. Caroline clapped her hands and moved side to side with the rhythm of the choir.

She even sang the songs that they were singing, but her eyes were on that young lady and her little girl, who looked like she was playing paper, scissors, rock with Michael. The young lady stopped Michael and the cute little girl from playing in church. Mike was too busy praising to notice what was going on. Michael turned around and made a weird face at Caroline, showing his thoughts about the cute young lady.

Caroline smiled and winked at Michael.

Caroline began wishing she'd never come to this church. This is ridiculous, she thought to herself. This is God's time. I can't be in church worrying about Mike and Ms. Prissy or whomever she is. Caroline thought, as she rolled her eyes at the same time the lady turned to see who Michael was making silly faces at.

Caroline tried to hurry and straighten her face and the sour look on it. Lord, I'm sorry I didn't mean to make that face. Ok, I'm sorry, again, I lied. I did mean to make it, but I didn't mean for her to look and see me make the face. Now, the lady is going to think that I have an issue with her.

The lady returned Caroline's frown with a smile. A crooked smile as she smirked and then continued to stand and clap her hands during praise. At the end of service, the pastor told Carmen to stand up and walk to the alter. "This is a living testament of what God can do in any of our lives. It hasn't been a full two years since the doctors told Carmen and her wonderful mother, Tangie, that it was almost impossible for Carmen to walk again. But won't he do it?" The pastor said to the congregation. "Yes he will," they replied. Some people were crying, including Tangie, and others were standing with their hands towards heaven, thanking God for what he had done in Carmen's life. It had been eighteen months, and Carmen had gone from a wheelchair and barely able to do anything herself, to walking with a walker, then a cane, and now, her body is totally healed, and she is back at one hundred percent.

"Don't ever take the doctor's answer as the final answer, church," the pastor said. "Our God is not a manmade God, but THE GOD, the one and only GREAT I AM, who wasn't shaped out of wood and stone as some people who "Make" their gods. He is not manmade, but he made man. All the wisdom, knowledge, and understanding that we have can, in no way, even begin to compare to his knowledge, which is all encompassing, and to his wisdom there is no end." The pastor began to speak to the congregation about what God can do, and Caroline found herself crying, because she had seen firsthand what God had done in Carmen's life.

"And to add icing to the cake, so to speak," the pastor said, still talking to the congregation. "Our beloved Carmen will be graduating high school in just a few short months." People began to clap and continued to praise God for what he was doing. "But wait a minute, church, she is not only graduating, but she is graduating on time with her class and with honors." The church was filled with amen, hallelujahs, thank you Jesus, and everyone was so happy for Carmen.

"I'm sorry, but one more thing before I dismiss you, church. I know that some of y'all are ready to go home and watch the game or get your barbecue on, your collard greens and candied yams." The congregation laughed. "You've had your spiritual, and I know that you're ready to feed your physical bodies, but I couldn't let you all leave without first congratulating Brother Robertson and the lovely sister Tangie on their engagement." Tangie waved her diamond in the air for all to see. "God has someone for everyone, so don't give up hope. God is doing something extraordinary with our single committee. I'm telling ya, if you haven't heard, you better ask somebody. Play with it if you want too," the pastor said. The pastor said the benediction and dismissed the congregation. Caroline didn't wait for Tangie, who was busy talking with other members, as they congratulated her on her engagement. Caroline tried to hurry to her car, but Mike called her as she was exiting the church. "Why the rush? I can't get a simple hello or how you doing, nothing? You were just going to leave?" "Hello," Caroline said. "Hey, there you are.

"Michael, I was looking all over for you. So this is where you disappeared to?" The young lady said to Mike, calling him by his full name. The young lady looked Caroline up and down and said, "Hello."

Caroline smiled and said to the young lady, "Hi, how are you?"

"I'm fine, but not as fine as this one," she said looking at Mike and undressing him with her eyes on church ground. "Right," Caroline said slowly. "So Mike, aren't you going to introduce me to your friend?" Caroline stood, holding her purse in front of her and looking up at Mike, waiting for Mike to introduce his friend to her. "Yes, I was just getting to that, Caroline, thank you."

The young lady gasped as she said, "Caroline, oh my goodness, it's nice to finally meet you. I've heard so much about you.

You and Mike use to date, right?" Mike rolled his eyes like, oh brother. Caroline chuckled, "And you are?" Caroline asked the young lady.

"Oh, I'm Jessica," she said as she held onto Mike's arm. "Oh thank you for messing things up with Mike, Caroline. I have been waiting forever to get this man on my arms. I wish that I could chat a little longer, but Mike and I are running late for a previous engagement. Bye," she waved her hand and turned Mike with her.

"Jess, wait a minute. Can Caroline and I have a minute alone?" Jessica stood with her hand on her hip and then she said, "Ok. Anything for you Mike," she winked and headed to her car and called her daughter, who was running in the church parking lot with Michael. Caroline turned away and begin to walk to her car.

"Caroline, wait up," Mike ran after her. "Mike, we have nothing to talk about."

"Look, I'm sorry about that but..." Caroline cut Mike off.

"Sorry about what Mike? It has barely been over twenty-four hours since we broke up, and you're already dating again? Or did you have her on the sidelines, just waiting. Is that why you wanted to end things with me?"

"End things with you? Caroline you broke things off with me, remember?"

"Yeah, well, it didn't take long for you to rebound did it?" "Caroline she's not a rebound; she's just a friend." "Yeah, just a friend that you tell all of our business to," Caroline said as she hit the unlock button on her key ring and put her purse into the car.

"Caroline, it's not what you think. Look, can you just talk to me for a minute," Mike said as he hurried around to the passenger side and got into Caroline's car. "Mike get out of my car. I have places to go and people to see." "What? Are you going to see him?"

"Does it matter? Go run along with little Miss prissy. By the way, is she even legal?" "Caroline don't do this." "Well, is she Mike?"

"Look, she's twenty-nine. Why does her age even matter?" "Because I don't have time for you or your little girlfriend games, Mike; that's why. Now, can you please get out of my car, so that I can leave?" "She's not my girlfriend, Caroline, and as far as little girl games, at least with her, what you see is what you get. You are the little girl, playing all these games and taking me on this emotional roller coaster that I am sick of, Caroline.

What am I supposed to do? Not live life until you decide that you want to be with me?"

"I'm not asking you to do anything, Mike," Caroline yelled and then started crying. "Why does she know so much about us if she's only a friend, Mike?"

"Caroline, believe it or not, I haven't seen Jess since the first time that you and I stopped seeing each other, when I saw Stacy over your house. Look, I met her through a mutual friend, and at the time, I needed someone to vent to, so she and I went out a few times and nothing happened. I took Michael to her daughter's birthday party, and they became good friends. Michael asked me if he could go to the Falcon's game with them today, and she had an extra ticket, so I told her sure I'd come. Anything that happened between you and me after that incident, I promise she doesn't know a thing about."

"Why is she here? At church, with you and Michael?" "Caroline, I told her to meet us here, so that we could all ride to the game together." "Beep, beep," Jessica honked as she pulled on the side of Caroline in her Mercedes Benz G class. Caroline hurried to put on her sunglasses, because she refused to let Jessica see her eyes red, puffy, and full of tears.

"Caroline look, I can tell her that I decline, and I will stay right here with you, until we figure out exactly what we're doing." "No you go, its fine, Mike. I know exactly what we're doing." "Well, can you tell me, so that we are both on the same page?" "We are seeing other people," Caroline said as she prepared to put her car into gear and waited for Mike to get out.

"So much for my good day," Caroline said as she sped out of the church parking lot, not looking in her rearview mirror at Mike, who hadn't got into the jeep with Jessica, but had got into his truck and went home. "Ring, ring, ring" Caroline's home phone was constantly ringing when she entered her home. She'd ignored her cell, because she wasn't in the mood to talk to anyone. Caroline just wanted to go home and get her mind right about what she should do. Caroline remembered what her pastor had said about soul ties, but what if it was meant for her and Stacy to take a chance and see where things went. Caroline felt guilty about pushing Mike away, because she knew that he's a good man and that he truly loves her. She hadn't been completely honest about her feelings with Mike, though, because although she loved him, it was for the wrong reasons. Caroline wanted Mike to be the one so badly that she suppressed her feelings about Stacy and did everything she could to convince herself that it wasn't love, but more lust with Stacy. She even convinced herself that she was a child and could not possibly have been in love. Maybe it was puppy love, like her mother and Ma Ann had told her so many years ago. Caroline's phone rang again, and in the midst of all her thoughts and everything that was going on with her, Mike, and Stacy, she screamed into the phone, without realizing that her thoughts had gotten the best of her.

"I'm still in love with Stacy ok," she broke down and started crying, without giving the caller on the other end a chance to say anything. "I broke things off with you and made it seem like it was your fault, because I couldn't stand to tell you that I'm still in love with him. I wanted you to be the one so badly, because you are a great man, and I admire you, but my heart is not in the same place as yours." She started crying harder as she slid down on the kitchen floor against the cabinets with her phone in hand, "Please forgive me, and I completely understand if you don't want to see or talk to me ever again. I want to love you so badly, because you are the perfect guy, and I might even be making a mistake, but I have to be honest with not only you, but myself. Being with you for any reason, except for the reason of love is wrong, because you deserve better.

I'm so sorry. Please forgive me." Caroline calmed down and noticed after she'd said her last few words that she was talking to a dial tone. Caroline looked at the number in her caller id and the number was restricted.

Maybe he was calling me restricted, because he knew that if I saw his number, then maybe, I wouldn't have answered. Caroline grabbed her cell, and she did have five missed calls from Mike, and she had a text from Tangie. Caroline knew that the restricted phone call was Mike, and that maybe, he didn't say anything, because Caroline had said enough for the both of them. Caroline's heart was broken, because she had grown to love Mike, and letting him go when she wasn't sure of what would happen between her and Stacy made her sick. She made up her mind that she was willing to take that chance, though.

15

"**C**aroline, can I see you in my office for a minute," Mr. Taylor said with a copy of the newspaper with Stacy and Caroline on the front cover folded in his hand. "Sure, Mr. Taylor," Caroline said, but had her eyes focused on someone standing inside of her office looking around. She couldn't tell who it was from Mr. Taylor's office, but she knew it was a woman. Mr. Taylor waited for Caroline to enter his office, before closing the office door all the way.

"What happened in Florida that I need to know about? Is this the tabloids making something out of nothing, or what I see is what I get?" Mr. Taylor paced his office floor, trying to make sense of the situation, at hand, before giving Caroline a chance to speak.

"Caroline, we've had this discussion, and I've told you to be careful and not to mix business with pleasure, no matter what your past history is." "I know, Mr. Taylor, and I've spoken to Stacy about this, as well, and I wasn't expecting for Stacy to kiss me. I sure wasn't expecting for things to get blown out of proportion, like it has, but I warned him that this could happen."

"Caroline, I need for you to be honest with me, because I have a lot riding on this. You know that I have been trying to get Mr. Lavado." Before Mr. Taylor could go into the whole Mr. Lavado investment speech/lecture again, Caroline cut him off. "I know. I know what you've been trying to do Mr. Taylor, but what if it hasn't worked so far, because you're going about it the wrong way?" "Caroline, it's just business, and that's the way things work. Look, Amanda Lavado is in your office, right now, and she asked to speak with you personally, so before you go making decisions about you and Stacy, you need to think this over very carefully and remember that not only I have a lot riding on this, but you have a lot, as well. Don't let your emotions overtake you. Now, go ahead and see what she wants, and I need to see you when you are done with Amanda, because we still have things to discuss." "Yes sir," Caroline said as she opened the office door and headed out of Mr. Taylor's office. All eyes were on her as she walked to her office. "Don't you all have work to do?" Mr. Taylor said as he watched Caroline enter her office. Everyone turned back around and continued to work. After Caroline went into her office and closed the door, Mr. Taylor went back inside his office and sat at his desk. "What happened to you, Caroline?" he said as he shook his head, while looking at the photo of her and Stacy kissing on the front cover of the newspaper. He took a deep breath in and a deep breath out as he pulled Caroline's employee file from his file cabinet and sat it on his desk.

"Hello," Caroline greeted Amanda as she entered her office. Amanda was busy looking around the office at all the contemporary art and the matching array of colorful decor that filled Caroline's office. "Very nice," Amanda said. "Thank you, Amanda. What can I do for you?"

"We'll get to that in a minute," Amanda said, while holding a briefcase. Caroline stood near her desk.

"Please have a seat," she motioned her hand for Amanda to sit down. "No thank you. This won't take long." Since Amanda wasn't sitting neither did Caroline.

Caroline's dad had taught her self-defense a long time ago and one of his rules was to never give your opponent the upper hand in any situation. Caroline wasn't sure what Amanda would try to pull, and she sure wasn't going to sit down and find out.

Whatever Ms. Fancy had to say, Caroline was going to hear it standing up. "Caroline, I'm not sure what happened between you and Stacy in Miami, and I don't want to know. Let's just say that whatever happened in Miami, let it stay in Miami. I know that you may think that you and Stacy have something, but I can assure you that it's nothing more than a childhood sweetheart. You see, I am the one who has been by his side all these years. I have had his back when he was searching for jobs or when his mother passed and even through all of this. I haven't questioned him on anything, because I trust him. We don't keep secrets from each other, and that's all I've asked of him.

"I know that he thinks that he loves you, but it's nothing more than curiosity. He wants to know if his first love is the woman he should be with before we make our vows, and I've given him time. I've always knew who you were, even before you knew that Stacy worked at the café. Anyways, to get to the point, stop playing with my fiancée's heart. You have a boyfriend, and it's clear that the only reason that you are trying to get close to Stacy is so that he can somehow persuade me to convince my dad to invest in this company.

"Don't get me wrong. I think the company is great. It helps educate kids and adults and provides resources for adults to get jobs, expand their education, develop a skill, and so on and so forth, and just when you think that you couldn't do anymore, you all have the art museum that also funds grants and scholarships for kids and some adults who wants to expand their careers." Amanda clapped her hands slowly three times, "I think all that is great Caroline, but the one thing that keeps away the phone call to my father to invest in this company is you."

Caroline took a step back and looked at Amanda, "And how is that Amanda?" "Stop playing games, Caroline. You think that I've been with Stacy this long to just allow him to be taken away by some teenage fling? Stacy is my man and just know that I am not letting him go so easily." Amanda sat the briefcase on Caroline's desk and opened it up. I am willing, right here and right now, to invest two hundred and fifty thousand dollars into this company. This is just pennies compared to what my father can give. I will continue to invest in GPSG as long as my fiancée is working for this company, so don't think that this has anything to do with you. I believe in my man, and I believe in his dreams, and whatever he needs I'm going to back him up. As far as getting my father to invest, now that is up to you. I have him on speed dial, Caroline. All you have to do is end this teenage love affair, and this company will have everything it needs for a very long time. I'm sure Mr. Taylor wouldn't be able to thank you enough. He wouldn't have any choice but to keep you on board then and maybe even move you up." "Wait a minute. What do you mean keep me on board? I haven't gone anywhere. Am I not standing right here in front of you in my office? Did I miss something? Have you and Mr. Taylor been discussing me without me being present?"

"Hold up, Caroline, before you get your panties in a bunch. Calm down, and no, we haven't been discussing you, but he and some of the other top executives have. You have made this company look unethical and scandalous by pulling whatever trick you pulled with Stacy in Florida, and Mr. Taylor is going to fire you. You see, I have friends in high places, and I know people, people who work closely with my father, and right now, he is not liking what he's seeing or hearing about this company. Whether you know it or not, my father is investing in this company, in a way, because he has people who work for him that are on the executive board and are major investors, and this little stunt that you pulled is having them second guessing about continuing to invest in this company. Caroline, you don't want to be the cause of this company to collapse do you? Everybody's talking about it. Why do you think that everyone was looking at you this morning? They know that it's just a matter of time before you get suspended and then you're fired."

"Ok, Amanda out of my office, you and your money. I've had enough of this small talk. I have work to do, so go somewhere. Don't you have a cheesecake or a muffin or something to go and bake? Please be gone," Caroline said as she fanned her hand at Amanda as if she was a fly.

"Don't get cute, Caroline, because although I work, we both know that I don't have to. You, on the other hand, if you get fired, then where will you go? What will you do? No one will hire you, because they will look at your background, and you won't have a chance. The only job you'll get in the TV industry is mopping floors at night, so don't try me. I'm your only friend, right now, Caroline, and I am trying to make this a win-win situation for everybody. Now, as I was saying, the only thing that you have to do is cut off all contact with Stacy.

"Get your assistant to work with him from now on. Don't call or text him. Don't even show up at the same Fundraisers where he'll be. Considering that you don't have any other options, but to do as I'm instructing, I've already called my father, and he should be arriving here um just a-bout," she looked at her Movado watch, "now." "Knock, knock, knock," it was Mr. Taylor knocking on Caroline's office door.

"Ladies, I'm sorry to interrupt, but Caroline, we have a business meeting to attend." Caroline looked out of the door at Mr. Lavado, along with three security guards standing on each side and the back of him. Amanda smiled and winked at Caroline and then she put her shades over her eyes and walked out to meet her father with her arms opened wide. "Daddy," she said as she hugged him. Caroline followed behind Mr. Taylor, thinking that she would join them in the meeting, but Mr. Taylor showed Mr. Lavado to the conference room, and he excused himself and Caroline for a couple of minutes.

After Caroline and Mr. Taylor went back into his office, Mr. Taylor told Caroline that he had to suspend her without pay, according to company policy. Caroline was in shock, because she hadn't believed any of what Amanda had said, although it served true at this very moment. "Are you serious, Mr. Taylor?" "I wish that I wasn't, Caroline, but the board voted, and most everyone agreed that you should take some time off until this mess calms down and everything is back to normal." Caroline couldn't believe that this was really happening.

She had busted her butt for this company. She worked at work and at home. She came in early and stayed late and did the job of two, sometimes three, different positions, and they were thinking about letting her go, just like that. This was a prime example of money talks and b.s. walks, because now, Mr. Taylor, Amanda and Mr. Lavado were in the conference room, discussing investment opportunities, and Caroline was walking to her car, suspended without pay over some total bull. Caroline was stressed to the max. During the month that Caroline was suspended, she stayed busy by meeting with caterers and event coordinators with Tangie. The wedding was in July, which was four months away. "You know that Jessica chick comes to the single committee functions with Mike now." Caroline looked at Tangie with a dull face. "I'm serious, Caroline," she has joined the church and everything. Everybody knows that when you see Mike, Jessica is some-where nearby." Caroline rubbed her head, trying not to hear the de-tails of Mike and his new lady and what they had going on. Caroline hadn't seen or talked to Mike in almost a month, and she hadn't seen or spoken to Stacy since Florida.

"So any news about your job? Have you spoken to Mr. Taylor?" "I have not spoken to Mr. Taylor, but I go back in a week, and I guess he'll let me know then whatever he has decided to do. I guess if push comes to shove, I can always move to D.C, and my mother can get me a job at one of her offices." "Caroline don't worry about it too much; things will fall into place. When I had to quit because I had to take care of Carmen, I was stressed out about how this or that was going to get paid, but I'm tell-ing you, nothing was ever late and we never went hungry. God was always on time. He did it for me, and he'll do it for you too. You're just going through a tough time, right now, but it'll all work out for the good in the end; you'll see." Tangie tapped Caroline on the shoulder through the fitting room curtain. "Zip this up for me, please," she said as she held the front of a beautiful white bride's dress and Caroline struggled to zip the back. Caroline looked at Tangie in the mirror.

"Tangie you look gorgeous." "Thank you, friend. I think this is the one. It's a bit too tight though. I'm scared if I move a certain way that I'll rip it." Tangie asked the sales associate if they had the same dress in a bigger size or if they did alterations.

The sales associate said no to both questions. Tangie wasn't leaving without that dress and she said, "There's only one thing for me to do then. I have to lose enough weight to comfortably wear this dress, be-cause I refuse to leave without it." Tangie bought the dress and she and Caroline left the store and headed home to drop off the dress and then they went to the gym. There were all kinds of eye candy in the gym this day.

"Girl, why haven't you told me about the gym before today?" Caroline looked at Tangie with a confused look on her face. Tangie pointed, "I mean, when I was single and ready to mingle. Why did we never come to the gym?" "Tangie, you weren't trying to come to any gym for one, and two, I run almost every day, or I'll do other cardio at home. I'm only here to support you. I'm not trying to pick up guys." "Girl bye, well you need to pick up a guy from somewhere, because I'm tired of hearing how lonely you are and how you want to date, but you don't ever get the opportunity to do so; well, opportunity is knocking all over this place, so get to answering," Tangie said as she gave Caroline a slight push and she bumped into a tall, caramel skin toned muscular guy about six feet tall. "Oh, I'm so sorry; please excuse me," Caroline said, looking back at Tangie, who was busy trying to figure out how to turn the treadmill on. "No problem, beautiful, excuse me," the handsome guy said as he sat down near Caroline on the bench press and began to lift weights. Nice guns, Caroline thought to herself as she sat on the other side of the man to get a slick view of him working out.

Caroline tried to get the pin out of the weights, so that she could work out on the leg press, but the pin was stuck on sixty pounds, and she knew that she couldn't lift sixty pounds. "Here, let me help you out," the handsome tall chunk of caramel said. "By the way, I'm Adam. And you are?" he said as he pulled the jammed pin out of the weights and handed it to Caroline. "Nice to meet you, Adam," she held out her hand, and they shook hands, "I'm Caroline." They begin talking and an hour later, Caroline and Tangie left the gym, and Caroline left with Adam's phone number.

16

Right after Caroline and Tangie left the gym, they went to the grocery store, and the grocery store was selling grilled hotdogs. Tangie went straight to the hotdog stand, "Two hotdogs, please." Caroline stared at Tangie, like really. "What? Don't judge me Caroline. I'm hungry." "Which is why we're at the grocery store, so that you can go home and cook something healthier, so that you can fit into your wedding dress," Caroline said under her breath, but loud enough for Tangie to hear her.

"I'm sorry, no hotdogs for me. I think that I'll pass." Once they were inside the grocery store, Tangie went into the fresh fruit section and grabbed a bag of tangerines and some bananas and then she took off to the snack isle. Caroline was busy getting romaine and tomatoes, so that she could make a salad when she got home. Caroline noticed that Tangie wasn't in the fresh fruit section anymore, so she went to the next isle, and there was Tangie with Twinkie's, oatmeal pie's, honey buns, and all kinds of Little Debbie's.

Caroline reached into her buggy and picked up the honey buns. "Tangie, what's this, and this, and this," she continued to ask every time she picked up a snack out of Tangie's buggy. "Oh girl, I'm getting those for Carmen and her friend's when they come over to the house. You know, kid's love their cupcakes and honey buns." "No ma'am, Tangie, you need to stop buying all this crap, and you know that you're going to be tempted to eat it. Carmen is young and her metabolism is up, but we are older, and those honey buns and cupcakes aren't going to come off as easily as they will an eighteen-year-old."

Caroline placed all the snacks back into the buggy. "Ok, but we have four months for you to lose fifteen pounds, and if you snack on this kind of stuff every time you get a sweet tooth, then you are going to add five to ten more pounds on, and you're going to have to take that dress back and look for another one. It already took months for you to find the perfect dress." Tangie was quietly mocking Caroline behind her back, like a kid mocking her nagging parent. Caroline caught Tangie mocking her and Caroline laughed.

"Ok, do what you want, but you're the one that's going to be wearing the super tight dress, looking like a mummy, trying to walk down the aisle with both of your arms stuck to your sides." "Caroline, go away. I know you're trying to use that reverse psychology or whatever it is, but it's not going to work. I can control myself. I have tangerines and bananas, see. If I want a snack, I'll have a fruit, and if I do eat a cupcake, it's not going to hurt. It's not like I'm going to eat the whole box." "Ok fine, but you want me to be your motivational coach and to help you eat a healthier diet, but you know you more than anyone else, and if you know that you can withstand that kind of temptation, then go ahead. If you believe you can, then I believe you can too." "See, now, that's the kind of support I'm talking about, because I wasn't hearing any of that other mess that you were just talking."

Caroline shook her head as she looked at the scale. Tangie was standing on the scale with a box of cupcakes in her hand crying. It had been a month since Tangie began her diet. "Tangie, maybe it's wrong, maybe the cupcakes are adding on some extra pounds here," she reached out her hand, "give me the box of cupcakes." Tangie gave Caroline the box, only there weren't any cupcakes inside. Caroline looked into the box.

"Tangie, where are the cupcakes?" "I ate them," Tangie cried. I tried on my wedding dress today, and I couldn't even fit it over my hips this time. Caroline, what am I going to do?" Tangie got off the scale and Caroline hugged her.

"It's ok, Tangie," she said as she rubbed Tangie's back. "You are going to get through this. Everyone slips up every now and then when on a diet, but now that you know what your weakness is, we have to find a healthier alternative, and before we do that, we need to find out what triggered you to eat a whole box of cupcakes in one day." Tangie shook her head, "I bet that you're going to say that you told me so, huh?"

"No, Tangie, I would never say that, but tell me what happened, because you were doing so well the last three weeks. You made great progress. You had lost five pounds, but now you've gained back ten. What happened?" "Stress." "Stress about what, Tangie? You are about to become Mrs. Robertson in three months, and your daughter is graduating high school soon and will be leaving for college in a couple of months."

Tangie interrupted Caroline. "See, that's just it, Caroline. It has always been me and Carmen, and soon she'll be going off to college, and I won't have my baby anymore. Who's going to be there to watch out for her or help her handle a difficult situation? I thought that I would be happy, but I'm not. I mean I am proud of her and happy that she's accomplished so much, but I'm going to miss her." "Aww, I know that you're going to miss her, Tangie, but trust me; Carmen will be ok. You taught her how to handle herself as a young lady, and you introduced her to God. Carmen has been through a lot, and she is a strong young lady with a good head on her shoulders. You both have been through a lot of good, bad, happy, and sad times together, but you have to know that what you taught her, she will remember.

"If she does need any advice, then you are just a phone call away, and not only that, but she's going to Spellman, and that's just twentyfive minutes away from you." Caroline's words lightened Tangie's heart and she laughed and wiped her eyes with a tissue. "You're right. Thank you, Caroline."

"No problem, and you know I got Carmen's back too. I'm always just a phone call away if you or she needs anything. Now come on, throw on your gym clothes, and let's go. We are going to stick to this diet, and you will lose twenty pounds by your wedding day. I'm not going to lie. It's going to be hard, but I believe that you have the will power to do it. You are going to have to lose about two pounds a week in order to accomplish this, but people have done it, and so can you.

Now, let's go."

"So whatever happened with you and that Adam guy?" Tangie set the treadmill and begin to jog. "Girl, let me tell you. So, you know that he told me that he was a financial advisor and that he worked for Mr. Lavado? Come to find out that he's a financial advisor, alright. Well, he has at least a hundred workers under him, all who are responsible for, get this, moving major weight." "Major weight of what? Like money?

Do they drive those armored trucks or something?" "Girl, let me put it to you this way. A lot of the Lavado's money is drug money." "Girl, no way. Caroline, do you really expect for me to believe that? Mr. Lavado is a respectable businessman, and besides, he's too old to be a drug dealer. This man is a billionaire, what does he need to sell drugs for?" "No Tangie, you are missing the bus. Mr. Lavado doesn't sell drugs, but most of his investors and people that he does business with are a part of a Mafia, and they have people who work for them that drop off kilos of cocaine and pick up the money. Mr. Lavado use to be a part of the same Mafia when he was younger, and because of certain people that he knows, he ended up with Lavado Bank and Trust." "Girl, what? I don't believe you, Caroline. I know that you and Amanda don't see eye to eye, but saying that Mr. Lavado is some kind of King Pen or head of some Mafia group, I just don't believe it.

How did you find all of this out anyways, because I know that Adam didn't tell you this?"

"You're right. He didn't, but somebody else did."

"Who?" "Amanda." Tangie began to laugh, "Ok, Caroline, you are really crazy now. Have you been smoking? Maybe you've had one too many of those energy bars. You need help. You and Amanda haven't talked since that little incident in your office. So how did she tell you this, again?"

"Well she didn't tell me exactly. See, I was at Adam's house for dinner one day, and he said that he had to take a phone call and that he'd be right back. I could hear his conversation, just as clear as day, and I was wondering if he had come back and was somewhere in his kitchen, because the kitchen is huge. It's like three bedrooms. Anyway, it was a baby monitor on the counter, and he didn't tell me that he had any kids, so that was a no go for one. If he's denying that he has kids, and he does, then that's an automatic turn off. But anyway, he had gone into his office, and he must have had her on speaker phone, but I heard her saying something about some guy was doing a drop tomorrow, and he was supposed to pick up three hundred grand or something like that, and I couldn't believe my ears, at first, but I continued to listen. I heard Adam saying that he was looking for something, which explains why he had Amanda on speaker phone. Now, I might be naive about a lot of things, but after watching what use to be my favorite soap, Gangsta Files, I know that a lot of people hide dirty money in businesses.

"I know what a drop and a pickup is, and I know what a kilo of cocaine is and its equivalent to money is. Anyway, to make a long story short, some guy was to meet with Adam's people, and Adam's people where dropping off twelve kilos, and they were picking up three hundred grand." "Caroline, how could you hear all that and continue to act normal?"

"Girl, let me tell you. I was saved by the bell. Literally, the doorbell rang, and I yelled up to him and asked if he wanted me to get the door, and when I answered it, two little kids were at the door, and the little boy, who's maybe about three, kicked me in the shin and said, 'where's my daddy?' Girl, my quick reflex kicked in, and before I knew it, I had slapped the little boy into the bushes." "Caroline!" "No, I'm just playing. I may have thought about doing it, but my shin was hurting too bad, and I was busy rubbing it and trying to grab the car seat with a baby girl about three months old inside of it. Anyway, the little boy ran upstairs, and I came inside limping, and Adam asked me if I was ok. I told him that his Bay Bay kid had kicked me, and he apologized and said that the kids were his brother's kids and that his brother should be home in a minute. I was concerned about the kids being on the porch by them-selves. I mean, whoever the kid's mother is, she just dropped them off at the top of the stairs and left. Girl, I felt some type of way about that, but anyway, the little boy kept calling Adam, Daddy, and I just couldn't deal with the lies, so I told him that I had to go, because it was getting late, and I had to be at work early the next morning. It wasn't late at all, only nine thirty, but I had to get out of that house. Girl, he called me later on that night, asking how my leg was doing and apologizing again and asking if he could come over and give me a massage."

"Did he ever confess that those were his kids?" "Girl no, he said that he had a twin, and that his nephew gets them confused all the time. Honey it was one lie after the next, so I'm done with Adam, and every-thing else he has going on. It's just too much for me. Besides, I'm not dating anyone in the mafia. Girl and the women that they mess with is just as dangerous. I'm not trying to get killed by some psychopath exwife or baby mama or whatever." Tangie was shaking her head. "Girl that is a lot to take in." "I know. It just makes you think what businesses are actu-ally legit and which ones are a cover up for something else. It also goes to show that it's not what you know, but who you know, because they know a lot of people from political figures to lawyers, judges, doctors, on down to cafe owners." Caroline gasped, "Do you think that Amanda's busi-nesses are a cover up? I mean, she does well and with two extra locations opened around the greater Atlanta area. I mean, is it all cafe money?"

"Caroline, don't go looking for trouble, because when you do, you will most definitely find it. Let whatever those people have going on be. Nothing has happened to them in all this time, and nothing will prob-ably ever happen. Besides, you don't know if Mr. Lavado has anything to do with this. It could only be the people who do business with him."

"Yeah, you are right. Whatever the case may be, I'm just going to leave it alone." "Yeah, and by the way, are you still coming out to Soulful Jazz? Its poetry night, and of course, my boo is hosting it. They have also started karaoke night on Saturdays, and the single committee is coming out. Are you going to come?"

"Not if Mike and his tag along is going to be there." "Girl please, so what if they're going to be there? You can't let that stop you from having a good time." "You and Brother Robertson are getting married soon, so y'all won't be a part of the single committee anymore." "I know, right, but we have already told the happily married committee to make room for us, because we are coming."

"So who will be over the single committee once y'all leave?" "I'm not sure yet. We are working on that now. If no one has come forward after we're married, we're not just going to kick them to the curb, though. We will still be over it, until someone else in the group decides to take the lead." Caroline and Tangie worked out for an hour and left to go home, and later, they met up at Soulful Jazz.

17

S oulful Jazz was packed, as usual. Apparently, more people liked poetry than Caroline thought. It was Caroline's second time coming, but the crowd had doubled. The patio and the inside were filled with people eating soul food, sipping complimentary champagne, and listening to the live band. Brother Robertson's sister, who owns Soulful Jazz, has a pit outside, where she slow roasts her barbeque ribs and pulled pork.

Caroline decided to go for the barbecue plate this time, which consisted of Asian Barbecued Ribs, Texas toast, Boston baked beans, and a red potato salad, which consisted of red potatoes, made with a roasted red pepper, mayo, dill, and scallions. The potato salad was different from the usual potato salad, but it was delicious. It had a touch of sweetness and a spicy kick. Brother Robertson said that it was a secret family recipe, and he couldn't tell what the secret spices were that gave the potato salad that extra umph. Caroline was impressed with the variety and expansion of the dinner menu since her last visit. Fusion restaurants were the new trend, and the Asian soul menu was impressive.

The Asian soul menu consisted of Asian style food, combined with soul food. It took Caroline five minutes to decide which side she wanted to go with her entrée, before deciding on the red potato salad. The red potato salad had nothing to do with Asia, but the kimchi-style cabbage looked yummy, and so did the Wasabi mashed potatoes. There were pictures of a few entrées on the menu that had Caroline's mouth-watering. Caroline hadn't eaten like this in a minute. She was as full as a tick and ready to enjoy poetry night with Tangie and the rest of the single committee from Tangie's church. Everything was going well, and Caroline was talking and laughing with a few of Tangie's church members, when all of a sudden, Stacy and two of his security guards walked in. Caroline was shocked to see him, because she hadn't seen him in a while, and she hadn't talked to him, either. Having no contact with Stacy was one of Mr. Taylor's rules for Caroline to stay employed with GPSG.

Caroline knew that had everything to do with Mr. Lavado and Amanda. Mr. Taylor was being their puppet master for a healthy price. Caroline smiled as she saw him walk by with the two security guards. Women throughout the restaurant were eye balling him, as usual. No one ran up to him for his autograph, but women did try to walk past him to get noticed.

Soulful Jazz is an upscale restaurant. Many celebrities frequented, so they didn't flock to Stacy, like many groupies did. Still, there were some women there who were making eye contact or waving, hoping to start a conversation with him. As Stacy waited on his food, he noticed Caroline, who tried to look away quickly after Stacy noticed her staring at him. He came to the table. "Caroline," he held out his arms to get a hug.

"Long time no see. How have you been? I've been calling and texting you, but no reply. Did you get your number changed? What have you been up to?"

Caroline couldn't believe that Stacy was playing dumb. Surely, he knew to stay away from her or she could lose her job, but it was too late. There was no telling who was at the restaurant, seeing them hugging and talking. Caroline excused herself from the table and asked Stacy to follow her. Caroline went near the restrooms, where no one could see them, and Stacy followed behind like a little puppy.

"Stacy, what are you doing here?" "I came here to get something to eat before my flight, later. You know that I've decided to take the job in Miami."

"Really? I didn't know that. I mean, Stacy that's great. You're doing big things now, and I always knew that you would. I'm very proud of you." Caroline got caught up in the happy news, and she hugged Stacy again. "Thank you, Caroline, but I couldn't have done it without you."

"Oh yes, you could have. You are good at what you do, and success was sure to find you." "Yeah, but you getting me the exposure that you did, and booking fundraisers, shows, and auctions really got me a lot of exposure." "I was just doing my job."

"No, you did over and above your job. You were the executive secretary, but you worked beyond the call of duty." "Thank you. I appreciate that, Stacy." "You are more than welcome." A waiter walked to the front with Stacy's food and looked around for him. One of the security guards took the food.

"Look, I have to go before I miss my flight, but I never got a chance to apologize for what happened in Miami. I was out of line, and I don't know what came over me. Do you accept my apology?" "Of course, I do."

"Okay, I have to go, but one last hug for the road? I don't know when I'll see or talk to you again. I know that we still work for the same company, but you're going to be twelve hours away." The coast was clear, so Caroline agreed to a third hug, only this time, she felt something. She'd closed her eyes with her head against Stacy's chest and inhaled his cologne, and before she knew it, she started kissing him. She had totally disregarded everything that Amanda or Mr. Taylor had told her.

When they kissed, it felt real, and it felt right. No matter what the rest of the world was saying, she knew that she couldn't let Stacy leave that night, without telling him how she felt. "Wow, what was that all about?" Stacy was surprised that Caroline had kissed him. "I'm sorry, I didn't."

Stacy cut Caroline off mid-sentence, "Don't be. You have nothing to be sorry about. I'm not sorry. Caroline." Now, Caroline cut Stacy off. "Stacy, I love you after all these years, and I wish that I knew how to turn it off, but I can't. I know that it's more than lust; its real love. You are the only man that I'm one hundred percent sure that I love, and despite Amanda or Mr. Taylor's efforts to keep us apart, I just can't turn and walk away from what we could have." "Wait a minute. What do you mean, Amanda and Mr. Taylor efforts to keep us away? I thought that you had a talk with Mr. Taylor and asked him to have your assistant to work with me from now on?"

"No, I never had that talk with him, because shortly after I got back, I realized that you are the man I want to be with." Stacy took a step back with his mouth open. The security guard looked at him and tapped his watch. Stacy held up one finger as to wait a minute. "So, you mean to tell me that you never had that talk."

"No, I never had that talk. I was told by Amanda to stay away from you or she'd, basically, get me fired, and Mr. Taylor told me that if I wanted to keep my job, then I had to cut off all contact with you, because you were a distraction, and you were having a negative effect on my job performance."

"Wow," Stacy looked in disbelief. "I can't believe this. Are you sure that Amanda threatened you? I mean, I don't put anything past Mr. Taylor, because he'd do anything for the right price, but it's hard to believe that Amanda would do that." "Yeah and that's not all, but I believe that Amanda and Mr. Lavado are in the Mafia, and a lot of the money that they have is from drug money," she whispered. "Shh," Stacy said, looking around. "Look, give me a call at this number later on, and we can talk, but it's even deeper than you think." Stacy gave Caroline the card to the hotel where he was staying in Miami.

He gave Caroline one last kiss on the lips, and he left. I knew it, Caroline said to herself. Caroline went back to the table, and Jessica was in her seat. Caroline looked around for Mike, but didn't see him. "Hey," Tangie pulled Caroline to the side.

"I have been looking all over for you. Where have you been? Were you with Stacy, because I know that he was here. I just saw him leave with a bag of food and two big, tall black guys." Caroline gave Tangie a guilty look. "Caroline, you have to stay away from that man, or he's going to cause you everything. Use your mind, because your heart will get you in trouble."

"Tangie, you know what I don't care anymore. I really do love this man, and I am going to see him, no matter what anyone says or thinks. I won't let Amanda or Mr. Taylor's threats keep me from being with the man that I know is the one for me, and I won't watch him walk another woman down the aisle when I know that it should be me." Tangie just shook her head.   12:58 a.m. is what Caroline's clock read on her night stand. Caroline had been trying to get some sleep for an hour, and so far, insomnia was winning. Everything that Stacy had told Caroline over the phone was too much to sleep on. Although their conversation was brief, it was an earful. Caroline felt as if, all of a sudden, she was a part of the cast in Gangsta Files. The only difference was that this was reality and not a TV episode.

Caroline turned on her lamp on her nightstand and grabbed her tablet. She couldn't sleep, so she thought that she'd surf the Internet. Her curiosity was full, and she knew that if there was one way to get questions answered, it was by the Internet. Caroline knew not to believe everything she read online, because a lot of things on the Internet are half-truths and whole lies, just like what happened with her and Stacy in Miami. "Oh the irony in that situation," Caroline said, thinking about how that incident in Florida, somehow, made her realize that she was still in love with Stacy.

Caroline went online to Google and typed in The Lavado Family. Caroline scrolled to images, and there were several pictures of Mr. Lavado and pictures of several of his banks. There were pictures of him, Amanda, and Mrs. Lavado, as well. Then there were pictures of Mr. Lavado with the Governor of Georgia. Most of the pictures were business related, with only Mr. Lavado and a few of Amanda or Mrs. Lavado by themselves.

Caroline scrolled all the way down, and she was about to exit the images, when something caught her eye.

There was a picture of a man, who looked exactly like Mr. Lavado, but younger. It was a mug shot. Caroline clicked on the image to get a bigger view, and then she clicked on the link at the bottom of the picture, and it took her to a Page, called Drug Traffickers exposed. The page was full of drug criminals, but not an average nickel and dime dope boy on the streets. It was exposing the big dogs.

These were convicted felons, who the Feds were either after or had seized millions of narcotics from. There were rewards for information, leading to the whereabouts of several Mafia leaders, and one was the man, who looked like Mr. Lavado. This man in the mug shot was arrested when he was twenty-eight. The U.S. Coast Guard seized over seven thousand pounds of cocaine off a ship that he was a crew member on. The seizure took place on the pacific coast, and the man was arrested while trying to board a raft to escape.

The name the man gave the authorities was Julius Esteban. Julius Esteban served nine years in a Federal Prison. When he got out of prison, he went back to Colombia, and now, he is said to be the mastermind behind drug trafficking from Colombia to the U.S. Although there has been no proof that this is true, he is wanted for questioning. No one knows Julius Esteban's whereabouts, and he hasn't been seen in the U.S. or Colombia. Many people say that, because Mr. Lavado and Esteban look so much alike, Mr. Lavado is, in fact, Esteban. Authorities say that Esteban and Mr. Lavado are two different people. Esteban was born, raised, and lived in Colombia, until he was taken to prison in the U.S. Mr. Lavado is Colombian American. Mr. Lavado was born in Miami Florida and raised in Atlanta, where he still resides. When Esteban was doing time in prison, Mr. Lavado was serving in the U.S. Navy. Because one person can't be in two different places at one time, it's hard to believe that these two men are the same man. Some people say that maybe they are twins, but that isn't fact, either. Mr. Lavado was the only child. Esteban was the middle child of seven children, all born in Colombia. Although these two men have striking resemblance, they are obviously two different people. Before Caroline knew it, it was three in the morning. She had been surfing the Internet, but Mr. Lavado was as clean as a whistle, except for speculation and what MeMe's people had made of he and Esteban being the same person. Caroline closed her tablet and put it on her night stand, then she turned off her lamp, hoping that, this time, sleep would find her. She thought about her and Stacy's conversation and how he'd broken things off with Amanda after the incident in Florida. Caroline had told Stacy how she had done the same with Mike.

Caroline told Stacy about Amanda coming to her office and trying to bribe her out of Stacy's life. Stacy had no idea about Amanda coming to Caroline's job or that she tried to give Caroline two hundred and fifty thousand dollars to stay away from Stacy. Stacy was under the impression that Caroline did not want to work with him anymore, so that's why he'd kept his distance. Caroline explained that she never had that talk with Mr. Taylor about separating them, and that she loved Stacy and wanted to be with him, no matter what. All these thoughts, including her and Stacy's new and exciting long distance relationship, filled Caroline's head, and soon, she found sleep.

18

It was, finally, time for Tangie and Mr. Robertson to tie the knot. The week was busy with rehearsal dinners, a bridal shower, and making sure that everything was set with the caterer and the wedding planner. Tangie had accomplished her weight goal, and the dress fit perfectly.

"Oh my goodness, can you believe it? The day is finally here." Caroline seemed more excited than Tangie, who was still wiping crust out of her eyes, while opening her front door.

Caroline came inside, hardly able to contain the excitement. "Wake up honey, you have a man to marry in," she looked at her watch, "exactly twelve hours."

"Caroline really? It's four o'clock in the morning. Why are you up so early and with all this energy?" "I'm just excited that my best friend is going to marry the love of her life today and don't forget that we have early appointments at the salon today. You better get ready, so we can beat that crowd."

"Caroline, our hair appointments are at six. We still have two more hours." Caroline's energy quickly rubbed off on Tangie, and the thrill and excitement of her wedding day overcame her. "Ahhh I'm getting married today," Tangie threw up her hands and ran in place filled with joy. "I know, I'm so excited," Caroline said as she and Tangie both jumped up and down, like two happy kids in a candy store ready to fill their bags with goodies.

"Well, since we're up at four in the morning, do you want some breakfast?" "No thank you, honey, it's your day. You don't have to lift a finger if you don't want to. Go ahead and get dressed, and we can get something either before or after we leave the salon.

It's whatever you want, Ms. Soon to be Mrs. Robertson." Tangie and Caroline screamed with excitement again as they walked to Caroline's car. "I am getting married, I am getting married," Tangie sang happily. After breakfast at the Waffle House, they went to the Hair Salon. When Tangie wasn't under the dryer or getting her hair washed, she was on the phone with Brother Robertson. Caroline talked to Stacy briefly on the phone, because he was about to board his flight to Atlanta to help celebrate Tangie's big day.

After a busy first half of the day of getting their hair done, manicure, and pedicure, and a full body massage, Tangie and Caroline headed to Tangie's church, where the wedding would be held. When they entered the church, the wedding planner was busy delegating tasks and making sure that everything was in order. All the bridesmaids were scheduled to be at the church no later than two p.m., since the wedding was at four. After checking out how the wedding preparations were coming along at the church, Tangie and Caroline went by the banquet hall, just a couple of blocks down the street, to see how things were coming along there. The banquet hall was already set up, and Brother Robertson's sister and her cooks were busy prepping food for the reception; the pastry chef was also there, decorating the wedding cake.

Tangie and Caroline arrived back at the church at five minutes until two, and the bridesmaids were pulling in at the same time. The pastor had arrived at the church around one thirty. All of the wedding party were there by three, and guests began to fill the sanctuary by three thirty. Tangie peeked out of a window into the sanctuary, and it was filled with people. Tangie was shocked to see someone she hadn't seen in years.

"Caroline, look," Tangie said, while holding a finger down on the blinds and peeking through. "Tangie, stop peeking. You know that you aren't supposed to see the groom before it's time."

"They aren't out there yet. The wedding hasn't even started. We still have a couple of minutes. Look to your left and tell me who you see." Caroline looked to the left, and in the middle section on the end, she spotted Niq. "Aww, look at her. I'd forgotten that you invited her and Pam. Tangie, that was so nice of you to invite them, in spite of what happened in the past."

"Yes, Lord knows that he has really done some major changing in my life. There was a time when I wouldn't forgive or forget, but I had to learn how to love people, like Christ loves me, and forgive people, so that I would be forgiven. You wouldn't believe the peace of mind that I have now, just by truly forgiving people who wronged me, and not only them, but forgiving myself for things I've done." Caroline nodded her head in agreement. "Amen, sister."

"Anyways, she looks good, doesn't she? Rehab has served her well. She has gotten a little more weight on her and just looking at her, she seems happy and at peace," Tangie said, still peeking out the dressing room window into the sanctuary. "Mama, we are getting ready to start," Carmen said as she came inside the dressing room to get Caroline and the bridesmaids. "It's that time," Caroline said, while holding Tangie's hand.

"I love you, and you look so beautiful, Tangie." "Thank you, Caroline," Tangie said, while still holding hands with Caroline. "Thanks for everything." "No problem." They patted each other with a slight hug, careful not to mess up their makeup or Tangie's beautiful, white bride's gown.

Caroline exited the room, just in time to see Tangie's mom walk down the aisle with Brother Robertson, and Brother Robertson's parents walked next. Carmen was one of the bridesmaids, and she walked the isle with her boyfriend. The other bridesmaids were friends of Tangie from church, and the groomsmen where Brother Robertson's friends from church. Caroline, of course, was the maid of honor, and she walked down with

Brother Robertson's best man and friend, Mike. "You look amazing," Mike said, as he took Caroline's arm, and they headed down the aisle.

"You look very handsome, yourself," Caroline said to Mike, who was sporting a white tux with a silver bow tie and silver waist covering. Caroline tried to pull her silver strapless gown down a bit at the bottom, because she felt it was a little too short for church. "You're fine," Mike whispered while slick checking out Caroline's butt. "Ok Mike and Caroline, you're up," the wedding planner said, while making sure that everything was going smoothly. Mike and Caroline smiled as guests waved and took pictures of them walking down the aisle.

The musician began playing "Here comes the bride," and everyone stood. "Baby girl, you look absolutely beautiful," Tangie's father said to her as he took her arm. The wedding planner whispered, "Ready?" "Here we go." The ushers opened both doors, and Tangie and her father proceeded down the aisle.

Everyone said their OH's and ah's and took pictures as they walked down the aisle. Brother Robertson was smiling so hard from ear to ear that you'd think he was the Kool-Aid man, himself. After the wedding, the wedding party took pictures with the photographer. The reception was to start at six pm. When Tangie and Brother Robertson entered the reception, the DJ said, "Everyone stand and congratulate Mr. and Mrs. Robertson."

Everyone stood and congratulated them, and then the waiters immediately came out to serve the guests, who were seated at round, tables with white table cloths and white and silver bow-tied chair covers. Caroline had been so busy with the wedding that she hadn't talked to Stacy, and she wondered why he'd missed the wedding and was now missing the reception. Caroline had several missed calls on her cell and a text message from Stacy, saying that he couldn't make the wedding, but he would make the reception.

"Can I have this dance," a voice said, while Caroline was reading her text messages.

"Stacy. Hey baby, I just got your message, but I'm glad that you made it." Brother Robertson and Tangie had just finished their first dance.

Stacy shook Brother Robertson's hand and congratulated him and Tangie, and he gave Tangie a hug and congratulated them again.

"My feet are killing me," Tangie whispered to Caroline. "I got you covered," Caroline said, as she discreetly pulled out a new pair of flip flops for Tangie to put on.

Although Tangie had changed out of her wedding gown, she wore a long silk gown that covered her feet, so no one actually knew that she wore flip flops. Caroline and Stacy danced with other guests, and they even did the electric slide. Women were eye balling Stacy, because they knew he was a famous artist, and some even asked Caroline if she mind if they danced with him. Even some of the older women danced with Stacy.

Caroline didn't mind; it was all fun.

Jessica was following Mike around like a hound, and even looked at him funny when he danced with one of the Mothers of the church.

The DJ played a variety of music from old school to new school. "Look at how she's eye balling the Mother of the church," Tangie said to Caroline, who was sitting next to her. "I can see if she was bumping and grinding all on him, but their just two-stepping and having fun."

Stacy was busy with one woman after another of all ages. He waved at Caroline in an attempt to come and rescue him, because he was all danced out. Caroline took his cue and went over to rescue him, and they sat down and ate and talked. Stacy's security guard stood to the side with his shades on and his hands cuffed in front of him. "Does he ever talk?" Caroline whispered to Stacy.

Stacy laughed. "Man, it's cool; sit down and get something to eat," Stacy said to the body guard. "These are my peeps." The security guard sat down and took off his shades and let the waiter know what he wanted to eat. The night was full of fun and laughter, and Tangie and Brother Robertson left the Banquet Hall with a truck load of gifts from their guests.

Later that night, Caroline and Stacy went back to her place. They sat on the patio and talked for a while, and Stacy made several attempts to make love to Caroline. "Baby no, I told you that I made a vow to God, and I'm not doing that until I'm married." Caroline was hot, and it was hard to fight her flesh, especially with the way Stacy looked into her eyes and kissed her so passionately. When it began to get late, Caroline told Stacy that he could spend the night at her place, but he had to sleep in the guest room.

"Really Caroline? You don't trust me? You know that I wouldn't do anything to you that you don't want me to." "Yes, I know, but I'm not doing it for that reason. I'm doing it so that I won't be tempted."

They went to their separate rooms, and Stacy began to text Caroline. "What are you wearing?" Caroline knew he wanted to hear thongs, boy shorts, or even better, nothing. She wasn't feeding into it, though. She texted Stacy back, "Granny panties."

Most men would have been turned off right there. "Let me see," Stacy texted. Caroline sent him a picture of a pair of granny panties out of the drawer. She sat the panties on the bed and took a picture and sent it to Stacy saying, "Goodnight." "You're mean," Stacy texted back.

"Goodnight." Caroline started to lock her room door, but didn't, because she trusted Stacy, and although he was stubborn, he would not attempt to have sex with her against her will. The next morning, Caroline woke up to the smell of eggs and bacon. Stacy was in the kitchen, cooking them an omelet and toast, and he'd even made fresh orange juice. "Good morning," Caroline said as she kissed Stacy.

"Good morning, baby." "And what did I do to deserve breakfast this bright and early in the morning?" It was seven forty-five in the morning when Caroline looked at the time on the stove.

"You are my lady, and that's all you have to be, and you can have anything you want, girl." Stacy kissed Caroline again and then sat her on top of the counter. He cut into his omelet and told Caroline to try it. "Oh my goodness, this is delicious," Caroline said. "Just like you," Stacy said as he kissed Caroline's lips, and their tongue quickly followed. Caroline put her hand around Stacy's neck, and he picked her up and held her with one hand and grabbed her plate with another.

He sat her plate down at the table and then he sat her at the table.

God help me, Caroline thought to herself. I can't fight this temptation by myself. Stacy knew exactly what he was doing, walking around with his six pack showing and his dreads tied back. At least, he had the decency to have on pajama pants. I don't know what I would have done if he was walking around in boxers.

Caroline didn't realize her focus was on Stacy's crotch, while she was in deep thought. Stacy bit off a piece of bacon and laughed, while standing in front of her and putting his plate on the table. "Eat up baby, I have a long day planned for us, and you're going to need your energy," Stacy said as he licked his lips. Caroline laughed and shook her head. Stacy knows that when he licks his lips, it turns Caroline on.

"What?" Stacy asked, knowing exactly what he was doing. "Absolutely nothing," Caroline smiled and said. "So what are we doing today?"

"We are going somewhere that we haven't been, well, I know I haven't been, since I was seventeen, and I was with you the last time that I went." Caroline gave Stacy a confused look. "I will give you a hint. They have rides, one that was your favorite, and you liked to hold up your hands when it would go down." Caroline mouth hung open.

"Oh my goodness, Six Flags? I haven't been there in, well, since the last time you and I went. I heard that they have all kinds of rides now. Yes, I would love to go." "Good and bring something sexy along too, because after we leave Six Flags, I have a romantic evening planned for us as well."

Caroline showered and got dressed. "So, what happened yesterday? You never told me why you couldn't make it to the wedding," Caroline yelled from her room to Stacy, who was busy getting dressed in the guest room. "Oh, business with GPSG," Stacy said. "On a Saturday?" "Um, Caroline, today is Saturday." "Oh right, my bad." Caroline had forgotten that she had taken off for the wedding on Friday. "So are you coming to church with me, tomorrow?" "Baby, you know how I feel about church. I love God, and I don't think that I have to go to church every Sunday to prove that. I'm just not into the whole church thing, like you are, Caroline."

"But, it's important to me, though. Won't you come? You'll have a good time. We will go to Tangie's church, because I know how you feel about my church and all the old people there." Caroline came out the room, just as Stacy was coming out the guest room. "Maybe next time, baby, but I leave early tomorrow morning, because I have to get back to Miami." Stacy kissed Caroline on the forehead. "Ok, but I'm going to hold you to that, Stacy." "Girl, you can hold me hostage for all I care, woo," Stacy said as he smacked Caroline on the butt and shook his head. "Ouch," Caroline said, rubbing her butt. "Stop playing, you know that you like it." Caroline smiled and shook her head. "Come on, crazy man, let's go." "Yeah I'm crazy about you." "No, your crazy don't have anything to do with me. I think Ma Ann may have dropped you on your head when you were a baby." Stacy laughed as he went to put their bags in the trunk and got in the car.

Caroline locked the door and headed to the car. She thought about Mike and how he always opened every door for her. She was more than capable of opening doors for herself, but it was nice to have a man to do it for her. It made her feel special. Nevertheless, you have to pick and choose your battles in a relationship. What will you accept, and what won't you accept?

I can live with him not opening the door for me; that's minor, Caroline thought as she opened the passenger door and got in. The security guard was in the parking lot, waiting for Stacy and Caroline to get there. He had talked with Stacy on the phone and told them where he was parked. It was weird to Caroline, having somebody to follow them everywhere they went. If they went on a ride, so did he.

If they went to the restroom, he went too. If they grabbed something to drink, he was right there, slurping along with them. Stacy and Caroline spent most of the day at Six Flags riding rides and taking pictures. Stacy signed a few autographs, and they enjoyed themselves, like two teenage kids. When evening came, the security guard escorted them to the Atlanta Symphony. There wasn't a concert going on, so Caroline was curious as to what was going on.

When she entered, a host escorted her to the dressing room, so that she could change clothes. After Caroline changed clothes, she met with Stacy in the concert hall, where they had a candlelit dinner on stage with members from the Atlanta Symphony playing soft music. It was so romantic. Stacy had a personal chef to prepare anything he or Caroline wanted. They danced to the sounds of the orchestra, and Caroline was swept off her feet.

As they danced, Caroline felt as if they were in a fairy tale, and they could just dance together until eternity. Stacy walked Caroline back to her seat and pulled out the chair for her. Caroline was impressed. She sat down, and Stacy got down on one knee. A million thoughts went through Caroline's head.

She and Stacy had been in a long distance relationship for three months, and he was proposing already? Half a year ago, he was engaged to Amanda. Caroline didn't know what to think. She did love him, and he loved her. Maybe, being at Tangie and Brother Robertson's wedding made him realize the time was right for him and Caroline to make it official.

"Caroline, I love you. You mean the world to me. I feel more than blessed that you gave me the opportunity to come back into your life. I know we haven't been in a relationship long, but it's been long enough. You are my soul mate, and we were meant to travel this road through life together. I want you to be my wife. I know that I'm far from perfect, but that in which I lack, I feel you make up for, because you are perfect to me. I love you, Caroline. Will you be my wife?" Caroline felt butterflies and she also felt as though her heart fell into her stomach.

Everything was right. "Yes," she said with tears in her eyes. "Yes, Stacy, I love you, and I will marry you." Stacy placed the diamond ring on Caroline's ring finger and kissed her. They both stood up and hugged, while members of the Atlanta Symphony Orchestra applauded.

Caroline felt on top of the world and wished this high could last forever.

"Champagne?" The waiter asked. "Why not?" Caroline said.

Caroline was never a drinker, but this caused for celebration. After listening to the live orchestra and eating dinner, Caroline and Stacy danced a final time and headed home. When they got back to Caroline's house, she asked, "So what do we do now? This is crazy. We just got engaged. I know, for sure, that my job and, possibly, yours is now gone down the drain. Your ex has threatened me, and there's no telling what we're up against now."

"Shh," Stacy said as he held a finger against Caroline's lips. "Don't ruin our moment, worrying about what the world thinks. I didn't tell you before, but I went to GPSG Friday to turn in my official resignation. I already have another job that I report to on Monday, and they pay more money, and I don't have to worry about money that I make being split three ways. I am no longer their employee, so they can't say it's a conflict of interest. I do want you to move to Miami with me, though. I mean, that's where my job is, and it will be my job for a while. You can easily transfer to the GPSG sister station in Florida, and we can live there."

Moving to Florida was a lot for Caroline to take in. Atlanta was her home, and although she was now Stacy's fiancée, they needed to decide on future living arrangements. Caroline told Stacy that she didn't want to make any hasty decisions and that she needed time. Stacy understood, and the next day, she saw him off to his flight back to Miami.

Caroline went to her church and wished Tangie wasn't on her honeymoon, so that she could call and tell her everything that had happened. Caroline was in desperate need of advice, and she couldn't hide her uneasiness from Mother Brooke. "Caroline, it's nice to see you, as usual," Pastor Brooke said as he shook her hand and other members.

"Caroline, are you ok?" Mother Brooke asked.

Mother Brooke saw that something was wrong, and she and Caroline went into one of the children's church rooms to talk. Mother Brooke made sure that the room was completely empty, before closing the door and locking it. "What's on your mind, baby?" Mother Brooke said, sitting in a chair next to Caroline. "Well, Mother Brooke, this should be one of the happiest times of my life, but I'm so confused, right now."

Caroline explained how she'd gotten engaged and how everything was so perfect and romantic. She also explained how she wasn't ready to move and how she'd been on her job, now, for eighteen years, and that she didn't know if she wanted to leave Atlanta. "Is it leaving Atlanta or your job of eighteen years that scares you, or is it the fact that you said yes to Stacy, and you aren't sure if you really want to marry him?" "No, I'm more than sure that I want to marry him. I just don't feel like I should have to move to Florida. Why can't he move back to Georgia?"

"Have you expressed your thoughts with Stacy?" "No ma'am, I haven't."

"Well, you need to. How will he know what you feel if you don't tell him? He may think that you're ok with moving. Y'all are engaged now, but one day, y'all will be married, and a marriage is all about communicating, and sometimes, making sacrifices. If you love this man, and he is to be your husband, why not transfer to the job in Florida? Be there for him and have his back. A man needs a woman who will support him. You can't let fear hold you back.

"If you truly love this man and are one hundred percent sure that you want to marry him, then step out in faith and move to Florida. If you are marrying him for any reason, except for the reason of love, though, then you better get out while you still have a chance, or else you are headed for disaster." Mother Brooke always knew what to say, and she always left Caroline with even more questions than she had to begin with.

Caroline did love Stacy, and nothing would make her happier than getting married and starting a family with the love of her life. But were they moving too fast?

Caroline didn't know what to think. What if Stacy only got engaged to her just to get in her panties? It sounded farfetched, but some men are known to go to certain extremes to get the goods. Questioning Stacy's reasoning made Caroline think that maybe they should slow things down. She was still going to be his fiancée, but she wasn't moving anytime soon.

Caroline stopped at the gas station on the way home, and Mike was inside with Michael grabbing a drink. "Ms. Caroline," Michael yelled and ran to give her a hug. Michael was now officially a teenager, but his eyes lit up, and he was happy to see Caroline anytime. "Hello Caroline," Mike said. "Hi, Mike."

Caroline tried to hold her purse a certain way, so that Mike wouldn't see the rock on her finger. "Hey, what are you doing this evening? We are having a cookout over at my parents, and we would love for you to stop by, even for a second. They've been asking me about you, anyway. You should come. They would love to see you." "I don't think that's a good idea, Mike, but it was nice to see you," Caroline said, trying to hurry out the door. Mike was fast on her heels.

"Aw don't be like that. It's just dinner with the fam and a good friend. You have to eat, right?"

Caroline smiled and nodded, "Yes, I do have to eat. I'm headed home to go cook, because I already have my chicken in the fridge thawing." "Now, look, I just saved you a day of slaving over that hot stove. Come on out." Caroline hit the unlock button on her key chain and was getting ready to put her purse inside, so that she could pump her gas. "Let me get that for you," Mike said as he opened her door. "Get in. I'll pump the gas for you." Caroline smiled, "Thanks." "No problem." "So, what will your girlfriend think about me being there?"

"Well, for one, she's not my girlfriend. She is someone that I occasionally go out on dates with, but I'm a single man. I go on dates frequently, thanks to my buddy at work. He doesn't like Jessica and thinks she's just a gold digger. I think that you were the only woman he actually approved of me being with." Mike finished pumping the gas and came around to Caroline's door. "Thanks again, Mike." "You're welcome, so I'll see you around five?" "Sure," Caroline said with her left hand under her arm and holding her head with her right hand. "Are you ok?"

"I'm fine; it's just hot outside," she lied. She wasn't ready for Mike to see the ring yet. She decided to take the ring off before going to the cookout, but then she felt as if she was being unfaithful by doing that, so she quickly put the ring back on. "Mike and I haven't been together for half a year, now. I don't have to explain anything to him. Why am I acting so weird?" She gave herself a final look in the mirror, before heading out the door. "Well, here goes nothing." When Caroline arrived at Mike's parents' house, they both came out to greet her. There were several cars parked in the driveway and along the street.

Most of the people were friends of Mike's parents, along with Mike's friend from work and his date. When Caroline was hugging Mike's mom, he noticed her ring. "Wow, did I miss something? I'm sure that I would have noticed that earlier today. Are you and Stacy engaged?"

Caroline swallowed hard and exhaled, "We are." Mike scratched his left brow, "Oh, well congratulations," he said awkwardly as he gave Caroline a hug. "Come on in and meet everybody." "Are you sure? I can easily leave if this changes anything."

"Are you serious? It's not like I'm asking you out on a date or anything. You're at a cookout with friends," Mike said as he opened the front door for Caroline to come in. Mike's dad went to the backyard to play baseball with a friend of his and the kids. Mike's mom went back inside into the kitchen, as she listened to the old school station and stirred her greens and checked on the macaroni and cheese in the oven.

"It smells so good in here." "Thank you, Caroline," Mike's mom said. Mike introduced Caroline to his parent's friends, who were seated inside, and then he introduced her to his coworker, who she hadn't met in person, but had heard about. After meeting him and his date, Mike asked her to come outside with him. He was on the grill, as usual.

Mike was a grill beast. He flipped over the ribs and chicken and closed the grill. "So, tell me all about it. How did it happen?" Caroline felt uneasy telling Mike, at first, but she told him, and even Mike agreed that it was romantic. "Wow, it must have cost him a fortune to do all of that," Mike said. "He went all out. He must really love you." "He does. So, tell me about you and your dating life. It's hard to believe that no one has snatched you off the market." "Well, being single has its perks, but hey, now and then, I do get lonely." "Well that couldn't be often, because Ms. Jessica hardly ever lets you out of her sight. I'm surprised she's not here today."

"Yeah, she's out of town. She took her daughter to see her father. He plays for the Kansas City Royals, and they had a baseball game today. Jessica is something. Persistence does pay off with not only men, but women as well." "What do you mean by that?" "Well, she knew what she wanted, and she went after it until she got it."

"Are we talking about you?" "Yes, after you kicked me to the curb, I didn't want a relationship for a very long time." "And now you do?"

"I don't know, but she does add a certain spark to my life, although at times, it can be annoying. Besides, you know the song, "If you can't be with the one you love, then love the one you're with," he said, looking into Caroline's eyes.

"So you do love her?" "In the sense that she is good with kids. She brings me and Michael food." "Oh she cooks for y'all?" "No, I didn't say she cooks. I said she brings us food. Mostly take out, but if she does bring food from the grocery store, I cook it, but that has only been like twice. She's cool people, once you get to know her though." Mike and Caroline went back in, and Mike's friend asked them if they wanted to play spades. Caroline was happy that Tangie had taught her how to play. After a game of spades, it was time to eat. Mike and his friend had won the game, but the ladies declared that it wasn't over.

By the time the night ended, Caroline and the other lady had won one out of four games. Mike laughed because whoever lost owed the other team dinner. Mike's friend left and said that he was going home to get his dinner now. Then, he corrected himself and said dessert, while licking his lips and walking behind his date. "So when am I going to get my dinner, Ms. Caroline? Or dessert?

Whichever one you choose to give me," Mike smiled, showing those pearly whites. "Um, I will let you know," Caroline smiled and headed out the door with Mike following close behind. "Thank you for inviting me. I had a nice time."

Caroline hit the unlock switch on her car and stood to the side, knowing that Mike was going to open her door and he did. "You are more than welcome and congrats to you and Stacy again.

I'm happy for you." "Thank you, Mike. That really means a lot to me coming from you." They said goodnight, and Caroline went home.

19

Caroline and Mike kept in touch and would call or text each other often. Mike understood and respected the fact that she was engaged to Stacy, and Caroline was happy that Mike had forgiven her for breaking his heart and that he was happily single. "Do you think that we didn't work out because we rushed things?" Mike said on the other end of the phone call with Caroline.

"I don't think we rushed at all, Mike. We started dating a year after you'd been divorced, and we just went with the flow. I don't feel like anything was rushed. I do feel like I wasn't honest with you about my feelings, though. It's like you are the obvious choice for any woman, and I wanted you to be my choice, but my heart was elsewhere. I did grow to love you and was faithful to you, but I couldn't deny what I felt for Stacy. I felt so relieved the day you called me, and I told you how I felt. I was disappointed that you didn't say anything, but I totally understood."

"Wait, what? You never officially told me how you felt. You just cut me off. I'm really just hearing all of this now." "No, remember, you called me, and I was crying, and I told you." Mike cut Caroline off.

"Caroline, that wasn't me. I wouldn't lie about something like this. Was it my cell number?" "No it was restricted." "No it definitely wasn't me then. I don't make restricted calls. Either you answer when I call you or you don't." Caroline scratched her head in confusion, trying to think who that could have been on the phone that day. Maybe it was Amanda, which would explain why she came by the office the next day, she thought. Caroline was silent for a moment.

"Caroline, are you ok?" "Yes I'm fine. I was just thinking." "So when was the last time that you talked to your parents?" "I talk to my dad all the time now, and most of the time, my mom is busy with work." "I thought that she retired?"

"She did, but I guess she couldn't stand the fact that she wasn't in a court room almost every day of her life, and now she's a judge." "Wow." "Yes, that's what I said." "So what is your daddy up to these days?" "Well, he said that his days of politics are definitely over." "I can understand that."

"Yeah, he said he's proud of his accomplishments, and he is quite content with reaping the harvest of retirement." "I know that's right. When it's time for me to retire, I'm doing just that."

"Yeah, so he spends his days remodeling their house or working in their garden. I'm actually thinking about going to visit them soon. I haven't seen them in about four years, except when we facetime or by webcam. We use to see each other at least once a year, but I guess that my life has been so busy lately that I just haven't had the time. To be honest, I just gave up, because I would always have to go and visit them, and they've only been to my home once." "I'm sorry."

"Don't be. I'm used to it. Work has always been their priority. I'm thirtysix years old. Why should I expect for things to change now?

Anyway, I have to go. I am late for an appointment." "On a Saturday?"

"Yes, on a Saturday, nosy. I will call you later."

"Aw I was hoping that you could treat me to that dinner that you owe me." "I know that it has been three months, but I have not forgotten about you, Mike. Maybe next Saturday, but this weekend I am a little busy."

"Ok, but next weekend, Soulful Jazz, your treat." "Gotcha."

"Alright and have a safe flight to Miami." Caroline laughed. She held her cell to her ear with her mouth hung open. "I can't get anything past you can I?" "No you can't." "You never lied about going to see Stacy before. Why did you feel you have to lie now?" "I don't know; it was silly of me, but yes, my flight leaves in a couple of hours, so I have to go." "Ok bye and don't do anything that I wouldn't do." Caroline laughed, "Goodbye Mike."

Caroline had actually planned on doing something that Mike wouldn't do. Which is why she didn't want to tell him or anyone else that she was going to Miami to see Stacy. It was no secret that she often flew to Miami to see Stacy or he would fly to Atlanta to see her, but she wanted this special trip to be a surprise. Plans for their wedding day was five months away, and she had plans for, at least, letting Stacy get to third base. She felt that if her friends knew where she was going, they'd know what she'd been up to, but really it was her own convictions.

Fighting temptation was hard around Stacy. They'd only went as far as kissing and touching each other with their clothes on, but never as far as what Caroline had planned to do. Caroline had bought some sexy lingerie and had planned on cooking for them and having a romantic dinner at Stacy's loft on South Beach. She had even gone as far as to think that maybe, they could just touch each other down there, without clothes on. She knew that if she told Tangie that Tangie would tell her that was impossible.

She could hear Tangie in her ear, "If he touches it with his hands, then you are going to want something else to touch it, and before you know it, you are going to break all your years of celibacy." No, she couldn't tell Tangie, she thought. It has almost been two decades; that's a long time, Caroline thought. Stacy brought something out in Caroline, though, and it was hard to extinguish that flame when they were together. It was Love and Passion combined.

When Caroline was boarding her flight to Miami, she saw Jessica sitting in a seat across from her. "Oh hi, Caroline," Jessica said, trying to sound happy to see Caroline, but really sounding fake. "Hey Jessica," Caroline said while putting her take on bags in the overhead compartment. There was an old lady sitting by the window next to Caroline, and Jessica asked if she wanted to trade. The old lady said she didn't like to sit by windows anyway, and sitting by the isle would make it easier for her to go use the restroom.

Jessica and the old lady switched seats, and Jessica was seated next to Caroline. It's going to be a long flight, Caroline thought to herself. "So you're going to see your boyfriend, huh?" "What's it to you?"

"Nothing. I was just trying to make conversation." "Shouldn't you be worried about more important things like, where's your daughter?" "No I'm not worried about my daughter. She is well taken care of by her nanny. I am going to Miami for a video shoot." Caroline had forgotten that Jessica was a hip hop video vixen. Caroline didn't know what Mike saw in her, except that she was drop dead gorgeous. Compared to Caroline, they were totally different. Caroline was small and petite with a nice shape and natural, long wavy hair.

Jessica was a yellow bone, who was about five nine, not adding the six inch stilettos on her feet. She had long hair, as well, but fake boobs and a butt enhancement that was ridiculous. Although Jessica was a video model, she did take very good care of her daughter and did seem like a good mother. "So what's the deal with Mike? Is he gay or something?"

Caroline could not believe that Jessica was asking her that. "Why are you asking me if Mike's gay?" "Well I mean, I have been after him for God knows how long, and usually, it's the other way around. I mean who can resist me," she said running her fingers through her hair and winking at the two men who were seated on the opposite side behind her.

"Why do you want Mike, anyway? He doesn't seem to be your type."

"Money is my type, Caroline. I always knew that if I was going to marry, then it was not going to be for love, but for money. That was until I met Mike. He has money, but he also has the goods. I guess that all the chasing and spending time with him has sort of made me feel attached to him. I think that I may even love him or, at least, that's what I've told him. I don't know if I love him or not. I've said it so many times to so many men in order to get what I want. I don't want to fall for a brother who is on the down low, though. I even asked him if he was gay, myself, and he said no. I was just wondering, because the only thing we've ever done was kiss. He never even smacked my butt or nothing," Jessica said as her Latino accent begin to come out. She was a feisty something. In church, she was this snobbish, sophisticated woman. Right now, she was being straight ratchet.

"Wow, you are two totally different people," Caroline said. "No I'm not. People just assume that I am one way until they get to know me.

Just because I'm beautiful doesn't mean that I think I'm better than you, Caroline." Caroline gave Jessica a funny look and thought to herself, is this trick trying to say that I'm ugly? At least I don't have a fake booty. Mine is one hundred percent natural. I don't have to wear a ton of makeup either, to say the least. Caroline couldn't think of too many other things to say about Jessica, except for the fake boobs, which looked awesome. Jessica did think more highly of herself than what she should, and someone should bring her down a notch.

It's not going to be me, Caroline thought. Not today anyway, so she kept all those thoughts in her head. On the flight to Miami, Mr. Lavado and Amanda was on the news. Jessica was still babbling on, and Caroline shushed her and told her to be quiet. Caroline put on her ear phones and listened to what was going on.

Levy Pharmaceuticals had made a major breakthrough in the treatment of cancer. The news was talking about some rare organic plant powder being used to virtually destroy some forms of cancer. Mr. Lavado and Amanda are part business owners of Levy Pharmaceuticals in which they have several doctors and scientist who work for them. The drug was approved by the FDA. Caroline couldn't believe it.

Maybe, that's what Amanda and Adam had been discussing over the phone. The rumor that Stacy had told her about Mr. Lavado changing his identity must have been just that, a rumor. There was no way that this man, who was doing all kinds of good, was also a Drug smuggler and head of a Colombian Mafia. Mr. Lavado was on TV, explaining how he lost his father and grandfather to cancer and how the breakthrough of this medicine was dear to his heart. "Well I'll be," Caroline thought to herself.

When Caroline arrived in Miami, she'd arrived at Stacy's loft on the beach. Caroline had her own key, so she let herself in. Stacy wasn't at home, and Caroline was glad, because that gave her time to shower and put on her sexy lingerie. After Caroline showered and slipped into something a little more comfortable, she walked around the condo to admire Stacy's art. Some old and some new.

"My man is so talented," she said, walking through Stacy's home gallery, where he kept a small collection of his art for guests to enjoy when they came over. Stacy's art has the tendency to captivate a person's mind to where they are lost in the moment of his creation. Caroline continued to walk through the loft, leaving a trail of smell good brought on by her favorite perfume. "Maybe Stacy is out getting lunch?" Caroline looked in the fridge and in the cabinets and nothing was in the fridge, except two beers and some bottled water.

Caroline grabbed a water and headed to the living room, where she was totally caught off guard. There was the forever portrait hanging on the wall above the fireplace. The famous portrait was sold to the old couple that Caroline and Stacy had met in Miami, so she wondered if Stacy had drawn another one or if he had bought it back. The earth tones in the portrait of Caroline blended in with Stacy's Rustic living room décor.

Caroline smiled and touched her heart, while looking at the portrait.

This painting symbolized their love. A love that was forever. Caroline took her time examining the painting, because although she was the first to see it, she never saw herself in the painting, until it was on the cover of the newspaper that also had her and Stacy kissing. It was funny how all she could see in the painting was her and what seemed like her hair blowing in the wind, when she saw it on the cover of the newspaper, but in person, she saw a tall, beautiful tree that stood out amongst other trees as leaves blew in the wind, and when you turned your head in a certain angle, you could see the word, forever, in the leaves. Maybe, Caroline wasn't looking at it right.

As she stood searching to find herself in the painting, she felt something warm on her neck, followed by a kiss in the same place. Caroline closed her eyes and then opened them again, and she saw herself in the portrait as plain as day. That's weird, she thought, but she was too busy enjoying the soft kisses on her neck and then her ears. Caroline turned around, and there was Stacy, looking as handsome as ever. He didn't have on anything fancy, just a white beater, some shorts, and some loafers, but he looked and smelled like a million bucks.

"I followed the scent of your perfume, and it lead me here. How long have you been here waiting? I would have waited here had I known that you were coming." Stacy grabbed Caroline's hand as they walked to the kitchen. "I went out to get a few groceries and came back home to all kinds of goodies," Stacy said, while giving Caroline a nice smack on the behind.

Stacy had gone into the kitchen with intentions of putting up the food, but the food sat on the counter, and he put Caroline on the kitchen island, and they begin kissing again. Caroline wrapped her legs around his waist and took off his shirt, admiring his ripped physic. His abs went from a six pack to what now was more like an eight. Temperature was rising with every kiss, and the more they touched, the more Caroline melted, until their bodies where in sync with one another. Stacy picked Caroline up and took her to his bedroom. He laid her down on the bed and asked her, "Are you sure that you want to do this?"

Caroline stood and slipped off her halter baby doll. When it hit the floor, she looked up at Stacy and said, "I'm ready." Stacy unbuckled his shorts and took them off, along with his boxers. Caroline's eyes got huge. Stacy was definitely packing more luggage than he was when they were teens, way more.

Stacy walked over to Caroline and laid her down on the bed. He began at the bottom with soft kisses on Caroline's feet and worked his way upward. The whole time, Caroline was battling the war between what her spirit knew was right and what her flesh felt was right. Caroline tried to justify in her mind that they were going to be married soon. That it was going to be a onetime thing. Tangie was right, she said in her mind, there was no way she could let Stacy get to third base, without hitting a homerun. Stacy reached Caroline's thighs and with every stroke of his tongue, she was ready to welcome him to come hither. Suddenly, Stacy stopped and leaned over Caroline starring her in the face. "What's wrong, Caroline?" She slowly opened her eyes. "Nothing is wrong, baby. Why did you stop?"

"Because, at first, you were looking at me, and we were making eye contact and then you start closing your eyes and shaking your head no, like you wanted me to stop. Are you ok?" Caroline sat up on the side of the bed. "No Stacy, I'm not ok. I'm sorry baby, I want to do this, but I have come a long way, and I just can't. I want our wedding night to be special." Stacy sat on the side of the bed next to Caroline, but he also was standing at full attention. Caroline looked at it, wanting nothing more than to jump on it and go for a ride into ecstasy, but she just couldn't. Caroline stood up with a sheet wrapped around her. "Stacy, I am so sorry."

"Baby, I don't understand. We are going to be married soon. What's the big deal? If it's about us not being married, then we can go get married right now and have our ceremony later. Baby, don't do this to me. Don't leave him like this," Stacy said, looking down at himself. "I'm sorry baby," Caroline said as she walked off with the sheet around her. "I will make it up to you. I will cook you whatever you want. Or if you want to go out then it's on me."

"Caroline, you can cook or take me out, but that ain't what I want to eat," Stacy said, while starring down at Caroline's goodies like he could see them through the covers.

"I'm going to go cook." Stacy laid back on the bed and banged his head on the bed, while cursing. He even took a few swings at the air as if it was a punching bag. After Stacy calmed down, he went to take a cold shower.

Later on, they sat at the dinner table and ate, but the whole time they ate, it felt awkward. They barely said anything to each other. Caroline knew that Stacy was disappointed that they didn't make love. Later that night, as Stacy slept, Caroline gently tugged him and told him what she wanted. Stacy was happy to oblige as he wrapped her legs around his face, and she returned the favor, until they both reached euphoria and fell asleep.

20

It was now Christmas time, and Caroline had planned a Christmas party. This Christmas was extra special, because her parents were flying into town to spend the holiday with her. Stacy was also flying into town Christmas Eve. Mike had been driving Caroline around all day, along with Michael. Caroline was out buying decorations, a real Christmas tree, food, and gifts.

Mike, Michael, Jessica, and her daughter were some of the guests attending the Christmas party, along with Tangie and Brother Robertson. Mike and Caroline were like two peas in a pod. They were best friends, next to Tangie and Caroline. They could talk about anything and even, occasionally, have dinner together, without it being any more than friends having dinner. Caroline always informed Stacy of whatever she was doing when it came to Mike, because she didn't want any issues. Stacy understood, because he had numerous lady friends that he'd acquired through business, not to mention he and Amanda would occasionally talk on the phone or even go out for drinks. Caroline wasn't completely comfortable with that situation, but what could she say? She was basically doing the same thing with her ex. Caroline trusted Stacy, but it was Amanda and her motives she was worried about. Caroline got home from a long day of shopping around nine p.m.

Mike put the tree up for her before he and Michael went home. Caroline decorated the tree. It was late and Caroline had a lot to do the next day, which was when everyone was flying into town. Mike and Michael offered to come over tomorrow to help decorate, and Mike even offered to help cook if need be. Caroline was only cooking a few items, but she had Soulful Jazz to cater for the Christmas party, and she bought a couple of cheesecakes, pound cakes, and pecan pie from Amanda's café. They may not get along all that well, but Caroline couldn't deny Amanda's gift of being an awesome pastry chef.

The only thing that Caroline had to cook was a pot of gumbo, which was mainly for Tangie, who was now pregnant and had been craving gumbo since September. Mike and Michael came by as planned to help decorate Caroline's house. By the time the three of them finished decorating, Caroline's yard was lit up with lights and many Christmas decorations. There was a nativity scene section with baby Jesus, Mary and Joseph, deer and angels, horses, and wise men, and Christmas lights covered the house. Many of the neighbors came by to take pictures of Caroline's house, and cars that usually bypass her house slowed down to enjoy the lights and decorations.

Caroline was exhausted from decorating all day, but she was very proud of all the work after she, Mike, and Michael had finished the job. Mike left to go pickup Jessica from the airport, who had just come back to Atlanta from a Hip Hop video shoot in New York with an upcoming male artist. Stacy called Caroline once he got to Hartsfield Jackson, so that she could pick him up. "Baby, I'm coming," Caroline said as she tried to put on her earring with one hand and put her pumps on her feet with another. "Caroline, are you sure, because I can take a cab?"

"No, no, no don't take a cab. I'm coming to get you. I'm in the car and on the way now," she lied. "Oh I know what that means. You're still at home, getting ready, aren't you?" "I am, but I am on the way, I promise." A light went off in Caroline's head. She thought to herself. Hey, Mike is at the airport picking up Jessica now. I wonder if he could pick up Stacy, too.

Mike and Stacy were not the best of friends, but they had learned to be, at least, cordial for the sake of Caroline. Stacy saw Mike as his competition, even though Caroline had promised that they were only friends. Mike knew that Stacy wasn't too fond of him, and the feeling was mutual. Mike had Caroline's friendship, but Stacy had her heart. Mike had learned to deal with it, because as some people would say, "You can't help who you love."

Both were running neck in neck with looks. Mike is tall and muscular, chocolate skin tone, and he keeps his hair cut low, and his waves are deep enough to make the Atlantic Ocean jealous. Stacy is also tall, but slimmer, with an eight pack for abs. Stacy has that V cut at the bottom sides of his abs that all the ladies love, especially when he did a summer photo shoot and was featured on the front cover of Men's Health. He did a nice beach pose in his trunks that showed off his abs, and then there's the dreads. The women loved his long dreads that he mostly kept tied back.

Mike has more money, but Stacy is very ambitious and hardworking and has come a long way from working as a cook at Amanda's café to making a healthy six figures a year. Mike grew up with wealth, as Caroline did, but Stacy is from the streets, so he's determined to reach for the sky when it comes to his career. Mike is a dedicated member of his church, who is saved and God fearing. Stacy hasn't been to church since he was a teenager and would rather be at work, making money, than sitting in a pew. Mike is a divorced single father, and Stacy doesn't have any kids, although he was engaged to Amanda for several years. Both men have their pros and cons, and both know what they have offer. "Baby, how do you feel about Mike coming to get you?" "What?" "Well, he's at the airport now, picking up Jessica, and I'm sure that it wouldn't be a problem for him to get you as well, since you all are coming back to my place. Baby, hold on for a minute; this is him now."

"What, wait? Caroline." Stacy looked at his cell phone and said, "Can you believe this?" As if the phone could respond. "Baby, Mike just passed you. He saw you as he and Jessica were driving by. He said that he can bring you by. He is near Delta pickup and drop off section in a silver Escalade EXT." Stacy looked up and saw Mike waving for him to come on. "Great," Stacy said under his breath. "I would've rather taken a cab." Just as Stacy was walking towards Mike's truck, he bumped into Caroline's mom, who was following their driver to the car, his hands full of Caroline's mother luggage. Caroline father had one carry-on bag. "Be careful with that bag," I have a lot of expensive gifts in there," she said to the driver.

"Yes ma'am," the driver said with a smile, but was really irritated. "Oh excuse me, young man," Caroline's mom said to Stacy, not realizing who he was. Stacy took a second look. "Excuse me, ma'am, Mrs. Victoria?"

"Yes, I'm sorry young man, but do I know you?" Caroline's father said, "Hey, well I'll be. Stacy, how are you?" Caroline's mother pulled her shades down over her eyes. "Well it is you. Stacy, my dear, how are you?" Stacy and Caroline's father shook hands and then Caroline's father hugged Stacy. Since they were being so warm, Stacy thought that he'd also go for a hug with Caroline's mother, but she just reached out her hand instead, and Stacy gave a fake smile and shook her hand. "Do you have a driver?" she asked. "I don't, but..." Caroline's father cut him off mid-sentence.

"Oh well, in that case, come ride with us. There is more than enough room, and besides, we have some catching up to do, young man. I hear you and Caroline have been reunited for quite some time now." "Yes sir, we have, but..." Just then, Mike walked up and asked Stacy if he needed help with his bags and to hurry up, because he wasn't trying to get a ticket.

Stacy didn't know what to do. Should he go with his nemesis or should he go with Caroline's parents, who were ready to grill him like a slab of ribs on the fourth of July? Stacy thought that he would be better off riding with Mike this time. He could tell that Mrs. Victoria still had her head held too high, and she thought that she was better than everyone else. "Hey, yeah Mike, I'm coming. Let me introduce you to Caroline's parents, though. This is Mr. Victor, and this is Caroline's mother, Mrs.

Victoria." Caroline's mother made a slight smile. "Nice to meet you, Mike," Mrs. Victoria said. "Will you be attending the Christmas party as well?"

"I will, as a matter of fact, I am on the way there now." "Oh good," Caroline's father said. "We will just follow you all to Caroline's if you don't mind?" "I don't mind at all," Mike said. When everyone arrived at Caroline's place, the catering party was there, and they offered people eggnog or champagne as they entered the door.

Tangie and Brother Robertson had already made it, and Tangie was on her second bowl of chicken and andouille gumbo. Caroline introduced everyone who hadn't met, and her dad gave her a big bear hug, almost smashing her with his six foot five, three-hundred-pound physique.

"Caroline, your yard looks lovely, honey," Mrs. Victoria said as she gave Caroline a smooch on each one of her cheeks and gave her a hug with a slight pat, careful not to mess up her Chanel makeup. "It must have taken you weeks to do that." "No, believe it or not, it only took about five hours with the help of Mike and Michael."

Mrs. Victoria looked at Mike and then looked at Michael, who was coming to get another cup of non-spiked eggnog. "Oh, you have a son?" "Yes ma'am," Mike said. Michael had been in the entertainment room playing video games since Mike went to pick up Jessica. Mike introduced Michael to Mrs. Victoria and Mr. Victor, who said he'd rather go by Vic.

"Well, I will just call you Mr. Vic," Michael said. "What a well-mannered young man," Mrs. Victoria said, impressed that Michael was a respectable young man and well mannered. Everyone socialized and danced, played games, and then it was time to eat. Mike said grace and everyone dug in. The food was so good it was silent for a moment. After a couple of minutes, Jessica broke the silence. "So Stacy, that was a nice photo shoot that you did this summer. Are you thinking about pursuing a modeling career, because if you are?

I know a few people." "No, I was just having fun, and I did the interview in relation to art and a lot of that business related stuff."

"No, no, no," Jessica said, as she waved her finger and smiled. "It wasn't all business. I have the magazine. There was some pleasure in it too. You talked about how you're always working, but manage to stay fit, and you talked about a possibility of pursuing a modeling career, and of course, you talked about your lovely fiancée, Ms. Caroline, and how she's the love of your life," Jessica said in English, but you could hear her Latino accent every time she spoke. "Well, it's something to think about. I mean you can never have too much money," she said as she smiled and winked at Stacy. "You are right about that," Stacy said.

"Stacy, so you are the artist having all of these young girls going crazy? I had no idea. I mean, I heard of SAG. You are like a celebrity." "I guess, you could say that," Stacy said to Mrs. Victoria. "Well I'll be, Stacy Alexander Graham. You sure have turned your life around and made a name for yourself." Mr. Vic hit Mrs. Victoria leg with his knee underneath the table.

"Victoria, don't start," he said. "Mother please," Caroline said. "No baby, it's fine," Stacy said. "Your mother is right. I made it out of the projects, and I am living my dream, and I am proud of it. I am not ashamed of where I come from, because I know where I am going." Jessica held up her champagne glass. "Good for you, Stacy. I say kudos. As the song goes, it's not where you from homeboy; it's where you at," Jessica said, quoting some lyrics from Lil Scrappy and Young Bucks Money in the Bank, and dancing in her seat. "To money in the bank," Jessica said, while feeling a little tipsy.

"Hey now, there's a toast that I can toast to," Mrs. Victoria said, while holding up the glass. "To money in the bank," she said proudly.

Caroline could not believe how Jessica had gone from riches to ratchet.

When she first met Jessica, she seemed classy and well put together, but the more Jessica talked, the more she showed off her true colors. Jessica sat at the table and talked about how she came from the hood, and now, she is a video vixen and a model. She did do a cover of XXL, and she is one of the most wanted women in the Hip Hop, Pop and R and B world.

"Well good for you," Mrs. Victoria said to Jessica. Then she looked at Mike, "So Mike, how do you feel about your girlfriend being the Jezebel of the music industry?" Mike almost choked on his glass of water that he was trying to swallow, when Mrs. Victoria asked him that off the wall question.

"Well, Mrs. Victoria, Jessica and I are just really good friends; that's all. We don't use the terms, girlfriend and boyfriend, because that could complicate things. Jessica does her thing, and I do mine, and we just hang out from time to time." "Oh, you mean, like you and Caroline?" she said, attempting to take another sip from her champagne. Mr. Vic grabbed the glass of champagne right before Mrs. Victoria could get her lips wet.

"That's enough Victoria." "Oh Vic please, but I'm just getting started. I want to know exactly what "Friends" means." She held up her hands in quotation marks. "It seems like Caroline is spending a great deal of time with Mike, while Stacy is running the streets, doing God knows what, and who could blame her. On one hand, there's a top ranking executive who is making almost four hundred grand a year, and then there's an aspiring model, who is barely making one hundred thousand a year. The choice is obvious who she should go with." "Okay Mother, that's enough," Caroline said. "I need to speak with you privately."

"No Caroline, whatever you have to say to me, you can say right here in front of everyone. We are not strangers here." Caroline held her head in her hands, trying to fight back emotions. "Baby, don't worry yourself. I got this" Stacy said as he got up. "I will never be good enough for Caroline to you. Will I?" "Baby," Caroline said as she lifted her head and grabbed Stacy's arm for him to sit back down. "I was never one of those brothers who took the easy way out. I lived in the projects, but I didn't let what I saw everyday dictate how I was going to live my life. I have always had a legit job and worked hard for what I wanted. I made a few mistakes when I was a teenager, smoking weed here and there, but I haven't rolled a blunt since I was nineteen years old. You never saw me on the corner selling drugs, and I never ran up in anybody's spot, trying to take what they worked hard for. You never even tried to know who I was. You just saw a face and matched it with all the other teens and black men you have thrown in jail as a defense attorney, and now you're a judge. "I bet you are throwing all the brother's in jail, especially if they don't fit your certain "background" or criteria," Stacy said, using his fingers as quotation marks. "I bet it kills you that I am going to marry your daughter, even though you tried to get rid of me decades ago. Well, guess what? Your little payoff didn't work."

"Okay everyone," Caroline stood up and said, "Party is over." "Baby, can you please give our guests their gifts on the way out. I'm sorry everyone." "It's okay, Caroline," Tangie said, "call me if you need me."

Brother Robertson waved goodbye to everyone and said Merry Christmas; everyone said Merry Christmas, except for Mrs. Victoria, who replied with a Humbug. Caroline just shook her head.

When all the guests left, Caroline pulled her mother on the back patio and spoke with her. "Can't you be decent for a full three hours? I can't even have a Christmas party without you passing judgment."

"Caroline baby, can't you see? I'm just trying to stop you from making a mistake and marrying this thug. I mean really, what can he do for you that you can't do for yourself? You make more money than he does, and from what I've heard, he goes for women with money. He's really nothing more than a gigolo. He doesn't really love you, Caroline, because if he did, he would let you be. He is not family material. With all these women throwing themselves at him, do you really believe that he will be faithful to only you? Can't you see that I'm just looking out for your best interest?"

"Like you did when I was seventeen, and you paid Ma Ann to take him away and never return for a healthy lump sum of money?" "Caroline, I did not pay them to go away if that's what you've thought all these years. Ma Ann was in debt, and her mother was sick, and I gave them an opportunity that she would have never gotten had I not helped them."

"Oh, let's give it up for the Almighty Queen Victoria," Caroline said loud and sarcastically, while giving a fake applause. "Mom, you're no savior. You are always only looking out for your best interest, like you've done all my life. You were never there for me as a mother. You were too busy working. You never had time to come to a game when I was a cheerleader or to Cheerleader competitions. You never sat down and talked to me about boys or growing up, like other girls' mothers did when I was growing up. Ma Ann was more of a mother to me. You always thought that if I had money, then I would be happy, but I wanted you. I wanted you to be there for me, to braid my hair or watch girly movies with me, to tell me that everything will be alright when I went through my first heartbreak, which was caused by you.

"Thanks to you, Mom, I have been alone most of my life, because I refuse to let anyone get close to me. If someone did show any feelings for me, I'd just push them away and bury myself in my work." Caroline cried. "It's funny how I've become the person that I resent the most." Mrs. Victoria stood there with her hand over her heart. She couldn't believe that Caroline had talked to her that way. Caroline stood looking at her mother, waiting for her to say something, yet she said nothing.

"Wow, well at least, I can say it's nice to hear complete silence from you for a change." Mrs. Victoria tried to grab Caroline, but Caroline snatched away and walked back into the house. Stacy was in the living room, talking to Mr. Vic.

They both got up when they saw Caroline. "Honey, are you alright?" Mr.

Vic asked. "I'm fine, Daddy. You and Mom can stay here if you like, or I can get you a room downtown at the W hotel."

"We came to spend some time with you, and that's exactly what we are going to do," Mr. Vic said as he gave Caroline a hug. "I am going to go outside and check on your mother." Stacy told Caroline that he was getting a hotel room for the night and that he refused to stay the night with Mrs. Victoria there. "Why would you up and leave me at a time like this, Stacy? Tomorrow is Christmas, and I wanted us to bring in Christmas together. I wanted it to be special."

"Caroline, I can't bring in the holiday like this. I love you, but you and your mother have some issues that you need to work out, and I feel like it's better if you all work them out, without me." "But you are a part of me, Stacy, and in a few months, we will be one. Just tell me one thing. Did my mother really pay Ma Ann and you to leave forever or was she helping Ma Ann to pay off some bills and to take care of your grandmother?" "What does it matter, Caroline? That was the past. Either way, your mother never wanted us to be together. She may have called it charity, but she wasn't doing us any favors. My momma was more worried about you and who would take care of you. She was going to go see about my grandmother and come back, but your mother paid us to go and never come back. Those were her exact words. I will be back tomorrow, but I refuse to sleep here tonight," Stacy said as he kissed Caroline's forehead.

"Merry Christmas baby," he said with hurt in his eyes. "Merry Christmas, my love," she hugged him and watched him walk out the door. She then turned and went to her bedroom and locked the door. She wanted to bury herself in her pillows, full of tears, but one teardrop did not fall from her eyes. She was sad, and yet, relieved that the weight that she had been carrying around all her life had finally been lifted, just by her telling her mother how she truly felt. She wanted her mother to knock on her bedroom door and apologize and hug her and just hold her, but she never came. That night, Caroline lay in the bed, listening to "What Do the Lonely Do at Christmas by The Emotions as she went through her emotions, until sleep finally gave her rest.

The next day, Caroline woke up to Stacy laying on the couch and her parents gone. "Baby, how long have you been here?"

"Caroline, I'm sorry. I had my security to come pick me up, but I didn't even make it all the way to the car. By the time I turned around and was coming back inside, I saw your parents leaving. I'm not sure if they went back home or what. Your dad said, see you later, and your mom just looked at me. I came to your door to knock, but I figured that you needed some time. I needed some time, myself. I sat up most of the night, thinking about us, and how much I love you, and you are right. We are going to be one, and I promise that I won't ever just leave again. I want to spend my life making you happy. "If you hurt, I hurt. I also didn't want you to see me last night, because I cried like a baby. I cried, because no matter what I do in life, some people will only see me as a boy from the projects. I cried, because in spite of what your mother thinks, you think the world of me, and I appreciate that. I love you so much for having my back, and I promise, from now on, whatever you want me to do, I will do it. If you want me to go to church, then that's what I will do, every Sunday, front row." Caroline laughed. "I'm serious Caroline.

I love you, Merry Christmas, baby," he said before kissing her. "Merry Christmas," she said as she softly kissed his lips back.

As Caroline and Stacy exchanged gifts, Caroline's parents pulled up. Caroline's mother asked Stacy if she and Caroline could have a moment alone. Stacy looked at Caroline to see if she would be ok, and she nodded her head that it was ok to leave her alone with her mother. Stacy and Mr. Vic stepped onto the back porch patio, which was nice and toasty inside. Caroline's mother gave Caroline a large box, beautifully wrapped with a bow.

"Open the box," Mrs. Victoria said. "Mom I thought that you came here to talk?" "My goodness, you have always been so hardheaded.

Caroline please... Just open the box."

Caroline took her time opening the box, which looked as if the wrapping must have cost a fortune. Caroline just knew that it was some expensive gift inside, because her mother thought that money and gifts made up for words unspoken, but this time, Caroline was wrong. As Caroline took the top off the box, she saw an even smaller box inside. Caroline took the smaller box and opened it. It was a single picture of her and Mrs. Victoria on the beach. Mrs. Victoria had on a beach hat and a bikini, and Caroline was no more than a year old, and her mother held her hand as she walked in the sand, touching only enough water to get her feet wet.

"Is this you and me?" Caroline asked. Mrs. Victoria nodded. "It is. I remember when I first had you. You were the world to me. I would take you everywhere and show you off to everyone. You were your dad's and my pride and joy. Even then, as a baby, I was very over protective of you as you can see in the picture. When your dad would try to put you on his shoulders and take you out a little further into the beach, I would pro-test. When we would take you swimming, I only wanted you to stay by the stairs, because I was too afraid that you would drown.

"Over time, I started being demanded at work, and before I knew it, I had spent all my life making a living, instead of making a home. I was raised that money was everything, but when I met your father, love caught me by surprise. My mother thought that because her life had taken a downward spiral with my father, that my life would do the same.

I worked hard, because I didn't want to become like my mother. She married my father for money, and he left her and me without a dime.

"My father was the first and only black man that my mother had been with, but she married him for all the wrong reasons. She was beautiful and could have any man she wanted, and my father treated her like a trophy wife, until he truly fell in love with someone else. Because of what my father did, my mom forbade me to date or marry a black man. I dated all kinds of men white, Asian, Latino, Indian so on and so forth, but I fell in love with a black man. I guess my mother figured that, since I'm half black, if I married white, then it would make everything alright.

"My daddy was a pimp, Caroline. My mother was nothing more than a piece of meat to show off, until he got caught up in his game one day, and he divorced my mama and married his bottom you know what. Since my dad was from the projects, I look at all men from the projects the same way. It's funny how that works, because your dad is from an upper middle class family, but my mom looks at him like he is still the scum of the earth, even with all his accomplishments.

"I am saying all of this to say that I am sorry for everything. I know now that my views of Stacy are no more than my views of my own father, who was never there. I also realize that I have been prejudice to my own race. I may have even won a lot of cases by having no mercy and just throwing them into the prison system without a fight. I thought that I had been looking out for your best interest all these years, but I haven't.

"I haven't been a mother to you at all. I let someone else raise you, right before my eyes, because I was too busy being angry. Angry at my father for leaving us, my mother for marrying a pimp, and at Stacy for having the audacity to love my daughter like she deserves. I know that Stacy loves you, but fear grasped hold of me, and I remember where he came from, and all I can see is what happened to my mom and me. I was so wrong.

"This man is a hard worker and has come a long way from Bankhead. I just want you to know that, yes, I could have filled this big box with all kinds of expensive material things, as I always do, when trying to makeup. I want you to keep this box and this picture inside, because it symbolizes my world, and as long as I have you in it, then I have everything I could ever want or need. But if you leave my world," she took the picture out of the box, "then my world is full of darkness and empty space. You are the best gift God has given me, and I want to be your mom." Caroline wiped her eyes, and they both stood up and gave each other a hug. Just then, the men came inside, and Stacy said that he and his future father in law were going to go catch a movie, while Caroline and her mom caught up. Mrs. Victoria apologized to Stacy for everything. She even apologized for giving them money to go and take care of his grandmother. She confessed that she was really trying to keep Stacy away from Caroline.

After everyone exchanged gifts on Christmas, Caroline and her mom watched Christmas movies on Hallmark and listened to Christmas music, while cooking dinner together. Caroline's mom even tried to braid Caroline's hair in a couple of braids, but that was a fail, so instead, Caroline braided her mother's hair, something her mom had never gotten done to her hair. Caroline's mom kept telling her how proud of her she was. She was even more impressed that Caroline could cook, something she hadn't even mastered the art of yet.

Later Christmas night, Tangie and Brother Robertson came by, so that Caroline could see Carmen, who had come home for Christmas. "Oh, I love your hair Mrs. Victoria," Tangie said. "I know, it's nice huh? And Tangie, call me Vickie," Mrs. Victoria said as she held the door open for everyone to come inside. Tangie didn't know what to think. Mrs. Victoria or Vickie, as she calls herself, was totally different from the party. Tangie pulled Caroline to the side and spoke under her breath. "Is this the same Scrooge from last night? Wait a minute, I know. This is the quiet before the storm, right?" "No, this is my mother, or should I say, my mom," Caroline said with a smile. Tangie looked at Caroline up and down, "Well alright, then," Tangie smiled and hugged Caroline, and Tangie's baby kicked. "Oh my goodness, I felt his or her little feet." "Yeah that means that you are next," Tangie said. "In a few months, this will be you, Caroline, hardly able to bend down or tie your shoe. I have to roll out of bed."

They both laughed. "No ma'am, that will not be me. I don't think that I'm ready for motherhood, yet. I will just spend my time spoiling yours or keeping yours whenever you and Brother Robertson want to go out."

Caroline took a quick second to think about becoming a family with Stacy.

She thought about him, her, and a little boy. She always said, if she had a baby, then she hoped that it would be a boy, because from what women have told her, boys are easier to raise. She didn't know how true that statement was, but she didn't want to take any chances. Somehow, between thinking about a family and a little boy, she thought about Michael, who was now a teenager, and then she thought of Mike. Just then, she received a Merry Christmas text from Mike, saying that he hadn't talked to her all day, and he hoped all is well.

Caroline texted Mike back and said Merry Christmas and all is well. She texted him that she had something to tell him, being excited about how she and her mom made up. Caroline did receive many gifts for Christmas from her parents. Her father brought in a big Santa bag, full of all kinds of goodies from household items, to electronics, clothes, shoes, and jewelry, and gift cards. Her dad gave her a big box, as well, and when she opened it, there was a key to a brand new Lexus NX with a note attached that said, "For our grandbaby, Love nana Victoria and papa Vic." Caroline looked around and said, "Ok do y'all know something that I don't know?" Everyone laughed, mostly at Caroline's facial expression. "We got the car, so that it will be easier when you and Stacy bring our little bundle of joy home. Go check it out," Caroline's dad said. Caroline went to inspect the car, which was very stylish. "Yes, this is nice, Caroline, and I told you that you are next," Tangie said.

21

"**W**hy is everyone wishing a baby on me?" Caroline asked Mike as they talked on the phone. Caroline was at home working, from her office desk. Mike was at his home, answering a few business emails as well. "Well, Caroline, you haven't had sex in two decades, and your biological clock is ticking, so it's bound to happen." "Excuse me, but did you just call me old?"

Mike laughed. "No, I did not. I said that your biological clock is ticking." Caroline laughed, "Whatever, Mike, you know what? We are not friends anymore, just by that one statement."

"What, are you going to cut me off, just like that, for telling the truth?" "Yeah, whatever, and when talking about sex, does oral sex count?"

"Um, I mean, you can't get pregnant that way, but what are you saying?" "I'm saying that we've had oral sex once a few months ago, and it was awesome, but I felt so bad afterwards, because I had waited all that time trying to do the right thing. I could hardly contain myself that time, so I told Stacy that it had to be a onetime thing, because otherwise, I would probably be pregnant, right now, for real." Mike shook his head on the other end of the phone. "I knew it," he said.

"You did not," Caroline said. "I did too," Mike said calmly. "It's been written all over your face since the day it happened, Caroline. I even know the day it happened. It was the day that you and I were on the phone, and you were acting strangely. You didn't want to tell me that you were going to see him, and you hadn't hidden anything from me before, so I figured maybe you had planned having intercourse with Stacy. You didn't want anyone to know, because you thought that Tangie or I would try to talk you out of it."

"So what do you have to say," Caroline said, waiting to get a lecture. "I have nothing to say, Caroline. I am not your friend to judge you. You are a grown woman, and you are free to do what you want. We all have our issues, and I'll be the last to try to judge anyone, because Lord knows, I have my issues."

"Oh come on, Mr. Perfect. You are clearly every woman's dream man. You are tall, dark, and handsome, and you have a great career. You love the Lord, and you are an awesome single father. Nobody's perfect, but you come pretty close. Clearly, you're every woman's dream man." "Not every woman," Mike said. There was a brief awkward silence and then Caroline announced the date of her and Stacy's wedding. "So February 14 is the official date." It took Mike a minute to realize what Caroline was saying. "I'm sorry, what?"

Mike had his own exciting plans for that special date and thought maybe, somehow, Caroline had found out his exciting news. "Wait a minute, has Michael told you the news already? I know that when he's over at his mother's house, he always comes by to see how you're doing, as well. Did he tell you that we were moving to New York?" "Wait, what? You are moving to New York? When were you going to tell me this?"

"Well, I was up for promotion for a couple of months, now, and a week ago, I got a call that if I wanted the position of Vice President of Menswear Product Development then the job was mine. I have by February 14 to be in New York to start that position. I was holding off to tell you the news, because I didn't know how you would take it. I know now that the wedding is the same day that we leave for New York, and I know how much your special day means to you, and I really wish that I could be there to support you, but that is the final day that I have to be in New York. I'm really sorry, Caroline." "Are you serious? Don't be sorry. Mike, this is an opportunity of a lifetime. I am really happy for you."

"Are you really? I wasn't sure how you would take it, because I know that I'm going to miss my best friend, and Michael is going to miss you as well, but I got to do what I got to do.

You know?"

"Yes, of course, don't be silly, Mike. I am so very proud of you. Besides, I love New York. Now, I have an excuse to be there. Whenever I want to go shopping, I can shop until I drop and then come visit you and Michael. It will be great." "It may be for you, but what makes you think that Stacy will let you visit us in New York alone?" "Oh I won't be alone. I am dragging him with me," Caroline laughed. Mike didn't think it was too funny. Even though Caroline was marrying Stacy in less than a month and he tolerated Stacy as much as he could, something about Stacy still didn't sit right with Mike. "So, how is Jessica taking the news?"

"I still haven't talked to Jessica since her little shenanigan at Christmas.

I told her that it was best if we just ended things, because our lives were going in two different directions. Don't get me wrong. She's very funny and beautiful, and she has a lot of street smarts, but she's just not my type." "How did she take that?"

"She was relieved actually. She told me that she had never chased a man in her life and chasing me was too much work. She actually thought that I was on the down low, and she thought that if I was, then she could make me straight." Caroline laughed. "Yeah, she told me that she thought that you were gay."

"No ma'am I had to let her know that I'm all man. I love women, but I love God more. It took me a while, but now, my life is finally on track. When I decided to follow God completely and whole heartedly, then that's when my blessings began to pour in. Not that I wasn't blessed before, but when you succumb to the will of God, he does miraculous things in your life. I got tired of fighting my flesh every time Jessica came around.

"I think it was more lust than anything between us. I had to plead the blood of Jesus every time she came around, and if she rubbed against me or something, then I would start quoting scriptures. She would look at me like I was crazy, and it turned her off immediately. She goes to church or whatever, but it's more of a religion thing with her. Any woman that I date must have a relationship with the Lord."

"Yeah, I totally understand that. Those are the types of battles that I'm fighting with my fiancée.

Most of the time, we do foreplay and that's it."

"Um hum," Mike said, listening, but not in agreement. "Caroline, let me ask you something? Do you feel obligated to have foreplay with him, because he's use to having sex and you're not?"

"Of course not, Mike. I love him, and when we kiss or hug, it's like electricity and I just want to show him how much I love him. It's not like we are having the actual act of sex." "But you are."

"What do you mean, we are? Foreplay is not sex. We had oral sex once, and that was a mistake. Besides, he's going to be my husband soon."

"Caroline, baby, stop being so defensive. Again, I am not here to judge you, but as your friend, I feel it's my godly duty to speak the truth. Okay, sex is sex. Whether it's done with a finger, a tongue, a penis, a toy, or whatever. It's all the same. If you disagree, then tell me this. What are you thinking about when y'all are fondling each other?"

"I don't know," Caroline said in an unsure voice. "Okay, well since I'm the only one keeping it real tonight, I'm going to tell you from past experiences what was on my mind. I was thinking about how bad I wanted it. How I couldn't wait to get her clothes off and how I wanted to bang her brains out, take it nice and slow, or whatever, depending on the mood. It's more of a lust thing, and that's what gets you all riled up in the heat of the moment. We both know what it says in the bible about if you lust after a person, right?" "Right," Caroline said dryly. "Aww, come on, don't be so salty, Caroline. So what does it say?" "Everyone that looks at a woman with lustful intent has already committed adultery with her in his heart," Caroline said dryly again. "But Mike, it's so hard." "You don't think that I know that? I just told you what I was dealing with, but she wasn't bringing out the God in me. She was bringing out the Mike in me, and Mike without God is no joke. I tell you what, just don't do it anymore from now on, and do like I did and quote scriptures or plead the blood of Jesus and see what happens."

"Okay, I will. I'm going to be strong from now on." "Yes, and you will be strong, because you have a best friend who is constantly praying for you. You want to always be with someone who is uplifting you and not someone who is pulling you down, whether it's financially, mentally, spiritually, or whatever." Caroline knew the "spiritually" was coming.

In other words, Mike was saying that Caroline and Stacy were unequally yoked, but he had said enough, and he didn't want to preach her to death. Besides, Caroline knew right from wrong, and she had her own convictions. "So anyway, good talk, but it's getting late, and I have to be at the office earlier than usual in the morning, because we have the current VP coming through, and I need to make a good impression, because as you know, I will be in those same shoes, so I have to say good night, my friend." "Wow it is late. I didn't realize the time," Caroline looked at her alarm clock, and it was 12:05 a.m. "Good night, my love."

22

Now, it wasn't unusual for Caroline and Mike to tell each other that they loved one another. They did it all the time. It wasn't even unusual for her to call Mike "my love", but it was something about that time she'd said it. Mike and Caroline both felt it, but they both ignored it. As the wedding got closer, Caroline decided to take some time off work in preparation.

Caroline took off a whole month, two weeks before the wedding and two weeks after the wedding. Caroline was under a lot of pressure from getting the perfect dress, to getting the right menu and location, guests and not to mention, there was a lot of tension between her and Stacy whenever he came to visit her or she flew to Miami to visit him. Ever since she had been holding out with no sex of any kind, Stacy would short talk her if she tried to ask for his input about the wedding, or he would always say that he was going to work or hang out with his friends, whether he was in Miami or Atlanta. Usually, Stacy would leave to work on his art, because he said it gave him more peace of mind.

Caroline remembered that Stacy had told her that before, but the funny thing was that when she was around, he created some of his best work. There was definitely trouble in paradise. Caroline wondered if another woman was keeping Stacy company at some hotel, like she was, when he was engaged to Amanda. Caroline thought about how not all women have restraint like she had, especially when it comes to a fine man, like Stacy. These thoughts almost drove Caroline crazy, and since Tangie was busier being a newlywed and making preparations for her new bundle of joy, Mike was her only outlet.

The day before the wedding was Stacy's bachelor party and Caroline's baccalaureate party. Stacy wasn't expecting a big bash or anything, just chill out with the fellas at a bar and have a beer or two. Since Mike and Stacy had learned to accept each other for the role that they played in Caroline's life, and they'd developed a tolerable relationship, Stacy invited Mike to the party. Mike didn't have any plans, and besides, he was leaving for New York tomorrow, so he decided to hang with the fellas. They all met up at a bar in Buckhead and had a few drinks for a couple of hours, until one of Stacy's childhood friends talked him into going to a club.

"Man are you serious? This is the last night of freedom.

Tomorrow it's clink, clink, life sentence. You know what I mean?" Stacy's friend said, barely tipsy and ready for some action. "Man, I have done everything I needed to do as a single man. I'm just ready to marry the love of my life tomorrow," Stacy said to his friend. "I feel you on that," Mike said. Then Mike raised his beer in the air as to toast and said, "To Caroline." All of the other men were looking at Mike weird, including Stacy. Mike cleared his throat and said, "I mean to Stacy and Caroline."

They all toasted to the soon to be newlyweds and then they took a sip of their beer. There were eight guys at the bachelor party, five of whom were already married. "Who all ready to go back home?" The bar was slow where they were and the guys' facial expression showed it. Stacy's childhood friend continued to talk. "Man, it's eleven o'clock at night, and y'all are acting like old men. I know this spot a couple of blocks down that be jumping on Friday's. Y'all should come with me and check it out." "No, I have to get back to the house," one man said. "So what, and I have to get up early tomorrow and make sure everything's one hunnard for my man's big day," Stacy's best man, and childhood friend said in his Ga accent. "Man, shut up, you sound like a female. It's getting late, I got to get back home," he said, mocking the other friend in a girlish tone. "Man, you are just scared of what your wife might say. Whoever isn't scared of your wife, raise your hand. No man raised their hand. All the men looked at each other and began to laugh. Another one of Stacy's friends said to Stacy's childhood friend, "Look man, it's not that we are afraid of our wives; it's more of a respect, and besides, what I look like walking in the house at four or five in the morning, when I got everything I need waiting for me at the house. I can turn up at home with wifey."

"Man, you sound lame. Do y'all honestly think that the women are thinking about us, right now?" "Naw, they ain't thinking about you, because you don't have a woman," another friend said. "My point exactly. I don't have a woman. I have women down the street waiting on me, and I'm about to hit this club now. Y'all can either come with me or head back to the house, only to find that your wives are out letting some guy named Chocolate Thunder shake his thing all in her face, while y'all sitting here like seven old geezers." "Well, I haven't had a good time in about a good five years," one of Stacy's other friend's said, "count me in." "Ok cool, I have one man with balls. Do I have two?" "Naw man, y'all go ahead I'm good," one friend said. "Yeah, I'm good too," another friend said. "Fellas, it is kind of early," Mike said, looking at his Rolex.

"I'm going to check out the spot with the fellas. This bar is kind of whack." "Yes, man, thank God somebody said it," one of Stacy's friends said. "Yeah, it is kind of whack," they begin to agree one by one. "I'm just going to call home and make sure my wife is alright, first," one man said.

Stacy's childhood friend tapped the man on the hand. "Man, put that phone down and stop calling your wife for permission." The phone continued to ring and went to the man's wife voicemail. "See, she didn't even answer. Did she? Man, your wife ain't thinking about you. Man we out." Mike, Stacy's childhood friend, and another friend began to walk towards the exit, when another friend scratched his head and said, "Man, they are right; this bar is whack. Stacy I'm out," he threw up the

ONE FOR THE REASON OF LOVE

deuces to Stacy and headed towards the exit. "Really, it's like that? So y'all just going to leave a brother at his bachelor party?" "Stacy they are right man. Where the party at?" one of his friend's said.

"Man, this is not the Stacy that I know. You are like the king of party. What's up with that?" "Man, I don't know.

I just have a lot on my mind, and I don't really know if..."

"If what man? Oh, I get it you're having cold feet. Man, that's natural. You'll get over that, but for now, I think that we ought to join the other half of the crew and see what this club like." After thinking about it for a minute, Stacy agreed, and as they walked out, Stacy's childhood friend stopped his Escalade and said, "Yeah, now that's the Stacy I know. Let's get it."

Stacy jumped in the truck with his childhood friend, and everyone else followed them to the club. "So, you were just going to leave a brother at the bar with no ride home or nothing, huh? Stacy said. "Man, calm down. I knew that you were going to change your mind. That's why I was in the truck, waiting for you to come out. Man, don't worry about nothing. You're going to have a blast; I'm telling ya."

When they pulled up to the club, they stopped at the door and let Valet park their cars. Security was at the front with a list. You could only enter if your name was on the list, or you'd have to wait an hour in line. Women screamed out SAG, and waved to Stacy as he walked to the entrance of the club. Some women didn't say a word, rather they smiled, winked, licked, or bit their lip, or flaunted their greatest asset.

"Man, the women love you," Stacy's childhood friend said. "I guess," Stacy said back. Stacy's friend went up to the security guard and said, "I have eight under the name of Polo." "Polo, my man, what's hannen?" The security guard said in his Georgia accent. "Man, they have been waiting on y'all in there, and you know how they get when they have been waiting." The security guard and Stacy's childhood friend, Polo, began to laugh. "Man, don't I," Polo said. "Gentlemen have fun." The club was an exclusive upscale club. No jeans or tennis shoes or t shirts were allowed. When they walked in, a young blond waiter walked them to VIP, where three strippers where waiting on them. "Here he is, ladies," Polo said. The women flocked to Stacy, like birds on breadcrumbs. The club was jumping. "Now, this is more like a bachelor party," one of the fellas said, and another nodded in agreement.

The fellas popped a few bottles of champagne, filled their glasses, and began to party. A waiter came by and brought over a bottle of Louis thirteen and said, "This is from the beautiful young lady in the VIP section across from you." Stacy tried to see who the lady was, but he couldn't from the strippers dancing on and around him. The woman looked like Amanda, but he wasn't sure if it was her. The lady in VIP across from Stacy began to come over with her four friends.

Stacy told security to let them into their section, and Stacy realized it was Amanda. Stacy excused himself, while the strippers went to mingle with his friends and a few of his friends mingled with Amanda's friends. Stacy and Amanda hugged each other, and she told Stacy congratulations, but he could hardly hear her. They went outside on the patio upstairs of the club to converse. "Thank you for the bottle. I couldn't hear what you were saying inside, though," Stacy said.

"I was just telling you congratulations. I am really happy for you." Stacy gave Amanda an odd look as if he didn't believe her. "No, I'm serious. I really am. I still believe that I should be the one, but if you are happy, truly happy, then I am even happier for you."

Amanda and Stacy stood on the patio overlooking downtown Atlanta and talked, reminisced, laughed and joked, before long two hours had passed, and they were still on the patio talking.

"I love you..." Amanda said, at the same time Stacy said, "I miss you..." There was a brief silence, and then they kissed. At that same moment, Mike was coming to tell Stacy that he was out, because the club was closing soon.

When Mike saw them kiss, he hid behind the doors inside and peeked at them around the corner. "What the hell are you doing, Stacy?" Mike said under his breath. Mike couldn't believe his eyes, because he really believed that Stacy loved Caroline. Any other man would seek this opportunity as a chance to get with Caroline, but Mike was more concerned about her heart being broken, and he pondered what he should do.

He wanted to tell her, so that she'd know what kind of man she was about to marry, but at the same time, he didn't want to be the one to bring her bad news the day of her wedding. Mike quietly went back down stairs, and Polo was coming up to get Stacy, but Mike told him that Stacy was in the restroom, and that he was coming.

"He must have mixed the white and dark together. I have told him about that," Polo said, shaking his head. "Alright, well, let him know that Imma be in the car."

Mike turned around to go back up the stairs, and Stacy and Amanda were walking down, holding hands, not realizing what they were doing. When Mike looked at their hands, they both let go of each other's hands, and Amanda awkwardly walked away. "Bro, it's not what you think," Stacy said to Mike. Mike threw his hands in the air. "Hey, you don't have to explain anything to me. Polo said that he would be waiting out front for you, though." Security was tight at this club, so the groupies that were wilding and trying to get Stacy's attention had no chance. For the most part, people were normal towards him, because many celebrities frequented the night club. Stacy got in the truck, feeling sick, but not from alcohol, but from stress. Polo began to laugh, as he hit Stacy in the chest with the back of his hand and pulled off with the other hand.

"Aye man, what did I tell you? I told you that you were going to have a good time. I done told you about mixing the brown with the white, too; now, look at you. You ain't learned, yet?" Stacy's mind was far from what Polo was saying, and it was all gibberish to him. Stacy had to make up in his mind as to what he was going to do and why he was doing it. Was he marrying Caroline because he felt that she belonged to him? Did he feel like he still had something to prove to her mother? Was it pride? Did he refuse to see her with Mike? Did he feel like the Vajayjay was his and marrying Caroline was the only way to state his claim?

All of this was too much. Stacy told Polo to stop the truck, and Stacy got out and threw up on the side of the road. "Aye man, are you alright? I'm going to hurry up and get you home, so that you can get some rest, because your soon to be Mrs. isn't about to kill me for having you out all night and making you late for your own wedding." As Stacy threw up, he waved his hand around to shut Polo up.

Polo gave him some napkins out of the truck to wipe his mouth. "Man, I can't marry Caroline." Polo shook his head.

"Man, does this have anything to do with Amanda?"

"Man, it has everything to do with Amanda. It wasn't by chance that she was there tonight. It was by fate. Man that was a sign from God that I am making a mistake. I'm not ready to marry Caroline or anyone, for that matter. I think that I have issues being alone, because I was the only child, and then when my mom passed, Amanda was there, so I poured my everything into her, and I never really coped with it. I feel like I'm marrying Caroline, because she was a part of my life when I was a kid, and she's the only other person that loved my mom as much as I did, and some kind of way, I feel fulfilled when I'm with her, but I guess not fulfilled enough."

Polo looked at Stacy as if he didn't understand. "You don't understand do you?"

Polo shook his head. "Man look, I don't know what it's like to be the only child, because it was eight of us. I do know what it's like to have all those siblings and still feel alone or like nobody understands me. That's part of why I wild out as a kid, because I felt like nobody cared. To this day, I still do stupid things, and later on, when I'm paying for what I did, I see that it's not worth it. Man, it's like this, what your mama and my grandma use to tell us about God is true. We can search the whole world, trying to gain fulfillment, but we won't ever get it, unless we seek after God. I think that God put Caroline back in your life to help get you on track with him.

"I remember your mama would always tell me that she was praying for me, and I use to laugh, but now, I believe her prayers and my grandma's prayers have gotten me through a lot. Man, I be out here in these streets wilding out, but I know who God is, and I know that I can't keep doing it Polo's way forever. Look, you have a good woman. Don't lose her reminiscing on your past. Think about your future. Do you love Caroline?" "Of course I love her."

"Do you want to spend the rest of your life with her?" "Yes." "Do you believe that you have what it takes to love, honor, and cherish her, while forsaking all others? Because if you can truly say yes to all of these, then marry this beautiful lady tomorrow, and get over this cold feet, as they call it. Now, come on and get back in the truck. I got a cutie with a big ole booty waiting for me at the crib."

Stacy laughed and shook his head. Polo was a trip. He had multiple personalities. He could be hood, he could be wise, he could be stupid, a preacher, teacher, or he could even be someone you should never take advice from, but tonight, he was simply his friend, and at the time when he needed him most, he came through. They both got back in the truck and rode off. When Stacy got back to Caroline's house, she was sound asleep. Stacy kissed her on her forehead and sat on the bed and watched her sleep.

23

oday was the day, and Caroline was so excited. She had got up at the crack of dawn to prepare for the big day. Stacy was still in bed, asleep. Caroline made breakfast and woke Stacy up. He had gotten about three hours of sleep, so he was still tired. "Baby, it's so early. We still have eight hours before the wedding. Let's go back to bed." "No sir, I have to go and get my hair and nails done, along with a few other things. I don't have time to sleep. You, on the other hand, only have to worry about getting your beard and mustache trimmed and throwing on your tux." "This is true," Stacy said, while yawning.

Just then, Caroline's doorbell ring. When Caroline went to open the door, no one was there, only a yellow package that said congratulations.

"Baby, are you expecting a package," Caroline asked. "No, who was that?" "I'm not sure, but I'm assuming it's a wedding gift. I'm going to open it and see what's inside. It feels like a CD or a DVD. Oh, maybe it's the cd I ordered online that has our first dance song on it." The package looked suspicious, and Stacy thought that maybe someone saw something last night and was trying to tell Caroline about it. "Baby, it's something that I need to tell you," Stacy said as Caroline tore open the package. "Ok baby, what is it?"

Caroline pulled out a DVD, but it looked as if it were a bootleg movie. Caroline put it into the DVD player and turned on the TV. Stacy stood in front of the TV, facing Caroline while scratching his head. "Baby, stop being silly. Get out of the way." Stacy moved and Caroline gasped and held her hand to her heart.

"I can't believe you." Stacy refused to look at the screen and came over to Caroline and apologized. "Baby, I am so sorry. I made a mistake. Please forgive me," he pleaded. "I love you so much." Tears began to flow down Caroline's face.

"Baby, how could you not tell me that you had this recording all this time? We should definitely use it at our reception. People are going to love this." "Wait, what?" Stacy looked at the TV screen, and it was a video of them playing together as kids, then the video switched to Stacy teaching Caroline how to ride a bike; the video had them at church with Ma Ann when the two of them got baptized, then it was a video of their favorite tree, and Caroline's first time making pancakes, which she destroyed.

Stacy could not believe it. Someone had taken a collection of videos from the camcorder and made a video of Stacy and Caroline's love. It didn't say who the video was from, and although both of them remembered each of the events on the DVD, they had no idea that the recordings were still around. Caroline's dad had flown into town, but her mother had stayed in DC, busy with a major trial of a young man accused of murder and had already served three years in prison. This was a major trial, and everyone knew about it.

As Caroline got ready for the day, the News Channel was discussing the coming trial and how tough of a judge Caroline's mother was. They said that if he was found guilty, he would most definitely be looking at a life sentence, especially with this judge. Caroline and her mom had come a long way in their relationship, but Caroline knew that her mom would not be able to make the wedding in preparation of the trial. Tangie came to pick up Caroline, and they went to get their hair and nails done for the wedding. Mike called Caroline to see how she was doing and to say his final goodbyes, before he and Michael moved to New York.

"Send me pictures," Mike said, "I'm really going to hate that I'm going to miss your big day." "It's ok, Mike. I totally understand. You just go to New York and make me proud. Not that I'm not already proud, but you know what I mean. I'm going to miss you, bestie." "I'm going to miss you too, my love," Mike said.

Caroline eyes begin to water. "Aww, you are thinking about marrying the love of your life, aren't you?" Tangie asked. Caroline shook her head no. "Well, what's the matter? Are you upset that your mom isn't here?"

Caroline shook her head no again. Tangie pulled into the mall parking lot. "Well, what is it?"

"I'm just going to really miss Mike and Michael. I have really grown to love both of them these past few years. I feel like I'm a part of their family. We do everything together. When I can't talk to you, he's my outlet. I just feel like a part of me is moving away, but at the same time, I'm starting a new life, as well, so I need to be happy, right?"

Tangie nodded her head yes, "Right."

"You need to be happy." "But I'm not." "Well, you and Stacy can always go to visit them, right?" Caroline nodded, but visiting was not enough, she thought to herself. She wanted to be with them.

It was an hour before the wedding, and guests were starting to arrive. Caroline was in her robe about to get her makeup done when Stacy knocked on the door. One of the bridesmaids yelled, "Stacy, go away. It is bad luck to see the bride before the wedding." "Well, I don't believe in luck," Stacy said through the door.

"Caroline, sweetheart, can you come to the door for a minute?" All the bridesmaids stood in front of the door to keep Stacy out. "Ladies, he's right. I'm sorry, we do need to talk. Can you all give us a minute, please?" The ladies left the room and Stacy came in.

The wedding dress hung on the wall behind her. "That's the dress. It's beautiful." Stacy was already dressed in his tux. "Caroline, sit down for a minute."

Caroline sat on the love seat, and Stacy sat on the coffee table in front of the love seat. Stacy grabbed Caroline's hands. "I love you so much, Caroline," he said as he fought back tears. Caroline began to cry as well, "I love you, too." Stacy put his left hand over his mouth and rubbed his goatee, "I just want to be one hundred percent sure that we are doing the right thing. Last night, something happened and..." "Shhh," Caroline said as she placed a single finger over Stacy's lips. "Last night is the past and today is a new day. I am not interested in what happened in the past, only what happens from this day forward," Caroline sighed. "Stacy, there is something that I need to say to you, as well, but I'll let you continue to say whatever it is you were saying." "No you go first," he insisted. "No, it's fine; you go ahead," Caroline said. "We can't get married," they both said at the same time. They both looked at each other, surprised, but relieved, at the same time.

"God, what are we doing?" Caroline said, looking up at the ceiling. "I know I don't understand it. I mean, we love each other, right?" Caroline quickly agreed, "Of course, but is it more than that?"

"I don't know. That's what I've been asking myself since last night. I mean, I know that I love you, but I think that I'm marrying you for personal issues that I need to work out. I don't want to marry you, being half the man that I need to be. I know what I need to work on, and that's being happy with being by myself. I need to find out who I am when I'm alone, and most importantly, I know that I need to seek God. You wouldn't believe who helped me realize this, either."

Caroline looked like "who?" "Polo." "What?" "Yes, I couldn't believe it either, but God has a way of doing things, and last night, I heard him, and I'm listening, and I'm not ready for marriage yet. I don't even fully know who I am, yet. I can't lead you or our family if I don't know where I'm going. I love you so much, Caroline, and it may sound weird, but that is why I can't marry you, because I know that I wouldn't be the man you need me to be. It's just one request I ask of you before I leave." "What's that?" "Can I see how beautiful you look in that dress?"

Caroline smiled and went into the changing room and came back out. Stacy had the biggest smile and gave Caroline the biggest hug. He kissed her on her forehead with a long peck before releasing her. Caroline pulled off her engagement ring and gave it to Stacy. He grabbed her hands and pulled them to his lips and kissed her hands,

"I love you."

He walked off, with tears running down his face. He stopped at the door an "He better treat you right, or I'm coming for him." And with that being said, he opened the door and left the church. The bridesmaids came running in. They had been listening by the door, but could barely hear.

"Caroline, are you ok?" One of the bridesmaids said. "Yes, I'm fine, thank you," she said while sniffling. "Go get him, baby," a voice said at the door. Caroline thought that it was Mother Brooke, but it wasn't. It was her mom.

"Mama!" She ran to the door and hugged her like a little kid. "Mom, what are you doing here?" "Nothing is so important as to keep me away from my baby girl's biggest day of her life." "The wedding is off, Mama."

"Go get him," Victoria said. "Mama, it's over, and I'm totally fine with it." "Well, what are you waiting for? Go get your man." "Who?" Caroline held her head to the side, wondering if her mama was thinking what she was thinking.

Neither of them said anything. They both just screamed with excitement, and Caroline ran outside in her wedding dress and heels and hopped in her mama's car and her mom drove her to Hartsfield Jackson airport. Mike's plane was scheduled to leave in thirty minutes. Caroline's mom hurried through traffic, like a NASCAR driver. Caroline held on for dear life and prayed the whole way there. When they got to the airport, Victoria let Caroline out in the pickup/drop off lanes. Caroline ran inside and asked if flight 037 had left yet, and the customer service rep told her it hadn't, but she only had a couple of minutes before the flight took off.

24

"*I* can't believe that you're just going to throw your life away. After all this time, you are just going to let her marry some other man?" Mike's father said to him in a frustrated tone. "I bet she has no idea that just as good of a position was offered to you here, does she?" Mike shook his head no, "Dad, the opportunity here is not as good as the one in New York. "I don't really want to talk about this, Dad. Can we just let this go? She loves him, and as the saying goes, if you love someone, then let them go, and if they come back, then they're yours to keep, and if they don't, then they never were. We had our chance as lovers, but we were better at being friends." "Bull crap," his father said, making some people nearby uncomfortable. Mike's mom apologized to the people and asked her husband to just let the matter go.

"No, I will not let it go, because I refuse to see my son live a life of regret. Look son, there were times in my life when I thought that money and being successful were everything, but it's not. Especially, if you don't have anyone to share it with. You'll end up with your money, but you'll still be alone, and money can't buy you love. It can buy an illusion of love, but not the real thing. The real thing just happens, and it doesn't happen to everyone. That's why so many people are out trying to buy it.

"They spend money on cars, clothes, houses, jewelry, hang out in the clubs, or whatever it is to gain attention, because they are seeking what only a few of us have, and that's the real thing. They go spending all their money, and the next thing they know, they are broke, busted, and disgusted, trying to find love in all the wrong places." "Grandpa is right, Dad. Caroline is the second best thing that ever happened to you." "Boy hush," Mike's dad said.

Mike laughed, "And who was the first?" he said. Michael stood up and held out his arms with his hands up, "You're looking at him." Mike and Michael both laughed. "It's good to see you smile, baby. I haven't seen that smile in a long time," Mike's mom said. Mike stood up, because they were loading first class. He hugged his mom and then his dad. "Think about what I've said, son. I love you." "I love you too, Dad," Mike said.

Mike and Michael grabbed their tote bags and headed towards the plane.

Caroline raced to the terminal, but Mike's plane had already left. She was heartbroken and sad. How could I think for one minute that he would put his life on hold for me? I should have told him how I felt. I was so stupid. I let fear and my past get in the way of what God had been preparing me for all these years.

All these years, and my future was right there in my face, and just like that, he's gone. Caroline didn't realize that she was actually speaking these thoughts out loud, until she saw an old lady shaking her head and rubbing her on the arm saying, "Hun, I'm so sorry. We were all rooting for ya."

"Thanks," Caroline said.

Caroline was already the center of attention, running through the airport in her wedding dress with the train of her dress dragging the floor. By the time Caroline made it back outside, all of her close family, friends, and even Mike's pastor was outside, waiting on her. Everyone had parked their cars and were waiting outside. Caroline ran to her mother and her mother hugged her as she cried. Caroline's mother rubbed her back and kissed Caroline's forehead.

"Now, now baby," she said softly as she smiled. "Excuse me, ma'am," a voice cried from the doors. "Excuse me, but you forgot something." Caroline thought maybe she'd dropped her ID or something, while running through the airport, so she asked her mom if she could retrieve whatever it was. "I've been humiliated enough, Mom. Can you please get whatever it is?" The voice came closer, within a few feet from Caroline. "You forgot something," the voice said again in a deep, but soft, joyous, tone. Victor was holding the door for Caroline to get in, but she stopped for a moment. She recognized that voice now that she'd stop crying and could hear clearly.

She stood with her back to the man, afraid to turn around, in fear that her hopes would be shattered, but then, she hoped, and she believed, and she had faith. At that moment, she cast fear aside for the final time and allowed faith to see her through. She said softly as she smiled, "Mike?" The voice came even closer to the point where it was right behind Caroline. "You forgot something," the voice said a final time. Caroline quickly turned around, and there was her knight in shining armor, dark as night, with pearly whites.

Caroline jumped in his arms. Mike laughed as she kissed him on his forehead, nose, cheeks, and chin, and then they stared into each other eyes. The sun shining down on them as to say this was their moment. "I love you so much," Mike said. "I love you," Caroline said, and then they kissed, while Mike still held her in his arms. Mike put Caroline down and held her hand as he walked to her father, who was hugging Caroline's mother as they watched. "Mr. Vic and Mrs. Victoria," he said. "May I," as he looked to Caroline. Caroline's parents looked at each other, and then to both Caroline and Mike and said, "You may." Mike turned around and got down on one knee and in front of family, friends, and people at the airport, he asked Caroline to marry him, right now, today. Caroline screamed and jumped up and down and said, "Of course." Mike's pastor, who was watching, along with others in the crowd, came to where Mike and Caroline stood and married them right at the airport in the pickup and drop off zone. Everyone cheered for the couple. The reception was held at Soulful Jazz, but before the

Newlyweds arrived to Soulful Jazz, they stopped by an exclusive jeweler to get their wedding bands, and they also changed into a semiformal, yet classy, attire for the reception. "Ladies and gentlemen," The DJ said as he held the Mic with one hand and held his other hand towards Mike and Caroline as everyone stood. "Introducing for the first time as man and wife, I present to you Mr. and Mrs. Michael Washington." Everyone cheered them on as they entered the reception. They danced their first dance, and afterwards, everyone got on the dance floor and danced as well. Mother Brooke told Caroline that she was the one who had mailed the DVD to Caroline with her and Stacy. The DVD was a collection of VCR tapes that were left at their old apartment on Bankhead. Ma Ann never came back, and many items in her home were left by the curb, and people either got it off the street for themselves or tried to sell it.

Mother Brooke had kept a few of her friend's belongings and figured that the boxes may have had important things that Ma Ann would need. However, in the past when Mother Brooke would talk to Ma Ann, Ma Ann would tell her that she didn't need anything, and that she was starting over brand new. Mother Brooke had never gone through the boxes, until almost two decades later, when Stacy had come back to Atlanta, and she'd found out that her longtime friend had passed. "I don't think she even realized that she still had all those old videos," Mother Brooke said. Mother Brooke told Caroline that she was happy if she was happy, and she'd always support her, and she blessed their union.

As the evening grew later, the crowd begin to disappear, and Mike and Caroline found themselves still slow dancing on the dance floor under the golden chandeliers. "So, what about New York?" Caroline said. "I don't need New York. I have everything that I will ever need, right here." She looked into his eyes and smiled as she lay her head on his chest. Caroline could not believe how her life had dramatically changed within five years.

Here she was now, thirty-seven years old, married to her best friend, her confidant, and most importantly, the love of her life. She was so at peace in the decision to marry Mike, and she knew that, without a doubt, God had been keeping and preparing her for this very moment. The both of them had their share in love and loss, and in the midst of them losing, with the help of God, they discovered themselves and found each other. As they left the reception and headed home, neither of them knew all the answers, but they knew that this was the best decision that either of them had made in their entire lives. When Mike pulled up in his driveway, he hurried out of his truck and opened Caroline's door, scooped her up, and carried her over the threshold.

"Welcome home, Mrs. Washington," Mike smiled from ear to ear as if he was the happiest man alive. "Thank you, Mr. Washington," Caroline said, while looking deeply into Mike's eyes, before they shared a long kiss. Caroline was so overjoyed that all she could do was smile and in her head say, "Thank you Lord. I almost allowed my past, my fears, and my insecurities to have made me miss out on one of the biggest blessings a woman could have." As Mike watched Caroline walk to their bedroom, he held his hands together and silently said,

"Thank you Lord."

Who would have known that each of their futures would be living next door? Who would have known that lending a helping hand would turn into such a sweet friendship? Who would have known that a friendship, so sweet, would blossom into love? Sometimes, while we are trying to figure it out, we settle just to have a body, anybody. But the same God who created Eve for Adam, because he knew that it wasn't good for Adam to be alone, he too, had a plan for Mike and Caroline, and that plan was for them both to find that ONE, for the reason of love.

About the Author

Shubricca L. Bell follows her Christian faith as she writes books that deal with the challenges of everyday life. She strives to let Christians know that, while they are expected to be perfect, they are human like everyone else in need of a perfect God to help them forgive, heal, and live. Bell, who graduated from the Art Institute of Atlanta in 2003, is a certified chef de cuisine. Born and raised in Atlanta, Georgia, she lived in the Midwest before moving to North Carolina. She has four daughters.

www.ingramcontent.com/pod-product-compliance
Lightning Source LLC
Chambersburg PA
CBHW031313120626
46554CB00001BA/396